Bay Hymns

Bay Hymns

Garr Lange

Rev. date: 04/08/2021

To order additional copies of this book, contact:
Xlibris
844-714-8691
www.XLbris.com
Orders@Xlibris.com
822527

To Dad

Acknowledgements

To all my patrons who made this book possible; to Kristin Hannah for her editorial comments and advice; to Greg, Rebecca, Sandy, Johnny C., Peg, Mary Lu, Dale, Steven, and Mary for reading earlier versions of this novel and making valuable comments that I took to heart; to David for his support and encouragement; to Jeff and Lynn for their friendship; to Mark and Greg for their continued involvement in my artist life; to Gary Skiff for his generous time and effort; and to Charles (C.C.) Long who asked…"What about that book about the gravel pit?"

Rock

Chapter 1

Jess had lived outside of time for too long. In his sleep connections were made and he awoke that morning wondering what day it was. Maybe he needed a calendar. Or a clock. Something without ticks.

And shoes. From the camper bunk bed, he glanced at the floor at his tired white bucks. His old golf shoes. He had removed the spikes, but the inlays still made a *clack*, *clack*, *clacking* sound whenever he walked down the grocery aisle. People would stop and point. Others would stare. It wasn't the kind of attention he needed, not in this town. Certainly not in Emerald.

The sunlight shining in through the camper windows suggested he ought to get up. His better mind asked, what for? His dog had run off, his girl had too, and he had no money. He rolled over and went back to sleep, comforted by the thought that these days of reckoning came few and far between.

Jess cast his fly toward the southern edge of the pond and sat down on the gravel bank. His line snaked across the top of the clear emerald green water and the fly came to rest without a nibble. A warm breeze circled the gravel ridge and rustled the leaves of a group of alder trees on the opposite side of the pond. Life was good, Jess concluded. What a way to spend a day. Under a bright Clay Island sun sitting next to his pond.

His pond?

He turned it over in his mind's eye, questioning it from every angle. He finally concluded that it was *a* pond, not *his* pond. It was an *unqualified* pond. Period.

Between casts, Jess thought of a scene, and posed a hypothetical to himself.

A man unwittingly stumbles upon what appears to be an old gravel pit. Tacked to the concrete wall, separating public from private property, a handwritten sign warns "No Trespassing, Beware of Dog."

Dismissing it, the unwitting man ducks under the heavy steel cable at the pit entrance and proceeds to a spot where an old camper rests on an abandoned '62 Dodge truck bed . . . abandoned, one presumes, since the pickup—without hood, without engine, without wheels—looked to be every bit abandoned. Curious, the man tries the knob at the old office shack a few yards away, and it's locked. No harm. Then he spots an immense mound of gravel bending ever so nicely into a grove of Douglas fir, Sitka spruce, and alder trees thirty feet above him.

Hmm, what is this, the unwitting man asks himself.

He climbs the gravel ridge and there she be, by god, the most beautiful unqualified pond he'd ever seen! Upon closer inspection, he finds it is filthy with, crawling with, stinking with . . . *Oh sweet baby Jesus, will you look at all of those flopping fish!*

Jess considered this. A humble man, no doubt. Married, three kids. Unwitting was the key.

Then from his backpack, the unwitting man takes out a collapsible fly rod and threads the line with nervous anticipation, leaving Jess to wonder, *Whose pond was it now?*

Jess!"

A familiar voice called out from the other side of the gravel ridge.

"Yo!"

"Don't you *'yo'* me. Help!"

Jess glanced over his shoulder and looked to the top of the gravel ridge. For a split second he spotted A. B. "Buck" Buchanan as he broke yonder horizon, clawing for a simple handful of unyielding stones. Jess didn't budge. He had seen his father climb that gravel bank a thousand times; he didn't need his help. When Jess looked back, apparently his father had lost ground. He saw nothing but blue sky when he should have seen a floppy blue hat with a beautiful collection of handmade flies clinging to it.

"Jessie?" his father called out.

It was a plaintive plea. Jess listened for another.

"*You sonuvabitch!*"

It was too much to ask. Jess laughed out loud and climbed to the top of the ridge. He looked down at his father, stuck midway up the slope with his knees dug into the gravel for grip. Sweat streamed down his father's great Buck jowls; a sliver of spit dangled from the end of his soaked Tiparillo.

Jess slid down the slope and offered his father a helping hand.

"Here, grab hold."

His father was a big man and Jess had trouble pulling him to the top. He fell on his butt a couple of times and laughed at what a production it had become to haul his dad up the slope. At the top, Jess made sure Buck was steady on his feet before he made his way back down to his pole that lay next to the water.

Buck crab-walked on all fours down the steep slope backward, not entirely sure if Jess would catch him if he lost his balance and started to tumble toward the water. Near the pond's edge, the slope flattened out, and this familiar ledge was where Buck sat down and attempted to light his spit-soaked Tiparillo. On the third try, he pitched it in the water and looked at Jess with a smile, revealing that familiar gap between his front teeth.

"Chum," he said.

Here, father and son struggled to say hello in words that didn't come easy. They hadn't seen each other all winter and now they searched for something appropriate to say, something not too sentimental yet still expressing those ties that bind. But those words hadn't been invented. Or if they had, they were lost to the two men sitting next to the pond.

Somewhere in his mission outside of time, Jess had forgotten what month it was. The first week of April was normally when his parents would come back from their winter home in Hawaii. But this was still March. Or so he thought. He wondered if something was wrong.

' How's Mom?" he asked.

Buck lit a fresh Tiparillo and let the smoke dwell deep.

"She ain't dead yet," he said, tipping his head back and slowly exhaling the smoke into the breeze.

Jess stood up and flicked the fly rod again. He reeled in the line trying to summon up another way to say hello to his father.

"You won't catch anything over there," Buck said.

Jess had spent a lifetime fishing in the pond, and if anybody knew where to catch trout, he did. And his dad knew that. He looked down at his father, expressionless.

"Where's your rod?" he asked.

But Buck hadn't come to fish in the pond. Instead, he had other things on his mind. First and foremost was this thought:

This son is mine!

In Hawaii, Buck finally realized what had been bothering him. Eighteen holes a day couldn't provide him with a sense of drama. Not like concrete. It was a question of form. Since his retirement, an all-consuming impasse had planted itself squarely in his gut. He was bored.

Retirement life didn't help. The repetition of perfect days nearly killed him. He took sick for something to do and nearly got closed out on his backside. Bad form. He quit drinking. A week later he decided he would rather be sick. He took up reading, but the good guys always died. Marie enrolled him in the grandpa crib club, but penny-a-point couldn't hold his interest. The days lingered; the minutes crept by.

On the day of his liberation, Buck sat by the pool humming a Jess Buchanan tune when Marie interrupted through the screen door.

"Junior's on the phone."

The patio umbrella shifted in the hot Hawaiian breeze. Junior never called in the afternoon and Buck wondered if there was a problem. He pictured his eldest son in his office overlooking Sunset Bay. It was a gray day with a little chop on the water, the kind of cold blustery day that Buck longed for in his heart because he had spent a lifetime under those Clay Island skies. He pictured this as an eighty-eight-degree Kohala sun roasted his back. He punched the talk button on the patio telephone.

"Son number one."

"Dad, I need some advice."

Junior never asked for advice. And he said it in a tone Buck hated now, so far away. Not even a decent hello. But Buck had lectured Junior on mixing business and blood; business was business and blood was blood. There should be no blood feeling in business and no business at home. It made for better feelings in both places.

"I've got something here I think we oughta take a look at."

Junior was good about that, making Buck feel as if he were still a part of the company.

"What'cha got?"

"A pour. A big one."

"How big?" asked Buck.

"More rock than we've got . . .," Junior said.

He paused for effect.

Uh-huh. Buck figured it might come to this someday. Junior thought stockpiling crushed rock was what they did only in downtime, and if he didn't have enough gravel to finish a pour, he'd have to barge it in. And that would be a very costly mistake.

"In the ground," Junior finished.

Junior paused again, letting the immensity of the job sink in. He didn't get excited over much, but this was a different story.

"It's more rock than we've got, *period*," Junior said emphatically, doing his best not to understate the magnitude of it.

Buck couldn't believe what he was hearing. More rock than they had in the ground . . . for one pour?

But Junior's concern was not Buck's concern. What Buck knew, and what nobody else knew, was that it *wasn't* all the rock that the Buchanan's had in the ground. Underneath the pond there was enough gravel to keep Buchanan Construction in business for years to come. It made Junior and Jess partners, and it was a thing that Buck was proud of, leveling the playing field the way he did.

After giving his dad a rundown of the job, Junior said he had to go. Buck hung up the phone. A few seconds later, Marie heard a crash and a jangle from out back. She looked out through the screen door and spotted her husband lying face-up on the poolside surface, convulsing in spasms of frightening laughter.

For the message in the bottle had arrived sooner than Buck had anticipated. A simple phone call had provided him with all the form he could handle. He was going home to watch this one—Gravel Bowl I.

A man rarely survives the execution of his will, usually he's dead when it's read. But after his heart attack, the doctor told Buck that he should take it easy and quit the stress of running Buchanan Construction. Since Junior had been overseeing the day-to-day operations for quite some time, it became a simple matter. Buck sold the company to Junior—*sell* being the legal term for what he *gave* his oldest son.

But to be fair, Buck also stipulated that Jessie inherit the old gravel pit since his youngest son had no interest in the concrete and asphalt business. To Junior and everybody else, it seemed like a small matter at the time. What would anyone want with an old pit and a pond?

Yet in the attic of his sensibilities, pokerfaced Buck Buchanan had set the stage for his Learian drama. He smiled like a gap-toothed banshee at the signing of the treaty—a cry of love echoed in his big Buck heart.

"Do you see that pond?" Buck asked Jess, drawing on a fresh Tiparillo.

Of course he did. Jess reeled in a little more line and waited for his father to continue.

"There's a story behind that pond."

Or, as Buck would soon point out, under it. The last remaining gravel pit on the island—in fact in all the San Juan Islands—lay right beneath their feet.

After listening to what his father had to say, Jess raised his eyes to the heavens and asked himself the question he now feared the most.

Whose pond was it now?

Chapter 2

It was a good thing his dad had declined that cup of coffee. Jess opened the camper door to find his long-lost love, BB Gunderson, spread naked on the bunk bed, her sweet muffin pointed at anyone who may have entered.

"Gimme that pole," she said.

Homecomings are sweet, where nerves explode, and passion and vulnerability run amok. On top, Jess straddled BB's legs, and BB caught his tears in her mouth.

"I've missed you *so much*," he said.

She rolled him over and cupped his face in her hands.

"You're a big baby for thinking I was gone for good. LA's a nice place to visit but I wouldn't want to live there. People are strange, you know that? When you're *straaaaange!*"

BB brushed the dark brown hair from his eyes and looked at him, putting her nose right up to his.

"Look at me, baby, I'm home. For good this time. I promise."

Jess wanted to believe it. Tried hard to believe it. But something in the back of his mind prevented him from fully enjoying her new outlook on love.

But did it matter? BB was on top of him now, and he was more than willing to take advantage of her—again.

As darkness settled, they walked down Old Pit Road singing duets in the quarter moonlight. BB crept neatly inside his voice, weaving in and out, harmonizing with it. Sometimes she took the lead and he tried to harmonize with her. On either side of the road the Douglas fir stood tall, a respectful audience.

Another song, her lead. It was another unfamiliar tune that Jess couldn't follow, and BB taught it to him. At the mini mart entrance the song ended on a harmony that made them both shiver. BB bought the spaghetti and mushrooms. He bought the tomato sauce and beer.

On the walk back to the camper, he admired her tan against her light blue UCLA sweatshirt, a not-so-gentle reminder of her life without him. He wouldn't ask questions; the answers would only hurt.

After dinner, they went skinny-dipping in the pond and froze their asses off. Later, while lying in the bunk, he looked up to the camper ceiling a foot away from his nose and thought—*Jesus, another day like this could kill me.*

The next morning, Jess opened his eyes to find Junior reading the *Seattle PI* sports page at the camper table. Junior was a big man, six feet two and well over three hundred pounds, but fifteen years past his prime as a defensive tackle in college. Time had melted much of the muscle mass. The table's edge caught him at mid-torso like the line of demarcation between the Battle of the Bulge.

"Who won?" Jess asked, in a hoarse whisper.

They had spent many years together at the same breakfast table and he had asked that question a million times. Junior looked up slowly.

"Talk says you did."

Junior was obviously ticked off and Jess wanted no part of it. Junior was nobody to mess with when he was angry, especially at this time of the morning. Jess jumped down from the bunk and headed for the door, stark naked.

"I gotta piss."

Jess ran barefoot across the gravel to the old job shack. Inside, there was a sink, a shower, and a toilet. Jess imagined himself a dog and took his sweet time delivering. It was a great piss, a minute of piss with the head intact.

Jess understood why his brother was mad, but he really couldn't process it now, not with BB lying in the bunk. He thought maybe he could sweeten Junior's lousy attitude by making him laugh. It was his best deflection tactic, and over the years he'd been pretty good at it. Jess tiptoed back to the camper, thinking of how he could lighten Junior up a little.

"Coffee?" Jess said, as he entered the camper and slipped on his boxers.

Jess looked to BB curled up in the covers, no visible help. He knew she was awake and only pretended to be asleep. She despised Junior and Junior felt the same way about her.

Junior chewed on his lower lip. When his brother chewed on his lower lip, Jess knew he was in no mood for bad coffee.

"C'mon man, leave that lip alone. Life ain't that bad," Jess said.

Junior studied his younger brother. He was a good-looking guy but he needed to clean up his act, cut his hair or something.

"I don't want your shitty coffee," Junior said.

"Wait a minute," Jess asked in mock seriousness. "You walk in here unannounced and bitch about my coffee?" he said, taking the instant coffee out of the fridge. "You ingrate."

Junior tapped his foot on the camper floor. He shook his head as he often did in the company of his younger brother, certain that their life spheres careened in perpetual misalliance. Junior nodded toward the bunk bed.

"Who's the slut?" he asked, knowing full-well who it was.

Jess hoped his brother's remark had fallen on deaf ears. But it was not to be, as BB shot out of the bunk and planted herself stark naked in front of Junior, shaking a vivid middle finger.

"*Fuck you, Junior!*" she screamed.

There's something about a beautiful body when it's angry, Jess observed. The skin draws tight and every muscle seems to strain for attention. BB presented an intimidating figure in that respect; no man could deny that. Her long blonde hair fell to her ample breasts, and all five foot ten inches of her athletic body waited for Junior's reply.

"I gotta go," Junior said, using the newspaper to shield his face.

Junior couldn't look up at her. But BB wanted him to, just so she could shame him if he did.

' We'll talk about this later," he said to Jess.

BB stalked back to the bunk and drowned herself in a sea of covers. Jess followed her because he didn't want his brother there either.

Junior worked hard to extract himself from the slot between the table's edge and the back cushion. Moments later, they heard him leave, breathing heavily— like a miler.

Jess sat on the bench seat across from the fridge and played his guitar. BB asked him to sing her favorite song. He strummed the chords to make sure he could remember them. Luckily, there were only three.

When emotion from a troubled heart
Becomes too much for you
That old emotion
Where heartache falls down in a river
And it's rushing over you
And you're saying

Roll me over tonight
Roll me over tonight
Roll me over in the soft moonlight
Roll me over tonight

After a verse and a chorus, BB got the boo-hoos from a song that was both sad and sweet. She wanted to hug Jess but she knew a hug might lead to something more, and she couldn't take any more of that. The camper windows were open and a warm breeze blew over her naked body.

Listening to Jess sing and play the guitar made her wish that he hadn't given up his music. When the Jess Buchanan Band was hot, it had been an exciting time in their lives. They traveled up and down the coast while Jess was being courted by all the major labels.

But something happened in between, and looking back on it, one could say it was his own fault. Jess was stubborn. If they wanted him to sing somebody else's songs, he wasn't interested. BB argued that it really didn't matter who wrote the song, if he made it popular, no one would care who wrote it. But Jess wouldn't "sell out," as he put it, and one night after a show in Tacoma, he packed up his guitars and announced, "I'm done."

It was the last time he ever played onstage. Now it was a subject he rarely talked about, treating it like some battle-worn vet who refused to relive the memories.

BB looked around the camper and realized she couldn't live there for long. She wanted a house. A nice house. And if Jess sold the old pit, they could afford to buy one. But Jess didn't care enough about money to have any. What he loved most in life was that pond. Growing up, he promised they would live there someday; and now BB thought, okay, under one condition. That they get rid of the camper. *Now.*

After breakfast, **BB** took the baseball gloves down from the cabinet above the sink and stood with her back to the gravel bank holding the catcher's mitt chest high. The first few throws Jess exaggerated, windmill lobs that she caught underhanded. On the next few throws, the arc gradually straightened and she smiled at the first *pop.* Switching to four seams, he turned the ball inside to an imaginary batter, a screwball thrown hard enough to hear the seams whistle with friction against the air. She caught it at an arm's length away, a good save. He nodded and smiled, then motioned across his body. It sent her into a crouch.

The first curve of spring didn't bend much, Jess was careful of the elbow. The second curve he hung badly. He went back to the fastball and aired it out three times in a row—*bang, bang, bang.* The last one left **BB** shaking the sting out of her glove hand.

On the next pitch, Jess spun a wicked curve toward the imaginary plate. The ball hesitated midway on its journey and took a sharp dive. It rebounded off the hard clay and caught BB flush under the chin. Ass over teakettle she went. He stood there in disbelief. She didn't get up. He ran to where she lay and knelt down beside her. Her eyes were closed and she looked dead. Slowly, BB raised her left hand to feel her chin. Dark red blood oozed between her long brown fingers.

'Ball," she said.

On the drive to the Emerald Health Clinic, Jess thought about his bad luck. Chalk it up to sin on the soul, or Mercury in retrograde, or anything remotely resembling it, but a gambling man, a *wise* gambling man, knew that when bad luck was present, he better get up off the table, take five and ride the mutha out, or his butt was crushed.

Ebb and flow. The patterns were irrevocably cut in stone and no man's will could alter it. The pages of history were littered with the unfortunates who had tested the waters and lost. Ignorance had a way of equating strong and weak, rich and poor, wise and unwise. The problem lay in the sensing of it. Like many before him, Jess realized he had been a little slow on the draw. He made a mental note: *Grease the holster.*

The receptionist at the clinic told Jess it might take a while. They had taken BB right in but they needed to take X-rays to determine if her jaw was broken. Jess took the news like a monkey on a string, shoulders all caved in. He felt as helpless as helpless could feel.

The receptionist suggested he take a seat. But Jess couldn't wait in that place they called a waiting room. Instead, he was going down to Bob's for a milkshake. One of Bob's special milkshakes.

It took twenty paces to clear the clinic alcohol from his brain. He sucked, emotions riding roughshod over his frittered nerve endings. He was lousy at little disasters.

The aroma from Bob's kitchen, along with Sunset Bay at low tide, made the coffee shop smell like a hamburger fart inside. Bob kept the door open, citing the heat. He was the big jolly man behind the lunch counter, a man who had known the Buchanan family all his life. Buck owned the building and Bob paid the rent . . . when he could.

Bob greeted Jess like a long-lost son. Lately, Jess hadn't had any money so lunch at Bob's was out of the question. Jess sat down at the counter and ordered the special shake, hoping it was still on the menu. Bob kept a fifth of Crown hidden under the counter and sipped from it all day long. He even gave some to his friends.

Two elderly ladies seated in the back booth spoke loud enough for everybody in the room to hear.

"Buck's son?"

"I believe so,"

"He's a *hippy*!"

"Look at all that hair!"

Jess wanted to say something. He was in no mood for their comments, but Bob caught his eye and shook his head.

"I'll cut it for him," said the one gray-haired lady.

"Not a bad-looking boy either," said the other.

"How can you tell with all that hair?" a man sitting next to them piped up.

Everybody in the coffee shop laughed. A few minutes later the ladies got up and shuffled over to the register. They gave Jess the once-over as they passed by—*harrumph*—and Bob cashed them out. He returned to where Jess sat.

"I'm like you," Bob said, and flipped his favorite silver dollar in the air.

Jess dug out a quarter and flipped it.

"Like hell you are," he said.

Jess left double the amount for his special shake on the countertop.

"Two quarters," Bob said, generously.

Jess waited in the lobby of the clinic, paged through every *Sports Illustrated* in the magazine rack, and he was down to the *Better Homes and Gardens* when Doc came out smiling.

"Good to see you, Jess," he said, offering his hand.

Jess' hand fit snugly inside of Doc's big paw. Doc Long was a bear of a man. At six foot seven, he looked down at everyone.

"Good to see you too, Doc."

But Doc was not the foremost thing on his mind. Jess' thoughts wandered into the glistening clinic corridor, probing the rooms with fevered imagination. A little thing but . . . *Did she die?*

"I saw your dad yesterday. Hawaii does him good," Doc said.

Did she die!

Jess' mind raced on. Blood streamed off a forgotten gurney while an old nurse shrugged and talked of potatoes.

A fuckin' curveball killed my baby!

He would burn the gloves, better yet, he would cut his right arm off at the elbow and raise it to the heavens . . . *"Here, take this!"* The image was not his, but of Kirk Douglas in *The Vikings.*

Then he thought he might be exaggerating a little since it was a slow curve, nothing that could kill anybody.

"I'm sorry," he mumbled, loud enough for Doc to hear.

Doc tried to console him.

"It wasn't your fault. It was just an accident."

Just an accident? It was not *just an accident,* thought Jess. He had simply thrown a nasty curve into the dirt and it had subsequently changed the course of history. He wondered if it would leave a bad scar on BB's beautiful face.

Right then the door to the hallway opened and the nurse appeared, much younger than Jess had imagined, leading BB by the hand in a true gesture of compassion. Jess felt like a total shit for thinking she was more concerned about potato's than his girlfriend.

BB's chin was covered by a mass of gauze and tape. When she spotted Jess, she smiled a twelve-stitch smile, a good effort considering.

As they were leaving, Jess stopped at the door and apologized to the nurse.

"I'm sorry," he said.

She had no idea what he was talking about.

"Really, I am," he said.

After the glass door had swung closed behind them, it left the nurse to wonder— *What in the world did he mean by that?*

BB needed a good bed, so Jess pointed her battered red Mustang toward the best bed he could pay for. He knew his parents would be thrilled to see her again. Besides, a little R&R at his mom and dad's seemed to be just the ticket to soothe a couple of injured souls.

BB had taken it like a hero, and now, fumbling for small talk through a swollen jaw, she was getting nothing in return but his guilty silence. It bothered her. Why should he be feeling guilty? She considered herself a pretty tough gal, and what was needed from him was a little manning up, one small gesture of true grit in the face of calamity.

"Stop the car," she said.

Jess looked at her wide-eyed, alarmed by the tone of her voice.

"*Stop the car!*" she repeated, a bit louder.

He did. They sat in silence while BB considered the correct approach.

"Get out."

It was not the approach she wanted and that was obvious, not with Jess getting out of the car like a good soldier. BB had returned from LA wiser in the ways of life, and his sensitive boy act wasn't cutting it with her anymore. He needed to grow up.

"Get back in here!" she ordered.

He slid in behind the wheel, his forehead beet red now. She noticed the difference and thought, *Now we're getting somewhere.*

"I wish you'd stop acting like a baby," she said.

Jess didn't know how to answer that. For what it's worth, he could have killed her, and didn't that account for something?

But Jess couldn't speak his mind because he was moving outside his body again. He drifted up to the car ceiling, leaving the movie guy to sit in the driver's seat. The real Jess looked down at a young man and a floor littered with Styrofoam cups and yellow hamburger wrappers. The movie guy—a young leading man type—drummed his fingers on the dash. Jess never drummed his fingers on the dash.

"What's that stuff on your face?" the movie guy asked BB.

Amazingly, he had touched the right nerve.

' It's a pimple," she replied, batting her eyes at him.

' That's a pretty big pimple," the movie guy said, putting the car in gear.

"It's a *mahhty bahg pahmple,*" she repeated in her best Southern drawl, an over-the-top imitation of Scarlett O'Hara.

The movie guy took this as his cue to drive away like they do in the movies—with a little chivalry.

The best thing about home was the smell of it. Jess sat in the leather rocker next to the large picture window and held part of the living room drape to his nose. He looked out over the golf course. Cars skittered across the great green lawn like hungry bugs on a filthy floor. Nobody walked anymore. It made him sad.

Not fifty feet from where he sat, Jim Calhoun three-putted the thirteenth green. It was nothing unusual since Jim couldn't putt to save his ass, yet he threw his putter toward the fourteenth tee and stomped off the green. His behavior reminded Jess that some people had no right to play the Gentleman's Game.

Jess recalled a time when life was one simple grandiose projection of himself striding up the eighteenth fairway at Augusta needing a one-putt to win the Masters. Dusk was a time for dreams, and Jess practiced that putt for years. But Jess never made it. His dream to play professionally. He knew his inconsistency would eventually do him in, and it read like the highway map of his soul.

The golf game was a dollar Nassau, two down-press automatic, double on sandies and birdies, and Buck had the shanks. The toll was adding up. He made the turn sixteen units down on a warm spring day feeling like hell in a dry spell. He drew a six iron at the par three, thirteenth tee. His home sat just off to the right of the green.

The nature of the shanks had him thinking about the out of bounds. The nature of his playing partners had him thinking about his house.

"Do you have insurance on those windows?" asked Leo, as Buck addressed the ball.

"Never been broke," he answered, and it wasn't a lie.

"First time for everything," Marv reminded him.

But Buck was lost in his swing preparation, hooding the clubhead so severely that the possibility of a shank to the right was nearly out of the question. Yet that is the nature of the shanks. They have yet to be understood.

Whack!

The ball began its trajectory dead right, slicing impossibly right upon right, careening toward the house, then the upper deck, then . . . *Crash!* . . . through one of the large living room windows, where glass rained down upon Jess in the rocker as he read *the Sporting News.*

Buck got mad. Not at a window that could get fixed, but at a ball that had no business going right when he had done everything possible to prevent it. Through clenched teeth he whispered the dirtiest of all expletives, the one he reserved only for himself in times when he truly deserved it.

Leo drooled on himself, he laughed so hard. Marv fell backward on the ground and held his stomach, he was laughing so hard. Buck leaned on his six iron and replayed the impossibility of his misguided shot. He hadn't considered that someone may have been sitting in the rocker next to the large window. Marie was out all day running errands.

At the sound, BB raced upstairs to find Jess covered in shattered glass, the rocker toppled over, an open magazine resting on his face like the white sheet.

She carefully removed the magazine.

"Baby?" she said, peeking under it, her breath tickling his brow. "Are you alright?"

Jess didn't answer, or couldn't answer, as he lay there dazed and confused. Blood oozed from his cheek, and BB ran out to the deck to call for help. She spotted Buck on the thirteenth tee.

"*Buck!*" she cried.

Buck had teed up a second ball and was about to hit it when they heard the scream. He looked up and saw **BB** on the top deck. He had to ask himself, *What in the world is she doing there? And what's that stuff on her face?*

"*BUUUCK!*" she cried again.

It was a blood-curdling scream that defied explanation. Buck had broken the window. So what?

"*Jess . . . rocker . . . glass!*" the three men heard from a distance.

She needn't say more. All three men took off on a dead sprint, not one taking time to jump in a cart.

They were quite a pair sitting there in their matching face bandages. Buck Owens crooned over the stereo, while Marie shredded itty-bitty chicken slivers so their jaws wouldn't have to work much to get it slid down the gullet.

Jess reflected on this day full of errant balls and recounted the worst of his sins to make sense of his woolly karma. There was the time he screwed Martha Willis in the tenth grade on a picnic table at City Beach. The screw wasn't so bad, but for some reason he never spoke to her again. Thinking back on it now, the silence, and not the screw, was the real sin.

Then there was the time he cheated in the Junior Club Championship. Though he won by eight shots, the stroke he cheated never quite settled with him. So, considering he hadn't been to mass in several years, considering he had almost killed a man in a barroom brawl, considering all this, he understood why this day was meant for him. A man couldn't carry that much burden around lightly.

But maybe BB was right. He *was* acting childish about this. It was silly to think that God took time to steer balls in mysterious ways.

What Buck had to say over dinner made perfect sense to BB, but she questioned whether Jess would ever sell the old pit. As Buck pointed out, it was simple economics if Jess wanted to play it that way. If he didn't sell the old pit mineral rights, and Junior ran out of rock, the cost of doing business would skyrocket for Junior. Gravel would have to be shipped in, unloaded, and then trucked to the batch plant. Profit margins would shrink considerably.

Buck thought it would take years before Junior would run out of rock in the south town pit, but now it made Junior's position enviable. Junior could easily underbid anybody if he owned the rock. But he didn't, so this made him a desperate man. And price could act very funny in times of desperation, Buck added.

To sell or not to sell was the million-dollar question, and after Buck and Marie went to bed, it left them alone, and BB had something to say. It was time for that heart-to-heart, to finish the conversation she had left behind when she moved to LA.

BB told Jess how she was tired of having nothing. She felt it was time they started to plan for the future, and the future for her didn't include living in a camper in an old gravel pit. She understood the way he felt about the pond since they had practically grown up there. But that was then. Now it was 1988 and they were both twenty-eight. In her opinion it was time to get real.

BB studied Jess' face as she spoke. If he sold the old pit mineral rights, she saw it as an opportunity to start life in a way that a young couple could only dream about. Otherwise, it might take years for them to save enough to buy a house. She wanted him to understand her point of view, to see that what she said made sense.

But he couldn't do that.

Instead, when she finished, he simply got up from the table and went to his bedroom after saying goodnight.

It left BB to wonder: *Was it a mistake to come back? Was it a mistake to think he may have changed his stubborn ways?*

She would let Jess sleep on it, and then tomorrow, after his meeting with Junior, she would realize the measure of a man, her man, and where she fit in his plans.

Chapter 3

At Billy Wilson's Dockside Café, Junior waited at the center table in front of the large view windows with the realization that the economic future of Emerald, Washington pretty much depended on Jess. A helluva thought. Jess was a damn fine singer and songwriter, but when it came to the concrete business, he didn't have a clue. It was an advantage Junior felt he needed to press, to talk some sense into the kid.

But he also knew that Jess was nutty about trees, and they'd have to knock down a few acres worth to make room for the runways. Junior remembered the time when Buck took a chainsaw to the blue spruce out in their front yard. Buck cut it down because it had grown so big and bushy, nobody could see the golf course from the living room windows. When Jess came home from school and saw what had happened, he acted like his dad had just murdered his best friend.

Jess sat on the stump in silent protest for a whole week, a fourth-grader's view of the world. Finally, Junior took matters into his own hands and fired the football at his brother's head from twenty feet away, just to get his attention. Even then, at point blank, two tiny hands would catch the football easily. Jess was gifted in that respect. He was a college wide-receiver.

"What're you moping about?" Junior remembered asking Jessie.

"Dad cut down the tree."

"So?"

"It was living."

"So what?" said Junior.

"It's not living now. Dad hacked it."

Again, Junior threw the football at Jessie's head, but this time he didn't see it coming. The point of the football caught him flush on the temple and the force knocked him off the stump and onto the grass. Junior thought he'd killed him. When he turned Jessie over, a deep blue welt had begun to form on the side of his head, and Junior recalled feeling that helpless feeling, when one's whole world gets altered in a moment's notice.

Junior didn't know what to do. So he did nothing.

Slowly, Jessie recovered enough to stumble inside the house. At the sight, Marie was so shocked to see the condition of Jessie's head that she never asked how it happened. And Jessie must have never told, at least Junior never caught hell for it.

A waitress appeared at the table. Junior ordered another cup of coffee and then rehearsed what he would have to say to his brother. Without that rock, Junior would be like any other contractor forced to snip gravel to the island.

He glanced around the room at the men whose lives hung in the balance. There were forty-three big hummers in his immediate employ, plus all the subs that would get work thrown their way. Each man seated in the restaurant had his own reason for why Jess needed to sell that rock, and Junior had a bad feeling about what could happen if his brother continued to entertain those wild ideas about trees and ponds and old gravel pits.

It was a great buy, the kind of buy that could change an attitude in a blink—leopard-skin deck shoes, $4.99 at Save Mart. Imitation leopard perhaps, but it's not how good you look, it's how good you feel. And Jess was feeling good from his vantage point, six feet above the tiger glides.

Emerald bustled under a gray sky. Dark clouds had tourists scurrying to beat the rain. Jess walked down Main Street on his way to the Dockside for a bowl of steaming mussels on Junior. In the back of his brain, Earl "Fatha" Hines tickled the ivories, *Live at the Hangover Club,* and his stride bounced to the beat of the music.

Jess rounded the corner and spotted maybe fifty pickups in the parking lot, all facing nose first at the Dockside entrance. The trucks looked like a school of sharks waiting for a feeding.

Inside, side bets flew around the dining room; two to one Junior closes the deal by 12:30, eight to five by 1:00. It wasn't a question of *if* the kid would sell but *when*. Only two men inside the room doubted the outcome: Junior and Billy. The other men didn't know Jess like they did.

The dining room hadn't seen this kind of commotion in a long time. White-shirted waiters and waitresses glanced at each other not knowing what to make of it. Billy made the rounds, talking and joking with everyone. He seemed to be enjoying himself, an easy thing to do because he was making money.

At 12:07, the gathering noted Jess' arrival. He was seven minutes late, so the bets were adjusted accordingly, and even then more bets were made on the adjustment. The hostess led him to the center table next to the eight-foot windows that overlooked the Emerald marina and Sunset Bay. Junior looked up from the menu as Jess sat down.

"Do you want to go somewhere else?" Junior asked.

Jess glanced around the room at a host of familiar faces. Most of the guys seated at the tables were Buchanan Construction guys, the Brotherhood, guys that he had worked with in the summers. And sitting with the Brotherhood guys were all their construction buddies, carpenters and plumbers and heavy equipment operators, and even some guys who didn't have skin in the game but wanted to get in on the action. Jess nodded and smiled at the group seated at the next table over.

"They don't bother me," he lied.

Junior put his elbows on the table to get a closer look at his brother's bandaged face.

"Your face doesn't look so hot."

"Thanks," Jess said.

Jess picked up the menu and Junior leaned back in his chair to study his brother. It was important to understand the way an adversary's mind worked, the feeling-out process. But in this respect,

Junior realized he was at a considerable disadvantage. As far as he was concerned, the kid was out to lunch.

"The rib eye's good. Put some meat on your bones," he said.

Jess made a mental note, *Don't let him order you around.*

The waitress stood next to the table, speechless. Billy told her not to get in the way; no talking to the men, just limit the service to a quick in and out without saying a word. It was the waitress' nightmare. She looked at Jess to take his order, not knowing if she should say something, and he made it easy for her.

"I'll have the mussels," he said. "And a Coke."

"You're too skinny for mussels," Junior growled.

"You're too fat for steak," Jess shot back.

Naturally, Junior ordered the rib eye, rare.

The waitress walked away unsure if she should put the order in right away because it looked like the meeting could take a while. She asked the manager, and he didn't know either. They didn't dare ask Billy because he would have laughed at them. She put the order in, and she guessed right.

The gathering held their collective breath, 12:18 and counting, pocketbooks riveted on Junior's next move. Here, brothers measured each other Buchanan to Buchanan, with nothing in between but a history of insoluble blood chemistry.

A row of beach cottages flew by at forty-five as Buck had the Lincoln out for a drive along West Beach Road. He glanced at the clock, 12:21. An old Hank Williams tune played a mournful accompaniment as he wondered about his plan, partitioning the legacy equally among the boys. It remained to be seen what they had learned. But that was also something Buck was concerned about. Maybe one had learned more than the other. He was concerned for the littlest pup.

The gathering watched in approval now as Junior, nose to nose with Jess, talked the tough talk. The point being that if Jess didn't sell the gravel to Junior, and the bid went to an outside contractor, the Emerald economy might never recover.

In a sweeping gesture, Junior pointed out all the men who could stand to lose their jobs. Junior's comments were so full of half-truths that Jess quit listening and turned his attention to the marina outside. Junior aimed a bullet at his brother's waning attention.

"Now think of that, *punk*."

Here, Jess stood up from the table and leaned over on leopard skin tippy toes, placing his nose inches away from Junior's.

"Small change, Fatso," Jess whispered.

Jess felt it might be a good time to leave, but then he noticed the waitress approaching with the steaming Penn Cove mussels in a large purple bowl. He sat back down. Jess was determined not to let Junior spoil a good bowl of mussels, especially since they were on him.

Billy saw the look on Jess' face from across the room and recognized it for what it was. Growing up together, he had seen that look a thousand times, and it was something to reckon with. At the last minute, he seized an opportunity to make bets across the floor. He bet that Junior couldn't close the deal by one o'clock, and everyone took him up on it.

The gathering figured Billy was an easy mark since Jess and Billy were best friends, so Billy played the part. Capitalizing on another man's ignorance was a way of life for a good businessman, and Billy rarely saw some of these less-than-gentlemen in his restaurant. They wouldn't be caught dead patronizing a place owned by a black man. But he took it all in stride since his public persona couldn't afford his private feelings. It would have been bad for business.

Junior shifted in his seat and adopted another approach. There was a certain honor among the Buchanan family, a commitment passed on from Big Al to Buck and now to his sons, a responsibility to uphold the family name by donating things, buildings like the library and city hall and the health clinic, and the post office, the most essential buildings in Emerald.

In return, since Buchanan Construction had laid every road, poured every sidewalk and curb, and all of it done with local tax dollars, Big Al and Buck figured it was their duty, or their *responsibility*, to give back to the community. In a big way.

Big Al had built the library and city hall, and Buck had built the new health clinic, the post office, and the little league ball fields. And Junior continued the program started by Buck where Buchanan Construction handed out full scholarships every year to four graduating Emerald High School seniors based on merit and character. Junior also provided full college or vocational scholarships for all the sons and daughters of his employees. *Now*, in Junior's mind, looking at Jess, he wondered, *what have you done?*

"Grandpa Al, do you think he'd want you to keep that rock all for yourself? What in the hell is the pond good for besides catching a few fish? The only person I see using it is you. How selfish is that?"

A good point. A fair point. But Jess had other plans for the pond that didn't necessarily imply selfish motives. He opened another purple shell and dipped the mussel in butter.

"You can use it too. Plenty of fish for everyone."

His reply caught Junior with a mouthful of beef. The big man almost choked on it.

"That's not the point," Junior said, wiping his mouth.

"Then what's the point?" Jess asked, smiling at him. "Why are we here?"

Figuratively, Junior threw up his hands. He had just spent the last five minutes making the point, and if Jess didn't get it, then what was he supposed to do? He tapped the table with his forefinger, "*The point is* . . . you've got the rock. I *need* the rock. We *all* need the rock."

Then he reminded Jess of another particularly important point.

"And you need the money!"

True, thought Jess. He needed some. Just not a lot.

Junior wasn't sure where all this was headed, but he kept talking so he wouldn't lose Jess' attention—an easy thing to do.

"Don't you get it? Dad's trying to take care of you. And I'm glad he is because I won't. There's gonna come a time when your five hundred bucks a month, your *gift* from Grandpa Al, won't cut it anymore. Then what are you gonna do? You got no car. You live in a camper for crissakes!"

Evidently there was something out in the marina that was more important than what Junior had to say, so Junior threw another salvo at his younger brother's wandering attention. But this one was aimed below the belt.

"You know, if Dad didn't take care of you, nobody would. You can forget the handouts, you bum. You're not gonna get another dime out of me."

The dining room was caught up in Junior's heated gestures and only now did they realize that it was a minute past one o'clock. Time had run out on everybody except for Billy. A new round of bets were made as the men roamed the tables in lively discussion. They jotted down wagers on notepads and napkins, some on the backs of their hands.

Billy decided it would be a good time to say hello and walked over to the table.

"Hey, Junior, hey bro," he said, offering his hand to Junior.

Billy had good timing because Jess was just about to inform his brother of what he could do with his sell-or-else attitude.

"How you doing, Billy?" Junior said, shaking his hand. "That was a damn fine rib eye."

"As always?"

"As always," Junior said, smiling up at him.

Junior liked Billy because he respected his position in life. Billy turned to Jess, who figured he'd better fire them down before he told Junior to go fuck himself.

"You know, bro, we do have other things on the menu besides mussels."

"Tell him, Billy. He won't listen to me."

"I like the mussels," Jess said, without looking up.

"No shit," Billy said. "So what's up with your face?"

"Long story," Jess said.

Jess gave him a look that said, "We'll talk about this later." Billy understood, and he walked on since there were many more tables he needed to greet.

'Gentlemen, have a nice lunch. This one's on me," Billy said, walking away.

Jess figured it was the least Billy could do since he was making a bundle on the sideshow. But before Billy could walk out of earshot, Jess piped up.

"BB's back."

The announcement caught Billy by surprise. He turned around and looked at Jess.

"I thought she'd never be back."

"Things changed, I guess," Jess said, shrugging his shoulders.

"Interesting," Billy said, shaking his head.

"Yup," Jess said, shelling another mussel.

Here, the memory of the night she left town came back to haunt Jess. They had argued all night, and she suddenly sprung it on him as she dropped him off at the house.

"I'm leaving," she said.

Jess didn't know what she meant. She was leaving . . . ?

"Town. Right now. Get out of the car. I gotta go."

"Where's this coming from?" he asked.

"I've been thinking about it for a while," she said.

"Well thanks for the warning."

'I didn't know it was gonna be tonight. But it is. Get out."

Jess knew the answer to his next question. Man, he was really gonna miss her.

'Do you want me to come with you?" he asked, taking a stab at it.

'Nope."

"No right now, or no never?" he asked.

"Never," she said, staring blankly out the windshield.

There was a pause between them, perhaps mutual thoughts of how their relationship was ending on such a rotten note. They were leaving a lifelong relationship behind.

"What are you gonna do in LA?" Jess asked.

"Whatever I want."

"So I'm holding you back?"

"I gotta go," she said.

Out of habit, BB leaned over to kiss him goodbye. But he pulled away, not quite sure of what this was.

"Goodbye then," BB said bluntly.

Jess thought it was too late to be leaving.

"Don't leave tonight, leave tomorrow," he said. "Give yourself some time to think about it."

"Are you shitting me?" BB asked him. "Now you're telling me how to leave?"

Jess didn't think of it that way. But she did have a point.

"So this is it?" Jess asked, not quite understanding what was happening.

She nodded her head. He got out of the car and held the door open.

"What are you gonna tell Pop?"

She knew her father was going to be disappointed, but he'd get over it.

"I'll tell him the truth. I hate this place."

This was news to Jess. She had never mentioned it before, how she disliked Emerald. But to hate Emerald was to hate a postcard, and the thousands of tourists that it attracted every year was proof. Did she hate the people who lived there, people like him?

"I'll miss you," he said.

BB wasn't about to let him interfere with what she was about to do.

"Shut the door," she said. "I gotta go."

He glanced at the time on the dash. He knew if BB hustled she could make the last ferry. He wanted to say something more, but what was there to say? So he shut the door.

BB whirled the Mustang around and hightailed it back to Pop's, where another scene took place, similar to the one with Jess. Jesus, she thought, why was it so hard for the men in her life to understand that she simply had to leave?

Billy and Jess' conversation had given Junior time to plot his next move. He had tried reason and a little intimidation, so what was left now to beg? Junior quickly dismissed that thought since begging didn't quite fit his negotiating stance. Besides, he didn't even know if he could get down on his knees anymore since his knees were so shot to hell.

In negotiations, it was important to know what the other guy wanted, so Junior asked Jess straight out.

"So, what do you want?"

"I don't want anything," said Jess, digging at his final mussel.

And that was precisely Junior's problem. How could he negotiate with someone who didn't want anything?

'C'mon, man, you gotta want something. Think of something that you really, really want. One thing."

'Okay," said Jess. "I want my dog back."

This was news to Junior.

"Where's Legs?"

"Gone. Almost a week."

"Have you asked around?"

"Nobody's seen him."

Junior thought for a moment. It was a stab in the dark.

"If I find him, will you sell me that rock?"

Jess bore his steely blue eyes into Junior's.

"If you find him and don't give him back, I'll kill you."

Junior was never one to back down from a threat, implied or otherwise. Especially one coming from his brother.

"If you don't sell me that rock, killing will be the least thing I'll do to you," he said.

In order to prevent an all-out brawl from breaking out in Billy's restaurant, Jess pushed his chair back and simply and quite assertively walked out of the restaurant. He did this knowing that he didn't have money for bail if he started a fight.

The results were mixed around the room. Some men won and some men lost. But no one lost as much as Junior, who sat at the table twirling his coffee spoon between his fingers. He glanced out the windows in time to see Jess walk down the ramp. Junior knew that Jess couldn't possibly know what he knew . . . that this situation created by their father may have ended the feeling of family as they once knew it.

Jess had suffered a lifelong negative stage presence in front of Junior's audience, and the elation that now settled over him in his samurai hour set him to whistling at slip 138 as he watched two young boys drop a hook loaded with bacon fat down through a crack in the marina decking. A sign above them read, No Fishing. Silently, Jess celebrated their gall.

The boys' noses were pushed to the deck looking through a small hole in the planks to watch schools of perch swimming beneath the dock. One of the boys lowered the hook down through the hole and they waited. Soon, the line tightened around his small finger and he fell back, tugging at it. Up through the crack appeared the mouth of a startled fat perch. The hole couldn't possibly accommodate its girth and the fish's eyes bulged in surprise. The boy who didn't have a hold of the line got up and stomped it back down through the hole. The other took a knife and cut the line, severing their alliance.

Jess continued down the dock and at slip 143 he walked past a nice-looking, thirty-something woman sunning herself in the back of a yacht.

"I like your shoes," she shouted up to him.

Amanda Hunt reclined in the stern of a sixty-four-foot Bertram cruiser and acted like she wanted to talk. Jess would oblige any beautiful woman who wanted to talk, so he turned on his heels.

"Thanks. Save Mart, four ninety-nine," he said proudly.

She was nice-looking alright. Her long auburn hair fell to her shoulders and she wore a hooded gray sweatshirt with *Duke Law* written across her chest. She smiled up at him.

"Good for you, tiger."

Tiger?

He smiled at the thought, *Would he dare?*

In the distance a fire truck blew its horn, sirens wailed, and traffic came to a standstill on Main Street. Amanda introduced herself and asked Jess if he would like to come aboard for a drink. He had a little time to kill, but killing time with a beautiful woman was not like killing time at all. So yeah, he'd have this drink and then he'd go back to face BB. He would have to pay for his unwillingness to negotiate with Junior, and he wondered if she would leave him again over it. Then he thought, if she did, at least he'd know how to handle it this time.

Notes from a '72 gold-top Gibson guitar driven through a Marshall stack soared mightily over the Buchanan driveway, startling Marie, who climbed from her Cadillac Seville wondering why her youngest son was back from town so soon. A note high on the guitar neck was held for a whole note, then reverberations echoed from the back pick, followed by that old Clapton signature riff, "Layla," for which a fifty-eight-year-old God-fearing woman couldn't distinguish from a skill saw.

Marie was happy to hear him playing again. Jess' guitars had sat neglected in his old bedroom ever since he quit the band. Marie took a moment to collect her thoughts before she entered the room. She would try not to sound too intrusive with her questions about how the meeting went with Junior, but curiosity is a mother's right, or so she concluded as another sad note rang loud over the neighborhood. Marie used this as her cue to enter.

She opened the door and what she saw she hadn't expected to see. BB cradled the note tenderly with her back to the door, her face pointed skyward in a heartfelt grimace. BB sensed something from behind and peeked over her shoulder. A surprised Marie witnessed tears streaming down her bronzed BB cheeks.

Marie is pure.

Marie took a tissue and wiped tears that BB couldn't explain, how things never change. Perhaps better days ahead, one might say if semantics were to enter into it. But of course, there was no need for semantics with souls like Marie Buchanan around to fetch brass rings from dharma merry-go-rounds.

They had killed a whole pitcher of hundred-proof cowboy juice and things were moving fast. The music had gotten louder and so had their voices. Amanda and Jess danced in the middle of the yacht's stateroom and were having a mighty fine time of it when the song ended.

"Your pick," she said.

He flipped through her collection of CDs, a step up from cassettes. This was a Friday afternoon, a good excuse to play a blast from the past when life was good and the music better. Amanda showed him how to load the CD in the changer, and then—

Bam! "In the white room, at the station . . ."

He was up in the middle of the room flailing at an air guitar as he rode that Cream progression in a time when Cream meant nothing more than the stuff that rises to the top of some farmer's milk bucket. Amanda joined in at the chorus and filled in words he had never bothered to learn. But his focus had turned to matters other than lyrics.

Boy, did she have a nice ass. A fine ass is a fine ass, and has been for centuries, especially when it's wiggled in your general proximity. Between songs, he communicated this flattery.

"You've got a sweet ass," he said.

Slaaaap!

Jess found himself flat-assed to cruiser fiberglass thinking perhaps he had chosen the wrong words to communicate his flattery. Embarrassed, Amanda fled to her bedroom again, wondering why she was acting like such a bitch.

It was a perfect note to exit upon, but a dark sky offered up a thunderous downpour that discouraged any departure for a man dressed in light cotton. Jess could hear the heavy raindrops hitting the boards of the dock in steady rhythm.

He decided after the rain stopped that he would run from this strange Amanda Hunt, away from her slippery angst and the drama it generated. She was drunk and so was he. He had meant to celebrate since Fridays were good for that, but here in this happy hour gone haywire, his only thought was to get the hell out, weather permitting.

Amanda felt guilty for thinking shameful thoughts about the brother of her ex-boyfriend, but Junior had made it clear where things stood between them. So where was the guilt? It wasn't like she wanted to hurt him. She had met his brother quite by accident. It made perfect sense to her while she was drunk. She put on more lipstick and resolved to do better as far as this Buchanan was concerned, since this one was so damned good-looking.

Amanda entered the stateroom wearing a sheepish grin and little else. She apologized to Jess for slapping his good cheek and promised not to do it again. Her manner had completely changed and Jess was confused. She brought over the pitcher of cowboy juice to refill his cup and said, "I promise not to spill."

What was not needed was more of that cowboy juice. Jess retracted his cup just as she was about to pour, and it spilled down his crotch like piss in reverse. Mortified, Amanda hurried off to the bedroom for a towel and reappeared with a hair dryer. Her intentions may have been noble indeed, but Jess felt a little uncomfortable with a strange woman about to blow his balls dry.

"It's okay, really," he said.

He caught her arm just as she made ready for the plunge. A silly thing, a little thing, in better times qualified by a sober mind. But this wasn't one of those times, and Amanda stood back, eyeing him cooly.

"Okay, have it your way," she said, and left the room again.

Jess realized he had a penchant for pissing off pretty women lately, a habit he couldn't afford to abuse. He toweled off the sofa and the floor and the music ended, filling the room with an unbearable silence. His thoughts were becoming crystallized again, a good sign that some of that cowboy juice was wearing off. He thought of Amanda's situation. Here she was, this beautiful woman cruising the San Juan Islands alone.

Alone?

He assumed she was. But the notion that she *might not be* suddenly occurred to him. Who was he to assume anything in this strange place with this strange woman who, for all intents and purposes, could be involved with some badass who certainly wouldn't tolerate his presence on his boat with his girl.

Jess was a terrible liar but making up excuses fast. He had come aboard for one simple reason—the lady had offered him a drink. Innocent enough. But he also understood that innocence waxes thin amid crimes of passion. The other guy still gets blasted in the end.

And night was falling, along with the rain.

Amanda entered the stateroom with even less clothing on this time—a tiny silk black teddy, suggesting another dramatic mood change. Jess could hardly keep up with the shifting winds of her emotions. If indeed there was a husband or a boyfriend involved, if indeed there was some other man, well, he figured that a woman doesn't wear a tiny silk teddy without a purpose.

Amanda chose another CD and Nat King Cole filled the room. She poured two brandies and Jess peeked at her ring finger. He noticed it was bare. Amanda sat down next to him on the sofa and tacked a naked heel against her secret place.

"Pity, the rain," she said, as she looked out at the windows covered with raindrops.

It must be said that the thought of leaving still ran hot with Jess. But he could sometimes play the fool when confronted by an attractive woman like Amanda. To reckon with someone like her was an invitation to a love wreck. She played a game he wasn't familiar with, few men are, but some men caught in this circumstance choose to meet it head-on. Call it stubborn pride, or manly foolishness, call it what you will, but in the end some men submit themselves to such reckless consequences. Otherwise, women like Amanda simply wouldn't exist.

"Are you alone?" he asked.

Amanda threw her head back and laughed.

"You don't think—"

Jess interrupted, "Yes, I do think. In fact, I think quite a bit. I think that at any moment some guy could walk in and it wouldn't look good."

"What does it look like?" she asked, driving at something other than cute rhetoric. "Are you interested?"

She placed her tongue on the roof of her mouth, a beautiful mouth, he noted. She caught him looking.

"So you *are* interested."

He glanced at the door.

"If you're involved with another man, I need to know right now."

She traced the rim of her snifter with her finger.

"You needn't be afraid," she said.

"It's not a question of being afraid," he said. "I hate scenes."

Amanda looked up and brushed his good cheek with the back of her hand.

"The men I know couldn't give a damn," she said.

"Men?" he asked.

She shrugged.

"Man, men, what's the difference?"

Jess looked at her profile. She was even more beautiful from the side.

"If it's sheer numbers we're talking about, it's the difference between me and a fuckin' army."

Amanda threw her head back and laughed and then reached into the drawer for another CD, Junior's favorite. Jess recognized it immediately, Tower of Power. He loved this album.

"*You're still a young man, baaaby . . . Don't waste your time.*"

Jess studied Amanda. The picture had changed from haughty and aloof to one of pitiable loneliness. Amend that. He couldn't find her pitiable because he was just three days removed from that same condition. He caught her hand as she walked by.

"I don't mean to pry."

She sat next to him and leveled a breast at his elbow.

"So you want a guarantee?"

"Something like that."

She put her arm around his neck and whispered in his ear.

"I know one man in this town. One notoriously preoccupied man. He won't bother us. Not tonight."

She kissed his cheek just above the bandage.

"I can't stay long," he said.

"We'll see about that," she said, kissing his other cheek, the good one this time.

Lenny Pickett continued his saxophone brilliance as the vaunted Tower of Power horn section led them sensually into that good bay night. Love ran hot inside the floating bedroom and the strangers met it in a passionate fury of anxiousness. Each took turns pleasing each other, and it wasn't long before they both felt spent and completed.

Jess was late getting in and BB entered his bedroom. She closed the door and sat just inside the doorway.

"You didn't call."

"No, I didn't."

"You were with someone."

"Unfair question, BB."

"It wasn't a question. It was a statement."

She could smell perfume on him as he unbuttoned his shirt.

"Was she someone I know?"

The possibilities churned inside her. They had argued this morning. But why this?

"No," he said flatly. "It wasn't anyone you know."

Jess had answered the question frankly, too frank for BB, who crumpled up on the carpet, sobbing.

"Let's not get dramatic," Jess said, without an ounce of feeling left after a long day of drama. His nerves were so shot to hell that he couldn't help it. BB had suddenly left him flat six months ago, what did she expect? On his way to brush his teeth, he stepped over her as she lay on the floor.

"Goodnight," he said.

Chapter 4

Gone. Long gone.

The absent Mustang gave Jess the impression that BB wasn't coming to breakfast. Hangovers and remorse are not pleasant company. They waged an ugly battle inside his head all day long.

That afternoon, as he rode his bike into town, Jess wondered about dogs and women. Maybe they had this one period in their lives where they needed to wander. Maybe BB and Legs had hooked up and were out discovering the world together—*A Girl and Her Dog.* He wasn't thinking of a *Lassie Come Home* treatment either. The bitches were hot, hot, hot! They made epics about ugly people and dressed them up like some Greta Garbo or Cary Grant. Jess figured they would have to do that for Legs since he wasn't much to look at.

Jess imagined what he would do if he saw Legs at the end of someone's leash, say, walking down Main Street on a fine spring day like today. Would he kill the guy? Maybe it wasn't a guy, maybe it was a girl, or a lady—tall, dressed to the nines. What would he do then?

Jess thought about how well the dates connected. How some people in this town may have known the truth about the old pit before he did. He would have to ask Junior about that, who knew what and when. Junior would tell him the truth. Junior wasn't a liar.

Jess was clipping along Old Pit Road at a good pace when a car passed him and then slowed down about a hundred feet ahead of him. He didn't recognize it from behind. It was a piece of shit, but a lot of people he knew drove pieces of shit. When the car started to back up, Jess got concerned. A few weeks ago he wouldn't have given it another thought. He saw two guys seated in the back with just the driver up front. Nobody he knew rode that way. Something was very wrong here and he steered the bike to the side of the road.

One of the guys in the backseat jumped out with a rifle. Jess shucked the bike and dove into the woods on a dead sprint. A shot rang out.

A fucking shot!

Someone had just taken a shot at him and this was getting ridiculous. Jess ran through the woods as fast as he could, and then when he got to where he knew no one was gaining on him, he dove behind a large cedar log. He held his breath so he could listen, and he heard nothing. He lay back down and thought about his next move.

He couldn't ride his bike anymore without risking his life. He would have to buy a car because someone had just taken a shot at him. But maybe it was a coincidence? Some thugs were out for a joyride, saw him get scared, and decided to take a shot at him.

No, on second thought, Jess couldn't blame that kind of shot-making on any kind of serendipity. It definitely looked deliberate to him. For all he knew, they could have been on their way to his camper door. Somebody was responsible for this and Jess had his suspicions. He made a mental note: *Somebody out there doesn't like me.*

BB was in the throes of another life crisis when Billy pulled alongside at a traffic light on Hillside Drive. She glanced sideways and honked to draw his attention. Another minute and they were pulled off to the side of the road, saying hello.

"I heard you were back. Why?"

"I hate LA."

"That's not what you said a few months ago."

He smiled. They had hooked up one night when he was in LA on business. But neither of them felt very good about it, so that's where they left it. He looked at the bandage on her chin.

"Jesus, you look as bad as he does."

He realized something was wrong once he said it.

"It's over," she said, looking down at the pavement.

"Big news," he said.

"People change," she said. "At least some people do."

They endured an uncomfortable pause together, perhaps to resolve all the what-ifs.

"So," she said, breaking the silence and looking up at him, "how are you?"

He grinned.

"It's a grind, BB. A continual grind."

They had parked on a hill where they could see all of Sunset Bay and all of Main Street. Emerald was a beautiful town, and BB really appreciated her beauty once she came back.

"Lady trouble?" she asked, knowing Billy's history.

"Don't have much time for that," Billy said, looking out over the bay.

She saw a glimmer of hope in her otherwise shitty situation. *Did she dare?*

"Why not make time?" she said.

There. There was no mistaking it. Billy was caught off guard. Hadn't they tried this once before?

"I'm looking for a place to stay," she added.

"You're not going home to Pop's?"

Worlds were being realigned with every utterance. BB looked him in the eye.

"I'm a big girl now. I do what I want."

Billy raised his eyebrows.

"Okay, follow me," he said.

Billy was doing well for himself. He had a brand-new house and a hot tub out back. But best of all, BB liked the breakfast nook. The room was encased in thick tempered glass, tinted so nobody could see her at the table drinking coffee in her underwear. It was the kind of room that Jess would have liked. But he wasn't a person to acquire things, nice things, things that you could point to and say, *"That's mine."*

Billy worked hard and made a lot of money. The other men in her life—Jess and her father—never had his drive to make money.

All her dad wanted to do was coach baseball and teach physics. It was something he was good at, but it left her with a desire for more, for what life could be rather than what it had to be. She wondered how her life may have changed if she'd gone to UCLA on that softball scholarship, if she hadn't been riding in Billy's Jeep that day, if Jess hadn't been driving and they hadn't rolled it over on a sand dune near Fort Casey on Whidbey Island.

Memories of high school and her father flooded her senses now. Like the time Johnson and Parker came running into her dad's classroom all excited.

'Pop, physics question," said Johnson.

"It has nothing to do with physics," countered Parker.

They had argued in the teacher's lounge and had come to Pop to settle it.

"It's simple physics," Johnson said.

A few students hung around after class and BB was one of them. She needed to ask her father if she could have the car that night. Johnson was eyeing her boobs while going on about simple physics.

"So it's impossible for a fastball to rise, right?"

Some of the students giggled because Mr. Johnson was so into it. BB caught him staring and he winked.

"Hello, Ms. Gunderson."

Johnson walked the halls like a proud peacock. But BB thought he was a pervert, always flirting with the girls. Pop thought he was bone stupid. Even BB knew the answer to Johnson's question and she was lousy at the laws of motion. She had caught Jess' four-seam fastballs at 90 mph, and if the ball didn't rise, it sure didn't plummet.

Pop looked at the clock and knew his daughter had to go.

"Daughter of mine, can I help you?"

BB said, "I'll wait."

Johnson baited her father, "C'mon, Pop. I'm right, right?"

Mr. Parker had to get to his next class and Pop knew he had to nip this one in the bud. Otherwise, these arguments could last forever.

"No, Mr. Parker is right," Pop said assertively. "Gravity can be circumvented with outside intervention—in this case, the protruding seams on the baseball. Thrown hard enough, the reverse rotation, the backspin, can make the ball rise, like the dimples on a golf ball. Of course, a golf ball will travel at 120 mph or more, but Roger Clemons could hit 100 pretty often with seams much larger than a dimple."

Pop was lying. No fastball could ever rise when pitched. The baseball simply weighed too much. But Pop wasn't about to let Johnson know that.

Mr. Parker said, "You owe me twenty bucks, Johnson."

Mr. Johnson looked at Pop as if he had done him a grave disservice. "That can't be."

"Twenty bucks, Johnson," Parker repeated, leaving the room.

Johnson wasn't about to let it go.

"I've heard different, Pop."

"Fair enough," Pop said, hoping to put an end to it.

Students were gathering around the two teachers and it didn't look good. But Johnson was unrelenting.

"They've done studies on it. They've proven it!" he said, getting red in the face.

Pop wanted Johnson out of there. He was obviously upset and wanted to argue, and it didn't look good in front of the students.

"Whoever did that study," Pop said, "hasn't faced a Roger Clemons fastball."

"And you have?" Johnson asked.

Johnson said it smugly and BB noticed her father getting red ears, a sure sign that he was getting mad.

"I'll go ask Flaherty. He'll know," said Johnson.

Mr. Flaherty was the other physics teacher at Emerald High School. He didn't know a thing about baseball, when Pop had been the single A state coach of the year three times.

"You do that, Mr. Johnson," Pop said, relieved that it was over.

Pop walked away, leaving Johnson to stand in front of the class after the bell had rung. When he realized that the kids were staring at him, Johnson left the classroom in a huff. Pop watched him go, shook his head, and turned his attention to BB.

"Daughter of mine?"

That's what Pop always called her, and BB hated it in school. The way he said it made it sound so pretentious. Pop thought it singled her out from the crowd, like an old-fashioned Indian name. After all, her mother had been one-eighth Nez Pierce.

But BB preferred the nickname Billy had given her in high school—*BB Guuuun*. He said it like an announcer on an action TV show. He repeated it now on his way out the door.

"See you later, BB *Guuuun*."

She would have all day to discover this big house. The thermometer outside read sixty-four degrees at seven-thirty in the morning, so it was going to be one of those rare hot spring days in Emerald. She would lay out and get bronzed, and then she would wear white tonight. Yes, she would bring Billy to his knees in a white summer dress.

Chapter 5

Traffic streamed through the light at the intersection of Hilltop and Main. Jess stood there for what seemed like hours, waiting for the light to change. Right then he decided that Emerald was getting too big. In a town of a little over four thousand people, he had to wait for the light to change before walking across the street. It was ridiculous.

Jess thought maybe it was time to move to the country, way out in the sticks, where he could write and drink all day. He could become an alcoholic like Hemingway but do it alone so he wouldn't hurt anybody. Strike that. It was a horrible thought.

He was moving outside his body again; Jess could feel it.

The movie guy stood on the corner with his head down. The camera eye focused on the furrow of his brow because the man was obviously worried. He was worried about his girl and his dog, and he was also worried that someone might take a shot at him. But this was a busy intersection, so that possibility was fairly remote.

A yellow Jaguar stopped at the corner and Billy Wilson jumped out. It was quite a coincidence because the movie guy really had to talk to Billy too.

"I've been looking for you," Billy said, with one foot in the car and one foot on the street.

"Here I am."

"You need a lift?"

"Not really."

"We need to talk," said Billy.

"Have you seen BB?'

"She's out at the house."

The movie guy figured as much.

"Is she okay?"

"She's fine."

"We're on the outs."

"So I hear."

Then a thought crossed the movie guy's mind, a thought he hadn't thought of until that very moment. *His best friend and his girl?*

"Are you sleeping with her?"

Billy didn't miss a beat.

"I did last night."

The note struck like a truck. The movie guy felt a sinking feeling in his gut.

"She'll cramp your style," the movie guy said.

"I got no style, man," Billy said. "I make it up as I go."

Billy said what he needed to say, and the movie guy shrugged. He had nothing more to say to this man, formerly his best friend. Billy nodded and slapped the roof of the Jag with his open palm and then sped off, leaving the movie guy to wait for another light.

BB wanted a candy bar, not a confrontation. But if you placed one thing before her that she wouldn't want to run into, well, she would run into it. This included Jess, who stood before her now in the candy aisle of the drugstore.

"I just saw Billy," the movie guy said.

BB hoped Jess wasn't there to apologize. She wasn't about to get all wobbly if he gave her one of his standard apologies.

But the movie guy wasn't there to apologize. He had slept with a stranger and she had slept with his best friend. Two different deals in his mind. He drew closer and spoke softly.

"This is probably the last time we'll get to talk for a while. You're hurt and I'm hurt. But we'll always regret it if we don't end it right. You're with Billy. I'm in the gravel pit. We both have what we want. I know you're not a gravel pit kind of girl."

"You're right about that," she interjected, with a bit of smart-ass that she would later regret.

The movie guy was on a roll and he was annoyed that she had cut him off when he was trying to be sincere. He regained his train of thought and continued.

"We've grown apart instead of together. We were together for a long time, so now we'll have to learn to live without each other. We'll always love each other, but maybe it's not the kind of love that we thought. Maybe it's another kind. Let's discover that one, BB."

Looking at them from the camera eye down the aisle, Jess was proud of the movie guy's speech. The script was always downplaying his intelligence, and he was grateful that he had an opportunity to show more depth of character. Or at least, show that he wasn't a complete moron.

But BB had nothing to say in return. The movie guy hesitated, perhaps waiting for her reply, and then he walked out the door, leaving her to stare at the candy bars some more.

She seemed so casual about it. That's what pissed him off the most. She acted like nothing was going to be different. Well, it *was* going to be different, beginning right now on his way to the marina. If Amanda didn't want to be with him, he would leave. If she wanted him to stay, then they'd rock that boat.

In fact, he wanted Amanda to be in the car that just passed by, the one that looked an awfully lot like hers. The blue Mercedes pulled over and screeched to a halt. Amanda rolled down the passenger side window while she waited for Jess to catch up.

"Need a lift?" she asked, leaning over from the driver's side to look up at him. "Where you headed?"

Jess wanted to say something closer to the truth, something like, *"We're headed to Dicksville, baby."* But then he thought it might be a bit bold for her elegant ways.

"We're going back to the boat," he said.

Apparently she didn't mind, because he barely had buckled his seatbelt when he looked up and there they were, at the marina. She put it park and announced, "I normally don't do this kind of thing."

"So what?" he answered.

"I don't want to be your slut," she said, elegantly.

Jess thought that she looked like Grace Kelly with auburn hair. The sunlight through the sunroof shined down, illuminating her green eyes.

"*Slut* is a pretty bold term for this, don't you think?" he said, trying to match her elegance.

He could tell she wasn't convinced, so he elaborated.

"But *slut* is perfectly fine with me. Right now, I need a slut. Or someone who can fuck like a slut. I need to fuck and you're the best person I know for the job. So if you don't wanna fuck, let me know now, so I can go fuck somebody else," he said with a wry smile, letting her know that he was just kidding her.

But Amanda wanted him to fuck him just as bad.

Whoa . . .

When Jess looked out the window and focused on the dock again, the last person he expected to see walking up the marina ramp was Junior. A group of elderly people waited at the top, sure that their presence and the big guy rolling up the planks couldn't possibly accommodate each other side by side.

Junior was a lousy swimmer, so normally he turned down invitations to hang out on boats. The last time Jess saw his brother on a boat, Junior threw a guy overboard for making a snide remark about Buchanan Construction.

But the last thing either Jess or Amanda wanted was to meet up with Junior. Jess told her to sit tight while he got out of the car. He met his brother at the top of the ramp.

"What's up?" Jess asked.

"Nothing much. I was just having a drink," Junior said, looking a little embarrassed.

"The Dockside is up there."

"I was on a boat."

"You hate boats."

"Not if I can drink."

"I could use a drink," Jess said.

"The party's over."

"Too bad. I could still use a drink."

"Let's go to the Dockside," Junior said.

He wanted to finish with, "on me," but he figured he didn't have to say it since it was always on him.

"Can't," said Jess. "I've got something to do."

Jess took off on a good clip, walking down the ramp to slip 143, pretending to go looking for Amanda. Junior watched him walk away.

"We gotta talk," Junior yelled after him.

Jess waved his hand in the air, acknowledging that he agreed. But there would be time for talking later. Now was not that time.

In the parking lot, Amanda slumped down in the front seat of the Mercedes so Junior wouldn't see her. She watched him climb into his truck and waited until he was gone. Then she ran down the ramp to meet Jess at slip 143 and planted a cool lover's kiss on him next to her yacht.

Amanda had felt a little sinful upon their last meeting, making love to Jess like she did. But now with Junior pressing her to leave town, well, she saw a whole new life for herself in Emerald. Besides, she really liked this Buchanan. The sex was great.

> Everybody
> Wants to tell me
> How to run my life

Jess wrote this lyric down on a cocktail napkin because it was true. Billy sat on the barstool next to him looking smug as hell. Jess had stopped at the Dockside to take the edge off a quaking heart since sweet Amanda had administered the timeliest of couplings, and there sat Billy at the bar, when he thought his former best friend would be elsewhere enjoying the proximity of his newly formed alliance with BB. Jess thought Billy would make a lot of money someday, and at these prices that day may have already come. Four bucks for a shot of Crown?

Billy lectured Jess on the way business works, but Jess wasn't about to let him get too far with his advice. It was his decision and his alone. Fuck Billy. He was screwing his girl and now he wanted to become business partners? Billy had big balls, no gigantic balls, to think that Jess would want to partner up with him. And Jess let him know it too. He let him know he didn't appreciate the fact that Billy was screwing his girl.

' Let's be grownups about this," Billy suggested, placing his hand on Jess' shoulder.

"I'm being very grownup about this," Jess said bluntly. "In fact, if you weren't such a sissy business type, I'd knock you off that cheap barstool for violating my woman, a woman you know nothing about, a woman who is way out of your league . . . " Jess was on a roll and riding it out in what he thought was suitable fashion.

His voice got even louder.

"It's called trust. I trust Billy. Billy trusts Jess. Now you've violated that trust and we will *never* be friends again."

Jess realized it might be a good time to leave because people had started to gather around them, listening to what was going on. It was the kind of attention he didn't need, especially now, with the way public sentiment was running against him. But then he thought, why not live up to his fucked-up reputation?

So without saying another word, Jess knocked Billy off the barstool with a solid left forearm that caught Billy just under the chin. The force raised Billy up off the barstool and he made a full backward flip before landing on his hands and knees. Jess stood over him, perhaps to see if he had hurt him, but more likely to see if he could get another good lick in.

But Billy *was* hurt. He gasped for air from the blow to his throat, feeling like his Adam's apple had been crushed. Before he left, Jess made sure Billy was breathing okay, then he walked out the door in full view of the restaurant employees. Not one said a word to him. In fact, some were even laughing, watching Billy get his ass kicked right there in his own restaurant.

Chapter 6

"You're a commie sympathizer, you sonuvabitch!"

Jess could barely stifle his laughter, it sounded so funny. This was 1988 and commies weren't considered bad guys anymore. Just guys.

He faced the Brotherhood, forty-two Buchanan Construction employees, and most of the questions he fielded from the group were pretty ridiculous. Jess told the men how much he would hate to destroy the pond. Apparently, it made him a commie sympathizer.

Jess sat in a folding director's chair and pitched pebbles near their feet. The small rocks arced over the thick steel cable and landed near Melvin Banks, who stood closest to him. As president of the Brotherhood, Melvin served as their spokesman. Jess pitched another rock and it landed with an audible *plink*.

"But as commie sympathizers go, Tolstoy is one of my favorite authors," he said. "And Dostoyevsky is a genius, don't you think?"

While they were not stupid men, they were not the best read. At mention of the commie authors, they suddenly became very quiet. No one wanted to field that question for fear of sounding stupid. Junior spoke up.

"That's a bunch of shit, Jess."

Junior was right. If they were going to discuss the relative merits of communism, well, they weren't going to get very far on this chilly island morning.

Jess didn't do his best thinking at this early hour but he was trying. He had been up with the stumps rehearsing the scene in his mind long before the Brotherhood had come rumbling down Old Pit Road. Subsequently, he'd had four cups of coffee.

"I gotta piss," Jess said.

Junior wasn't pleased with his timing.

"Piss in the gravel. You stay here."

Junior was a bulldog and Jess couldn't help but love him for it. Instead of walking back to the old job shack, Jess walked over to the concrete wall and pissed on his side of it. He looked back at his brother and smiled. Junior had the look to scare men who were less than self-confident, but his tough-guy attitude didn't bother Jess.

Melvin took this opportunity to speak up.

"That kid needs a lesson in respect. Didn't your dad ever teach him that? That's a poor excuse for a raisin'."

Junior's look suggested that Melvin had pissed him off for the last time. Jess shook it an extra-long time as he listened to his brother's words fall, the space between the words punctuated by imaginary beats of a bass drum with a ton of reverb.

"Banks. . . (booje, booje) . . . if you think . . . *(booje)* . . . that Buck . . *(booje)* . . . doesn't measure up . . . *(booje, booje)* . . . in your eyes . . . *(booje, booje, booje)* . . . then I suggest . . . *(booje)* . . . Banks . . . *(booje)* . . that you leave us . . . *(booje, booje, booje)* . . . because you . . . *(booje)* . . aren't man enough . . . *(booje, booje)* . . . to measure Buck . . . *(booje, booje, booje)*."

Banks shrank into the background as Jess sat back down in the director's chair. Junior spoke up.

"All we want to know is that you'll bargain in good faith. That you have every intention of selling."

There were murmurs. To Jess, it sounded like an urge from the primal gut bucket.

"*Aarrgggggh.*"

Jess shifted in his seat. Every man had his price. The destruction of his sacred ground, what was it worth?

"How much are you willing to pay?"

Junior looked at him shamefully. Price wasn't a matter of discussion in front of the men. Jess was fully aware of that, but he needed to put the pressure back on his brother where it belonged.

"That's between you and me," Junior said in his lowest register.

"Then why are they here?" Jess asked.

Melvin stepped forward.

"It's in our best interests."

Jess wasn't impressed with his answer.

"That's *exactly* why I'm here too," Jess replied, emphatically. "I'm looking out for your interests and your children's interests and their children's interests, and so on and so on. People like me have to stop people like you from destroying everything in your path."

From a short distance away, Shorty Dewitt leaned on his pickup, separating himself from the other forty-two men. He understood Jess' problem, and it was the same problem that had cursed Buck. To destroy the pond, what was it worth?

At that point, Junior realized that bringing in the Brotherhood had been a bad idea. They weren't getting anywhere.

"Okay, guys, let's get to work. Hell, it's almost eight," he said.

The men grumbled as they walked to their trucks. Junior steered Melvin to his pickup since Banks was obviously upset about something. Junior had some harsh words with him and then came back to where Jess sat in the director's chair.

"What was that all about?" Jess asked.

"Banks thought we could hammer out a deal right here. He's just an idiot," Junior replied, wearily.

"Want a cup of coffee?" Jess asked, as he folded up the chair and headed for the trailer.

Ah, what the hell, Junior thought. After dealing with a guy like Banks, hanging out with his brother would be a pleasure.

Junior sat at the trailer table and couldn't believe what he had just heard.

"Billy?"

"Billy," answered Jess.

"No shit."

It never ceased to amaze Junior what people would do.

"I'd torch his restaurant," he said, without much exaggeration.

Reality suggested that Jess couldn't do anything but beat Billy with his hands. And he had already done that.

"Maybe you're better off without her," Junior said, mustering up a little sympathy.

They each took another sip of coffee and let the *maybe* linger.

"Where's Legs? Anybody heard?" Junior asked.

Jess shook his head.

"Maybe he's run off with some bitch," Junior said, knowing Legs' history.

"He usually comes back after he does that."

Jess was worried about Legs and Junior could see it in his face. His brother loved Legs. They went everywhere together. An idea struck Junior as funny.

"Billy's got your girl. Maybe he's got your dog too."

The idea wasn't so funny. Jess pictured Billy with BB and Legs like they were posing for a family photo, and the thought made him want to puke.

Time was running short for Junior. He had a meeting that afternoon with his bonding company and he needed answers. If he had to barge rock in, there was a chance he couldn't get a bond for a job that size, and he'd be out one airfield.

"Give me a number. Anything," Junior said, getting right to the point.

"Make me an offer," Jess said.

There was a long pause as Jess sipped his coffee, waiting for Junior's reply.

"Tell you what," Junior said. "I'll give you the business after pouring the runways. The whole thing. I walk away, you take over."

"I don't want the business," Jess said, evenly. "You know that."

In high school, Jess had spent his summers pouring sidewalks for the county. Enough to know that he wanted no part of the business. He respected and understood the service it provided, but somewhere in his soul he couldn't rationalize tearing up his sacred ground for little more than a few bucks. Well, a million bucks or so.

"Too many lives depend on that rock," Junior said. "You don't have a choice. You have to sell. Dad wants you to sell. Then it makes us partners. If you don't sell, we all go broke. Buchanan Construction is out of business."

Jess had discussed it with his dad. What his brother implied simply wasn't true.

"You could barge the gravel in."

Junior laughed.

"Do you know how much that would cost?"

So be it, thought Jess. It might better reflect the true cost of mining the gravel.

"Okay, let's say I do that," Junior added. "What would stop anybody else from doing the same? All they'd have to do is set up a batch plant and now we've got competition. They're not here now because we've got the rock and they can't compete. But take the rock away and, buddy, we're just like all the rest."

Junior wasn't made to see certain things in certain ways. To whitewash his own selfish interests in a bucket of common good was appalling to Jess. But he let Junior continue.

"You need a lawyer. There are some good ones in town. Find yourself a lawyer who can make the deal. You should get what you deserve. Go talk to Dad. He might give you an idea of what the rock is worth."

"Lawyers?" mused Jess.

"You gotta do it," Junior said. "Maybe Dad can recommend one."

Either way, Junior had to go.

"Keep an eye out for Legs, will you?" asked Jess.

Junior got up from the table and made his way to the door, pushing Jess aside.

"I hope your guys don't have him," Jess added.

It was a parting shot meant to give Junior something to think about. Junior looked back at Jess.

"My guys want a job. Why steal a dog and lose their job?"

Jess shrugged.

"If they wanna shoot me, they'd shoot my dog."

"Look," Junior said, holding the door open, "they may be stupid but they're not dumb. Legs has run off. He'll come back. He always does."

He closed the camper door, and on the walk back to the truck, Junior wished Jess would come to his senses. Otherwise, he would have to find some leverage. He'd have to find that dog.

With the stereo turned up and blasting out the back door, BB ran naked out to the patio and jumped into the hot tub. Billy had asked her not to go out naked, at least not until he had built a fence, and she wondered why. If the neighbors saw her naked, so what? BB didn't feel like she needed to hide from these people.

But whether she needed to hide or not, a man peering into Billy Wilson's fenceless backyard certainly received an eyeful that morning. What he saw he couldn't repeat—a blonde-haired beauty with a bandage on her chin was doing things to herself like you read about in the magazines. Up until that moment, he had always believed those *Penthouse* fantasies were a lie, but now William Anderson had one unfold right before his very eyes.

Anderson went to the hall closet and took down the binoculars. He focused in on a beautiful buxom blonde frolicking in the hot tub, and the distance was perfect.

BB played with herself. She imagined she was a flight attendant and suddenly the buzzer went off. She went to the rear of the plane where two muscular men sat on either side of the aisle. Her naked body bridged the seats on either side of the aisle while the two men did nasty stuff to her.

Anderson wanted to die right there. He wanted to know who this woman was, frolicking in the proverbial bubbling brook behind Billy Wilson's house. Later that evening, he would do that. After all, Wilson still had his hammer.

The thought of Billy on top of her made him sick. Jess knew he was only torturing himself, but it was the only way he could work through all the emotions. Maybe Billy and BB were more alike than he thought. They both loved money; they both loved to buy things, expensive things. So yeah, maybe they did belong together.

The tip of his pole dipped and bobbed excitedly. Jess was in no mood to catch fish. He reeled it in and gently removed the fly from the small trout's mouth, then gave it a stern warning.

"The next time you see this," he showed the hook to the young trout's right eye, "don't bite. If it looks like a hook, do like all the others and just ignore it. Don't they teach you this stuff in fish school?"

He tossed it back in the water and it swam away, merely startled by the interruption. He figured a fish had about a five-second memory span. He had caught the same one again not ten seconds later, usually the little ones. When he did that, he figured somebody down there wasn't doing a good job of educating the young.

What Jess really wanted was to make a movie. The movie would be about the pond, or the pond would figure in it significantly. But it was a catch-22. To make the movie, he would need money. To get money, he would need to destroy the pond. *Concessions*? He could try to find another pond to destroy, but there wasn't another pond like this one. He was a connoisseur of ponds, he had scouted many throughout the state, and he had concluded that this pond was one in a million.

He thought he could take photos and maybe remake the pond and its surrounds after the excavation, landscape the place right down to the very seedling. Could he restore the old pit to its original state? "You mar what you mark" was how the old saying went, and from his viewpoint, it was true. If he couldn't remake the pond, could he live with a fake pond for the rest of his life, especially after he had destroyed the most beautiful pond in the world?

And all I gotta do is . . .

Chapter 7

"Harris, I wanna report a missing dog."

Detective Ed Harris looked up from his desk at Junior Buchanan, who stood on the other side of the glass. The eyebrows on the big man were pointed in a V. He looked serious, so Harris took him seriously.

"Okay," Harris said.

He reached into a drawer and took out some papers—missing people papers. Harris thought, hell if the big guy felt it was this important, then he'd give it the special treatment. He walked to the bulletproof-glass window with the papers.

"Dog's name?" he asked.

"Legs," said Junior.

Harris didn't write it down.

"Last name first."

Junior thought for a moment.

"Legs."

Harris wrote, *Legs*.

"Middle initial?"

"L," said Junior.

"First name?"

"Legs," replied Junior in all seriousness. "Legs L. Legs. That's it."

"Race?" asked the detective.

The form called for something.

"Dog," Junior said.

"Can you be more specific?"

"Golden Labrador retriever."

Harris wrote *Dog* and then modified it to *golden retriever.* Through the bulletproof window Junior read what Harris had written and corrected him.

"He's a Lab."

Harris thought for a moment.

"Aren't golden retrievers Labradors?"

Junior didn't want to confuse the issue.

"I give."

"Is he your dog?"

"No. He's my brother's."

Harris wrote *relative* in the blank because he was stuck. What do you call a dog on a form for missing people? People didn't have names like Legs L. Legs. It sounded more like a movie dog to him, Legs L. Legs, Rin Tin Tin.

If this was a movie, Harris was game. He always wanted to try acting. He meant to try out for the community theater, but he never found the right role. He thought of himself as a Nicholson type, or a guy like the guy who played John Glenn in *The Right Stuff*. What was his name? *Harris, yeah, Ed Harris.*

"Harris?"

Harris looked up from the missing person form to find Junior Buchanan with his face smashed against the bulletproof glass. Behind him, a guy held a gun to the back of his head. The man shouted something unintelligible, and Detective Harris went into action. He scooted around the corner and shouted to the others.

"Cover the doors. We've got a hostage situation out front."

The others looked up from their paperwork.

"Cover the doors!" he shouted.

From the tone of his voice, the other cops knew he wasn't kidding. They drew their pistols and went for the doors.

Someone shouted, "Get the rifles."

Harris walked calmly through the glass doors into the lobby. A bystander stated the obvious.

"He's got a gun!"

Harris recognized the situation for what it was. Buchanan was scared. His eyes wore a blank stare, his body trembled, and there was a crazy man behind him looking like *Helter Skelter*. The crazy man shouted at Harris.

"Get Buford out here now. Don't fuck around, don't do nothin' bu'cept get him out here or this fat man is dead."

Harris didn't miss a beat. He went back through the door and quickly returned with Buford in tow, his gun drawn, pointed at the prisoner's right ear.

"You make a move, guy, and your guy is dead," he said evenly to the crazy man. "Then I'll shoot you too."

The crazy man considered this. He considered it surprising that this little cop would do this. It was the only move he hadn't thought through. He was stumped, but still crazy, and that accounted for something.

Then he noticed three rifles leveled at his head from the exit doors. He rightly concluded that these guys weren't fucking around. He knew from experience that when cops were fucking around they would yell stupid shit, idle threats. But the cops in this Podunk station weren't making a sound as they waited for him to make a move. Again, the crazy man was stumped. He hugged Junior tighter, using him as a human shield. Junior whimpered.

"Shut up!" the crazy man said, and thrust the gun deeper into Junior's belly.

The detective saw an opening. He would try and talk this guy down. He spoke calmly.

"You're a dead man and you know it. You've got a split second to get us all, and this ain't the movies. Put the gun down."

The crazy man wanted to do something, but he couldn't think of anything to do. He had never been in this situation before. He looked to his buddy for an answer but Buford was scared stiff with the little cop pointing the gun in his ear.

"For the last time," said Harris, "put the gun *down*."

The crazy man wanted to make it look good. He wanted to count to five, but he could only make it to three before his nerve got the best of him and the gun dropped to the floor.

Junior let out a loud cry of relief and the entire police station reverberated with his uncontrollable sobs. The other policemen waited for Harris to pick up the gun, then they pounced on the crazy man and threw him to the floor. They had looked to Harris for the go-ahead signal, and Harris felt good about that, finally gaining some respect for what he was. A good cop in search of the right role.

Jess read every ad in the classifieds and there wasn't a car under 200 bucks that moved under its own power. *Damn*, he didn't have 200 bucks. He couldn't buy a car. He would have to risk his life and ride his bike some more.

Smooth vibrations settled in on this, his third beer. He would need wheels to set his plan into motion. He would also need to keep the walking and riding to a minimum. He tried to spell minimum and he finally gave up, not after three beers, not while he was bemoaning the fact that he couldn't buy a car.

He looked around at the tavern walls. The bar was little more than the town drunk pump. Faded cardboard signs announced the beer specials. The women depicted were of an era gone by. He wondered, had it always been that way? A guy couldn't have a beer without looking at girls in bikinis?

From the other side of the bar, he overheard a conversation between the bartender and the guy who had just walked in. He figured the guy for a Harley rider because everything he wore announced it. He talked excitedly and used his hands to illuminate the points of his story. Junior's name was mentioned repeatedly, and it didn't make sense to Jess. What was Junior doing in this guy's world? Something was wrong here. What was he saying about his brother?

Jess interrupted.

"Excuse me. What's this about Junior Buchanan?"

The Harley dude was dressed in leathers and a black T-shirt. He looked at Jess out of the corner of his eye and continued his story. Jess moved closer. It was a saga of guns and the police and Junior caught up in the middle of it all.

"And ol' Buchanan just stood there blubbering, man, you oughta seen it. Like some big fat Baby Huey . . . shit, oh dear, just cryin' his eyes out."

The Harley dude slapped the bar with his hand and laughed gleefully.

"When did it happen?" Jess asked, without a hint of emotion.

It was a simple question requiring not more than a few words to answer. But the Harley dude took umbrage. He eyed Jess as if he had seen him before, like maybe in school. But the Harley dude had rarely gone to school, so he couldn't be sure.

"Who are *you*?"

The bartender interjected and told the guy who Jess was. The Harley dude looked him up and down.

"I don't care who the fuck you are, or who the fuck your brother is, he was shakin' in his boots, scared shitless."

Jess heard the story, and judging from its origins, the truth was definitely in question. Even so, Jess could picture what may have happened.

"You get scared to stay alive. What's wrong with that?"

The Harley dude laughed a mocking laugh.

"He's a fuckin' pussy!"

Jess drew closer.

"Until you've had a gun pulled on you, you don't know what you'd do."

The Harley dude was insulted.

"I had plenty o' guns pulled on me n' I never shit once."

It took a moment for Jess to decipher all of what the Harley dude had said. His two missing front teeth made his elocution lack in clarity.

Jess knew he could take him in a fight but why waste the effort? Just because he was calling his brother a pussy? People in Emerald were tired of hearing about the Buchanan's like they were the Cartwright's or something. He remembered his father's words, "Some people will resent you just for being who you are." It had kept Jess out of scrapes in the past, and he would remember it now, since he needed to get up the hill to the police station.

He walked over to the Harley dude and whispered, "If someone pulled a gun on you, you'd shit yourself. But I'll keep it our little secret."

Jess kept walking toward the exit, fully expecting the guy to come flying at him from behind. He was ready with an elbow to the throat if he heard footsteps. He pushed the door open and bright sunlight greeted him without an incident. On the bike ride up to the police station, he was running a buzz, and glad for one thing: he wasn't driving.

At the top of the hill, police cars surrounded the Emerald Police station entrance. Jess pushed his way through the crowd and walked inside. A little towheaded cop spoke to a cute young reporter who was taking notes. Jess interrupted.

"Excuse me. My name is Jess Buchanan. I'd like to see my brother."

Harris stopped talking long enough to dismiss him with a frown.

" I was standing right here," he said to the cute reporter, pointing to the spot.

" Can I see him?" Jess repeated.

The detective smelled alcohol on Jess' breath and he wasn't about to be upstaged by this Buchanan.

" Listen, pal, I just saved your brother's life. I do my job and I do it well. If you'll wait a minute, I'll tell you where your brother is. Until then, shut up."

It was a good speech, possibly appropriate. But Jess wondered why little guys always had to act so big. The towheaded cop was having his day in the sun, so Jess sat down on a bench while Harris reenacted the scene for the pretty young reporter. Jess sighed, remembering Warhol's remark about fifteen minutes of fame. Or was it five? Either way, the cop was really putting on a show.

Harris finished with the pretty young reporter and led Jess to the back of the station. The police chief's door was shut, and through the window blinds Jess could see Junior sitting in a chair next to the chief's desk. Harris knocked and opened the door. Junior looked up. His face was red and puffy from crying. Jess walked through the door and Junior was relieved to see him. Jess put his hand around his brother's neck and gave it a squeeze.

"You okay?"

He didn't get an answer, just a funny look as if to say Junior didn't know. Jess took control of the situation.

"Are we through?"

The chief looked to Harris for an answer.

"We're good," said Harris. "But you'll need an escort. There's a lot of people out there, radio and newspaper and all."

Jess put his hand on his brother's shoulder.

"You up to it?"

Junior wasn't sure. He stood up, still a little wobbly.

"I don't wanna talk to nobody," he said.

"I'll take care of that," said Harris.

The cop led the way, and just before they hit the exit door, he asked Junior, "Are you okay to drive?"

"He's not driving," Jess said. "I am."

"You've been drinking."

"Arrest me."

Harris cleared the way as Jess walked Junior to the Lincoln, holding him by the arm. It gave the newspapers the opportunity of a lifetime. They thrust cameras in their faces and Junior growled, "Get the fuck away from me."

Jess brushed one photographer aside and helped Junior climb into the passenger seat. Then he slid in behind the wheel.

"Keys?"

Junior dug them out of his pants pocket.

"Don't wreck it," he said, handing the keys to Jess.

Jess started the car and announced, "I'm driving and you're buying. We're going on a road trip."

It sounded fine to Junior. His brother was crazy too, so why not go with the flow and continue the madness?

"You got any cash?" Jess asked out of habit.

Then he remembered who he was talking to.

"Just drive," Junior said wearily.

Jess put the car in gear and glanced in the rearview mirror. Harris motioned for them to back up.

"Destination: Bangor, Maine," Jess said, backing the car up and brushing aside a few gawkers in the process.

He really didn't mean it was where they were going, just the direction they were headed in.

The sun had sunk below the North Cascade mountaintops when they finally pulled into the Summit House Motel in Leavenworth. Junior was sleeping like a baby in the passenger seat, all talked out, talked until the event had become just one more memory in those historical events of a lifetime.

Jess did his best thinking in the mountains. He considered how the fallout may hurt Junior's reputation. He hoped Harris hadn't described the situation to the pretty young reporter in the same manner his brother had recounted it to him, a frightened man's version of a dangerous situation. "This ain't the movies," Harris had said. Good for him, thought Jess. Junior had the presence of mind to remember that line.

Chapter 8

At breakfast in the Summit House coffee shop, Junior was back to his old self, baiting Jess into a nine-hole golf match for the mother lode. He would put up the company, and Jess the old gravel pit, winner take all.

Neither of them had played the course and they would have to rent clubs. Junior held the advantage in an even match since he had been playing regularly, and Jess knew it. They would have to settle on a format—strokes or holes. He hadn't played since last summer and Jess realized his only prayer would be in match play. If he lost a hole in match play that was one thing. But if he lost a hole by three shots, which was entirely possible, he would be out of it in stroke play.

"Match play," said Jess.

"Strokes," countered Junior.

"No deal."

Junior leaned back in his chair and stirred his coffee. Most golf games were won and lost before a ball was even struck and the advantage went to the best negotiator. It wasn't in Junior's best interests to settle on hole play, but he did anyway.

"Okay, we'll play holes."

"I need strokes," said Jess.

"Out of the question."

"Three," Jess said, in the hopes he might get two.

"We'll play even."

"Like hell."

"I wouldn't give Dad three," Junior lied.

"He's better than me right now. I haven't played since last summer," Jess said honestly.

Junior leaned forward and put his elbows on the table.

"Then you haven't seen him play lately. He can hardly hit it. Maybe it was the heart attack, I don't know. But he hits it about as far as a lady."

This was news to Jess. It's true he hadn't played golf with his dad since the heart attack, so he made a mental note: *golf with Dad.*

"What's your handicap?" Jess asked. "No bullshit."

"Four. You can look it up when we get back. And I can't play to it."

"Right."

"And you're about a four," said Junior.

"Fourteen maybe," Jess countered.

Jess knew it would get a reaction.

"Shit, you're better than me," Junior said, lying.

"Since when?"

The waitress came with the eggs and Jess leaned back in his chair and glanced over to the next table where a young girl smiled at him. He gave her a wink. She giggled and looked away.

Junior knew that if he could get his brother to agree on no strokes, he could beat him. He had been playing exceptionally well lately, and if he could keep it around par, he'd win. Jess had the ability to hit it long and straight, but he could also hit it a mile crooked. If they both played their best, Jess would beat him. But the chance of Jess playing well was pretty slim since he hadn't been playing.

"No strokes," said Junior.

"Two," Jess said, backing off a shot.

Jess knew he couldn't get three shots, but if he got two strokes, it would give him an advantage on a couple of the most difficult holes right off the bat. He figured Junior would shoot a couple over par at most, and Jess felt he had a few birdies in him. But he could knock it into the woods too. When he wasn't swinging well anything was possible, and the rust was bound to show up sometime.

Junior finished his pancakes and eggs and pushed the dish away.

Jess was barely halfway through his breakfast when he heard the final number.

"Okay, one shot."

The gauntlet was thrown down. Was Jess man enough to accept it? If he could hit some practice balls on the driving range maybe he could remember his old swing, a swing that could shoot under par on most days. He took another bite of hashbrowns and pushed his plate away.

"Okay, you're on," Jess said, offering his hand.

Junior had a determined look on his face along with a little bit of egg.

"You die," Junior said, as they shook on it.

"I'll bury you," Jess countered. "And wipe your mouth. You got egg on it."

The father of the family who sat at the next table over had been listening to their conversation unbeknownst to the brothers. He understood this to be quite a match. His family was on vacation, so why not show the kids the golf course that afternoon? He would love to follow the action.

On the driving range, both Junior and Jess realized that the rental clubs at the Leavenworth Golf Club were terrible. Junior held a driver that was bent in the middle of the shaft. Jess watched him hit a ball. It sliced off to the right, only 150 yards out.

"Not so good," he said, smiling.

"Hit your balls and shut up," said Junior, teeing up another ball.

There was nothing like a little competition to bring out the best in everyone. Jess hoped Junior was feeling the pressure of a bad bet. He addressed his ball with a driver in his hands as Junior watched. The club head splattered upon impact. Junior laughed.

"Tough shit. Play it as it lays."

Jess knew he couldn't win without a good driver. He marched up to the pro shop with the broken club, leaving Junior to shout in the background, "No way. Get back here!"

Assistant pro Andy Taylor stood behind the counter as Jess walked in with a piece of the driver head in each hand. Andy looked the part of a club pro—straight teeth, all smiles, blue cardigan sweater that matched his golf slacks. Jess had his game face on and the assistant pro didn't quite know what to make of it. Was this guy mad?

"I'm a good golfer and I've got a big game out there," Jess said to him calmly. "And this driver won't do. Would you have a better one stashed away somewhere, maybe in the lost and found? I need a good driver."

Andy was relieved that the guy wasn't angry, but he was sorry he couldn't give him a better club. The rentals were the rentals, and they were pretty much all the same. Andy, of course, was a good golfer himself, and knew what it was like to play with lousy clubs.

"I'll take a look," Andy said, going in the back where the clubs were stored.

Andy was not a generous man by nature, but what he did for this stranger on a fine spring day in the North Cascade Mountains was exactly what he wouldn't do for anybody else. He came back with his own driver in his hands and gave it to Jess.

"It's got a titanium head and an extra stiff graphite shaft. I made it myself. You won't break this."

Jess looked at the club and his heart skipped a beat.

"Is it yours?"

"I call it the Big Bopper. Swing it easy," Andy said.

The man's graciousness left Jess nearly speechless.

"How can I thank you?"

"Gimme half your winnings," Andy said with a smile.

Jess would have liked to tell Andy that he was playing for a million dollars, but he couldn't say it and have Andy believe it.

"You're on," he said, and shook his hand.

"Swing it easy," the pro reminded him, as Jess walked out the door.

And that's just what he intended to do. Smooth, easy, fluid were the keys to his swing.

Bang!

The first ball Jess hit with the driver was a mammoth drive—dead straight. It landed well over 300 yards. Jess calculated that the one drive was all he needed. Now Junior knew his length was there. The par-fives were all reachable in two. Jess checked the scorecard and saw the ninth hole was 510 yards—*birdiesville.*

"Illegal club. I protest," Junior said in all seriousness.

Junior had a point about the questionable fairness of the club, so Jess did the gentlemanly thing.

"You can use it too."

Junior was hitting the bent driver pretty well, so he didn't need the other driver.

"No way. Illegal club."

Junior's tone suggested it was the end of the argument.

"If you want to lodge a protest then do it now, before we tee off," Jess said.

The first hole was short and narrow and the tee was open. They didn't have time to argue. Junior put his bag on the cart and sped off.

"Hurry up, let's go."

Jess realized that Junior would try to hurry him along all day to take him out of his game, a game based on rhythm and tempo. *Swing easy*, he repeated to himself as he marched deliberately to the first tee.

He was now in the zone.

To the men gathered inside Buchanan Construction's pit office, the question seemed simple. Was Junior capable of putting the necessary pressure on his brother to sell? The scene at the police station seemed to suggest otherwise. Whimpering like a baby was not the image the Brotherhood wanted to see from the man responsible for their livelihoods, so a little pressure of their own was what they decided to exert, a little reminder to the kid that they don't fuck around.

But Shorty Dewitt objected, "You can't do that."

The men were surprised to hear him speak. It was a rare occasion when he did. Then he surprised them again.

"What you have in mind is against all law, God and man's."

Of course, Melvin Banks wasn't concerned about the legality of the issue. Melvin gave Shorty a hard look and spoke for the rest of them.

' Either you're with us or you're against us. We've got mouths to feed."

To Shorty, the thought of injuring a man or damaging his property didn't appeal to this God-fearing man. He couldn't go along with anything that might involve violence because he had seen enough violence for a lifetime in Vietnam. Certain smells on a warm spring day could bring it all back, make his insides explode—and that smell invaded the pit office just when the men were about to take a vote. Shorty pushed his way through the door and sank to his knees outside. Vomit streamed from his mouth. While his stomach convulsed, his mind was in that distant jungle again.

'What's wrong with him?" asked one brother to another.

'Bad sandwich maybe?" guessed the other.

The Brotherhood closed their collective lunch boxes to begin the last half of the day. They had unanimously agreed upon what was to be done, all except for the lone dissenter who was down on his knees in the island weeds wondering what had gone wrong with mankind.

"This match is under protest!" Junior shouted.

He said it at the ninth tee—the final hole—where Junior led by one with one to play. It was in response to Jess' decision to hit the Big Bopper. Jess hadn't hit it up to that point because the course was short and narrow, and he didn't need the length. All day he had hit his three-wood dead straight, 250 yards, middle of the fairway.

But here on the final hole, Jess had no choice but to go for the green in two and maybe eagle the hole, or at least to birdie it. He was sure he would need at least a birdie to have any chance at tying the match. So before he hit the driver, with the ball teed up and Jess about to take his stance, he asked again, "Is this an official protest?"

It was a good question, thought Junior. Did he protest knowing that if he won or tied the hole he was the undisputed owner of all the gravel he needed to retire in happiness? According to Buchanan family rules, an official protest would have to be settled by a third party, regardless of the outcome. To protest or not to protest was the question, and Jess asked him again, "Do you protest?"

Junior drew the bent driver from his bag. He had parked the cart nearly on top of the tee box as an act of intimidation. That, and as a general rule, he hated to walk.

But Junior also hated the fact that he couldn't protest this match. Not with one hole to play, not with a one-hole advantage when the worst he could do was lose the hole and tie the match. If he couldn't defend his lead, then he couldn't call himself a golfer. Or a man. He would birdie this hole and beat Jess out of what was rightfully his in the first place.

"Junior?"

"No protest," said Junior, exhaling. "Hit the damn ball."

Jess smiled as he addressed the ball, pointing the Big Bopper down the middle of a very tight fairway. There were trees to the left and out of bounds to the right. He tried to remember the same swing tempo that he had on the driving range. He would not permit himself to think that a wayward shot could decide the rest of his life. Andy Taylor's words of advice rang in his ears: *swing it easy.*

Bang!

Call it a repetition of wonder since the ball exploded off the driver in one of those purely connected experiences where the word *crushed* seemed to apply. The ball traveled three hundred yards and landed in the middle of the narrow fairway. Jess quickly picked up his tee and Junior nearly trampled him on his way to hit his own drive, a drive that carried the future of one Albert Buckminster Buchanan Jr. and all his employees with it.

Whack!

It could be said that Junior's tee shot landed where no man should tread, for he is way out of bounds and shouldn't retrieve such a ball that lay so deep in the weeds that light may never again touch its dimpled cover.

Yet, if by chance a passerby should happen upon a black Titleist 1 with a J marked on its cover, perhaps that passerby might like to know that there lies a misbegotten shot worth the fortunes of many innocent and decent lives, when two irresponsible souls let athleticism decide the outcome of such important matters of family and business.

Scissors

Chapter 9

Jess sensed something was different, and it was different alright. When they pulled into the old pit parking lot, he looked at his camper covered in soot and black with ashes. Nearly all of his belongings lay in a charcoal heap, including his bike that he left leaning against the cab of the abandoned truck. A note scrawled in soot on one of the side panels of the camper said, *SELL*.

Junior and Jess sat in silence while the Lincoln idled, both struck dumb by the scene. The car was in gear and Junior had his foot on the brake. He gingerly placed the shifter to park. Jess got out and ran to the camper to inspect the damage, hot with anger. There was no denying who was behind this and Junior was quick to point out that he had nothing to do with it.

"They work for you!" screamed Jess, as Junior walked up behind him. "I can't believe you burned down my house!"

Junior was quick to disavow any prior knowledge. He had instructed Melvin to burn down the job shack because it needed to go, but not the camper. Hell, it was the only thing his brother had to live in.

"Don't blame this on me!" Junior said.

An ugly pause ensued. Inside that moment spoke the voices of past, present, and future. Junior stalked back to the Lincoln determined to find out who was responsible for this. He shouted to Jess, who stood next to the stump outside his front door, or what used to be his front door.

"Let's go."

He motioned for Jess to get in the car.

"I'm not going anywhere," Jess said, rubbing the soot off the stump with his T-shirt, and sitting down on it.

Junior realized he had to get to the bottom of this or things could spiral out of control in a hurry. Who did this and why? Was it simply a miscommunication or was somebody going behind his back and taking matters into their own hands?

'I'll be back," Junior shouted, and sped off.

Go ahead, thought Jess. But he wouldn't be there. He might stay long enough to find some undamaged memento—an old picture of BB, an untarnished guitar string. A lot of songs went down with that Guild guitar.

Oh well, he would mourn and pay his respects on the funeral pyre of his worldly belongings, and then maybe drop by the Kingdom Come for a few beers. BB had some things that he was keeping for her but he couldn't remember what they were. Well, it didn't matter anyways. They were gone now.

Shooooo . . .

Shooooo . . .

Shooting rocks rolled down the gravel bank like teardrops tapping on his cold, cold heart. Jess listened to the falling rocks like a child watching for shooting stars. Fire had tilted his view of the world and he would note that life wasn't fair. He wanted to believe in karma. He wanted to believe in it because he was fed up with all this bad shit that was happening to him.

Jess felt like life owed him for recent events and he was mad that this bad luck and reckoning had lasted for so long. But he knew that eventually the tide would turn and events would revert back to the golden ratio. It was simply the law of averages.

But in a small town like Emerald, and his place in it, provided that he might not have to sleep outside on this chilly night. He began to walk. He wanted Amanda. He headed for town. He walked down Old Pit Road and out to the highway.

About 500 yards down the highway was the Kingdom Come,

where he could stop in for a few pops and then continue on his way down the hill to the marina. As he walked, Jess accounted for his belongings through mental pictures, a pitiful state. This was the emotional edge he rode as he walked past the sign that read: Welcome to Emerald, Population 4227.

And then he felt a calm drop over his senses. It was the movie guy again.

From a helicopter hovering fifty feet above the old pit, the director dangled from the cockpit and shouted for the action to begin. The movie guy sat on the stump next to a charcoal heap and rested his elbow on his knee like *The Thinker*. He looked glum. The camera eye panned the scene and the director slid back into the chopper and shouted to the pilot, "Great, just great!"

Jess walked on, resolved to be with a woman, any woman. He needed to screw somebody, and he needed her *now*.

In the full moonlight, Junior hauled his Silverstream trailer out to the old pit and parked it next to the torched camper. It was the super plush model because Junior never bought anything but the plushest. He figured it would be a definite improvement over that old camper. As he reached down to unhook the trailer, the thought occurred to him to leave the truck too since Jess's bike had gone up in the fire as well.

"No big deal," he said, loud enough for the gravel animals to hear.

It was his favorite saying. He walked away from it all, out to the road, and down to the mini mart where Darrel Ivie was just about to close up. Darrel was kind enough to give Junior a ride back into town since they had been in the same class together at school. Junior felt obligated to talk to Darrel since he was giving him a ride, but half the former classmates Darrel asked about he couldn't remember. They obviously ran in different crowds.

"Yeah, the marina, you can drop me there," Junior told him.

"Sure, go right by it. Amy and I live on Bay View. You know my wife, Amy Gilligan?"

Junior had no idea who Darrel's wife was, and once more, he didn't care. He just wished this guy would shut up and drive.

' Sure, you remember Amy. Cute redhead?"

Junior stared blankly out the side window.

"No. I don't remember her."

Junior had too much of Darrel by the time they arrived at the marina and he was quick to jump out. He thanked Darrel, then shut the door, a little too smartly for Darrel's tastes.

"Any time, asshole," Darrel sniffed.

Darrel spun the tires, stung by Junior's snub. Later, he told Amy about Junior. Darrel didn't know that Junior had been a guy Amy had screwed in high school. Outside of the fact that it was a pretty good screwing, Amy was pissed that Junior didn't remember her.

He couldn't even remember my name?

Amanda was surprised to see Junior. The nature of their relationship had been a strange one since Junior was a private man and he wanted to keep their affair low-key. But it was getting even stranger now that he had broken it off. She had seen more of him lately than she had seen of him when they were together. She had been with the man for nearly three months, yet she had never met his family. How could Junior take her seriously when their relationship seemed to be one of convenience? And here he was again in the middle of her stateroom, wearing an expression quite like she had never seen before. Had he come begging?

"Somebody burned down my brother's camper and he's blaming me. He lived in it," he said. "Or used to."

Junior couldn't have guessed what this news meant to Amanda.

"Was he hurt?" she asked, her first thought.

"He was with me. Up in the mountains."

Junior wanted to tell her much more, but his emotions were all jumbled up, and he really didn't know where to start.

Amanda had no idea that Jess lived in a camper. He could have stayed with her. In fact, she would have suggested it if she had known. But knowing him the way she did, he probably *liked* living in a camper.

"Where is he now?" she asked, innocently.

Amanda had to keep the truth from Junior so he wouldn't become suspicious.

"I don't know. I took my trailer out to the old pit and he was gone. I left it for him. My truck too."

Junior managed a smile as he imagined Jess' expression when he discovered his new home and his new ride.

"A present for your guilt?" Amanda asked.

Junior got mad.

"Don't lay that crap on me. Jess thought the same thing. What's with you guys?" he said.

Amanda wanted to explain to Junior that she wasn't a guy, something Junior had a hard time believing. He wanted a buddy, not a lover, and she wasn't the buddy type.

"You said somebody did it," she asked, in a tone more suited for the courtroom. "Who's the somebody?"

Junior sat up straight on the sofa. What had become of his former sweetheart grilling him in the heat of the night like some defendant?

"They left a message," he said.

Amanda was a tough lawyer who had earned her reputation in the King County Prosecutor's Office. She was confident in her skills as an interrogator, and a potential client was in trouble. She needed to ask some difficult questions since her suspicions pointed to the man sitting right in front of her.

"I know you did it."

If Junior had come for a little sympathy, he wasn't about to get it from her, and that was obvious. He wanted to tell her everything, but he realized he was too tired to really care. He could go to sleep right there on that familiar couch without much prodding. But Amanda would have none of it.

"You're not staying here tonight," she said.

Junior snapped to life.

"I haven't asked."

She crossed to the other side of the stateroom.

"What did the message say?"

He looked down at the floor.

"Sell. It was written on the side of the camper."

"And that's it?"

"That's it."

She had to laugh. These small-town men and their small-town ways. It wouldn't take much police work to find out who had motive.

"And you don't know who did it?"

"This deal concerns the whole goddamn island. It could be anybody."

"Who stands to gain the most?" she asked, pointedly.

"I don't know."

"I rest my case," she said.

He'd had enough of this.

"I had nothing to do with it, dammit!" he lied, loudly.

If not sympathy, what he really needed was wheels. He wasn't getting anywhere with her, so he abruptly changed the subject.

"Can I borrow your car?" he asked.

Amanda was formulating a plan and it required research. She would offer her shingle to Jess because he needed her counsel, ethics be damned.

"When can I get it back?" she asked.

"Tomorrow, when I come into the office."

His office was within walking distance, a half mile down Main Street. She tossed him the keys.

"It's parked in the second row."

Then she turned haughtily in profile. To Junior, it was a provocative pose. She was by far the prettiest woman he had ever dated. And the smartest.

"Now get out of here," she said.

He jingled the keys.

"Thanks."

Junior stepped outside, and just before he closed the door, he heard her say, "No big deal, right?"

He smiled. She was even beautiful when she mocked him.

It was late and Amanda stood up on the bed to see who had knocked on her bedroom window. She spotted Jess peering in at her. She gathered herself, put on a robe, and ran outside. She kissed him passionately thinking if he needed relief, she knew how to give it.

She opened the stateroom door and they fell onto the carpet, taking off their clothes in a race to see who could get naked first. Amanda slowed the pace down. It left her to think about how she could take control of Jess' business affairs and counsel him. At some point she would have to tell him about Junior, but now was not that time, not with the cute little cleft in his chin rubbing against her inner thighs. She purred loudly. All in due time.

Jess felt he should let Amanda devise the strategy to best handle Junior, but he had to think it through. It was a relief to know that she knew his brother, or at least, that she knew of his reputation. Anyone representing his interests would have to understand the nature of this relentless man. They were also a tight-knit family and that would figure into his decision as well.

Jess sat in Bob's coffee shop and wondered what to do next. He declined Bob's offer for the special shake because he needed to be clear-eyed and sober as a judge when making decisions that concerned so many lives. Besides, he was still trying to shake off the hangover from the night before.

At the Kingdom Come, Jess had stopped in for a few beers before he walked to the marina. But after a pitcher of Rainier, it was clear he should leave because the climate had changed to chilly. Normally he would be surrounded by friends, or at least people he knew. But last night Jess sat alone at the end of the bar, the others giving him the eye, talking about him. He didn't think the sale of the old pit would distance him from his friends like this, but he was wrong. From the guys, he received nods in place of handshakes. The girls all stayed away, which was unusual. If Jess was there without BB, usually a group of girls would gather around him since he was Jess Buchanan, former rock star.

Jess ran into two of the younger guys in the Brotherhood on his way out the door. He looked at the clock on the wall, ten o'clock, break time. He nudged one of the guys as he passed by with his elbow, a guy he knew from working with him in the summers.

"Thanks for the campfire. Next time I'll bring the marshmallows," Jess said.

The guy acted like he didn't know what Jess was talking about. But he was such a bad actor it was obvious he was acting. The guy and his buddy laughed out loud and Bob took notice.

"What do you guys want?"

"How about a marshmallow on a stick?" one said to the other.

Bob didn't like to see this in his shop, the gloating.

"You boys oughta be more careful," he said, giving them the eye. "People have ears in this town."

They shut up and ordered.

"Ten coffees and ten glazed doughnuts to go. Cream and sugar."

After Bob rang them out, he reached under the counter and poured himself a shot of Crown in his coffee cup. He knew Jess had bought himself a boatload of trouble. Bob didn't want to see him get hurt, but if he was dealing with the Brotherhood, it was a distinct possibility. Bob had firsthand knowledge of that. He'd been paid a visit on a loan he couldn't repay on time. A couple of the younger guys scared hell out of him by telling him what they would do to him if he didn't come up with the money. He took a big swill from the special coffee to settle his nerves. *God bless you, Jess. And good luck.*

Chapter 10

Jess turned into the old pit and spotted Junior's truck and trailer gleaming in the sunlight. On the windshield of the truck, underneath a wiper, was a note written in his brother's handwriting that said *"Thought you might need a place to stay. The truck gives you no excuses. Let's deal. Jr."*

That was correct. This would give him the mobility he needed to go find his dog. It was beginning to look like Legs was gone for good, but he figured everybody in town knew Legs belonged to him. If someone had seen him running loose, they would have said something. Or if someone had kidnapped him, eventually word would get out. Nobody could keep a secret in Emerald.

Jess stepped into the Silverstream and couldn't believe that they made trailers this nice. The whole kitchen area was trimmed in mahogany, and the bedroom had room enough for a queen-sized bed. He had never owned a bed that big before. He and BB were used to twin-sized beds where they practically had to sleep on top of each other. He thanked Junior in absentia, then turned on the TV, made something to eat, and found out what it was like to live like the rest of America.

Junior had been working on a plan that involved the navy and their flight patterns. He had been put on hold while he waited for Lieutenant Pederson to come to the phone. Confidential sources told him that Pederson was the man responsible for the navy's flight training routes at Whidbey Island Naval Air Station. Jets were what he needed. Loud jets.

"Hello."

'Lieutenant Pederson, Junior Buchanan here. How are you today?"

'Just fine, sir."

Junior wanted to break the ice by sounding congenial, but the navy had obviously trained Pederson well. He was all business.

'I understand that you're—"

'Yes, sir. I've been briefed on the situation," said Pederson, interrupting.

Junior wanted to impress upon the lieutenant the gravity of the situation.

"I don't want to tell you how to do your business—"

"Then don't," Pederson said, cutting him off again.

Pederson wasn't shy about putting Buchanan in his place. But he also knew that it was a big deal to the higher-ups, so he softened a little and was forthcoming with a little more information.

"If you're on a need-to-know basis, we'll employ swoop attack. It's where we drop right down over the target. Piece of cake for these hotshots, sir."

The navy understood that it made for good public relations to have a local contractor do the job. An infusion of military dollars into the local economy would certainly help the community's acceptance for having the jets fly overhead, day and night.

"So when can you do it?" asked Junior.

Lieutenant Pederson took exception to the inference that the United States Navy worked for one Junior Buchanan.

"That'll be for us to decide," said Pederson, with an edge in his voice.

Junior could spot ruffled feathers a mile away. This man needed a perk.

"Lieutenant Pederson, are you married?"

Pederson thought it was an odd question but he answered it anyway.

"No, sir."

"Do you have a lady friend?"

Pederson lied.

"Yes, sir."

Junior cleared his throat.

"Then you and your lady friend will be my guests at the Dockside Café here in Emerald for an evening of dining pleasure. It's a wonderful restaurant. At your convenience, of course."

Lieutenant Pederson didn't know whether this violated any codes of conduct. He couldn't think of any specific rule that might prohibit him from accepting the invitation, so he accepted the invite, wondering who he might take.

"Thank you," he said. "Is that all?"

"That's all, lieutenant."

Junior hung up the phone, pleased with himself. What a great plan—*swoop attack!* He was amazed by how easy it would be, when all they had to do was give Jess a taste of what it was going to be like once that airfield went operational. *Swoop attack!* Of course!

It was time for Buck to take his heart medicine. The pills made him so tired that he wanted to stop taking them, but he loved living so much that he was afraid to stop taking them. Even with the headaches.

Buck suffered from cluster headaches that no man could describe—the pain. They began like a hot knife melting through his forehead, then slowly the pain would twist somewhere above his right eye, and eventually it would develop into an agony that made his head feel like a metal garbage can full of smoking ice. He had been told that oxygen would help, so at 2:30 in the afternoon he'd retire to his study to sip oxygen alone, away from his wife Marie and her fretting.

And here came another one. Buck gripped the armrests on his recliner and tried to think soothing thoughts—a warm beach in Hawaii, pretty girls in bathing suits. The pain would escalate exponentially, and in the space of a couple of minutes it would go from zero to force ten. He grimaced as he might in a tremendous wind, forcing his body to go through contortions that an observer might think were gruesome.

In the hallway outside the door, Marie heard the muffled screams of her husband in violent pain. She clasped her hands together and brought them to her mouth, biting her own knuckles in a fit of empathy for this man she loved so much.

Jess sat on the top of the gravel bank and watched the sunset as the cool night air chased the warmth of this lovely spring day away. The sky was full of bright neon colors, and thoughts, sad thoughts, raced through his mind. BB was gone. Legs was probably dead. He could be too if he didn't watch his step.

A moment later a hellacious noise from above burst upon him. He ducked instinctively, his heart racing. It had come so fast that in his moment of paralysis—when fear suspended all time and thoughts were focused on one simple thing: survival—it was in this moment that Jess decided he was tired of playing the victim. Or the fool.

Indeed, fear was a prime motivator for getting off his ass. He realized this message was sent specifically for him, and it didn't take much to figure out who was behind it. In the silence that followed, he realized he needed to make a decision. And soon.

An EA6B Prowler jet could be heard in the distance as it made its way back to Whidbey Island Naval Air Station. It wasn't noticeable to most people in Emerald who were accustomed to hearing the jets as they practiced their maneuvers at night. But to Junior, who heard the faint roar from miles away, it was music to his ears. On the couch, in his underwear, he smiled and glanced at his watch. It had taken the United States Navy exactly nine hours to respond. *Nice work, guys.*

Jess sat on the charcoal stump and thought about how he wasn't eating right. He was practically living on coffee and beer, and he couldn't remember the last time he had eaten a vegetable. His monthly allowance was nearly gone. Five hundred dollars a month was barely enough for groceries and beer. But he had gone easy on the groceries this past month and still he had only sixty-two dollars left to spend on beer. He couldn't understand how he could spend so little and not have anything to show for it.

Jess wondered how much Junior made in a year. A hundred thousand maybe? He wouldn't know what to do with a thousand dollars, let alone a hundred of them. Junior acted like he would be ruined if Jess didn't sell the rock, and Jess knew it was a lie. Junior could make money standing stark naked in a snowstorm. But then, maybe the Buchanan family had used up all their divine allotment of prosperity and now it was time for them to become common wage earners again, a tale of shattered aristocracy, Emerald style.

He laughed out loud and doused the lantern. He stepped inside the trailer and put away the dishes. Then he decided not to stop there, and he cleaned the whole trailer, top to bottom. As he worked, he thought about how he needed to take control of the few lifelines he had left, at least the ones in his immediate grasp.

He stood up after towel-drying the floor and a few seconds later, another roar came from overhead and he hit the floor again. The jet's turbulence shook the trailer from side to side like it was in an earthquake. A moment later he realized that this jet thing was getting to be a real nuisance. He got up and dusted off his hands, and then he laughed at what he had done. Of course his hands weren't dusty. He'd just wiped the floors!

Chapter 11

Amanda was having lunch at the Dockside when she saw Junior walk in. He said something to the hostess and Billy came downstairs. They exchanged pleasantries, then went upstairs to Billy's office. She glanced out the window and saw a burgundy Dodge pickup swing into the marina parking lot. Out jumped Jess. Amanda left a twenty on the table and rushed out of the restaurant in order to meet him at the top of the ramp. The waitress followed her out and caught her just outside.

"Ma'am?"

Amanda stopped and turned around. The waitress had her sweater draped over her arm.

"You left this," she said, holding it up.

Amanda smiled at the girl, who looked to be still in her teens.

"Thank you. Your customer service is impeccable. I'll tell your manager."

Delighted, the waitress handed the cashmere to Amanda and added a knowing smile. The waitress had noticed that when Jess Buchanan walked down the ramp Amanda Hunt's eyes were on his every move. Jess was a handsome guy and a former rock star, and the waitress thought more power to her if she was involved with him. Then, through the Dockside's large view windows, the waitress watched Amanda catch Jess from behind just as he was about to enter the covered slips. It was obvious they knew each other intimately. She grabbed him by the butt.

"Whoa there," Amanda said.

Amanda had a hold of his left butt cheek and gave it a good

squeeze. He turned around and waited for her to catch her breath. In that moment Jess thought: *As BB is beautiful, Amanda is elegant.* After she had caught her breath, she planted a lover's sloppy kiss on his lips.

She led him by the hand inside the stateroom, where they ended up down on the floor again. Something about their relationship had them perpetually down on the ground in search of wonderful and spontaneous sex. It was something Jess thought about much later in the form of a question to himself: *Did she ever shampoo the rug?*

What Junior proposed to Billy was this. . . talk Jess into selling the old pit and he would make it profitable for him. Billy looked at Junior like he was crazy. But after seeing that look in Junior that he knew quite well from childhood, Billy assumed he was serious as hell. Junior had come to pay for a complimentary dinner, and while he was at it, he pitched Billy on a whole different view of sanity.

"That dog is leverage. He loves that dog. You know that."

"Legs?" Billy asked. "What's up with Legs?"

Billy knew Legs, and they were very dear friends.

"Wait. You want to kidnap Legs?" he asked Junior.

Junior put his hands on the desk solemnly.

"Somebody's already done it."

Junior was trying to make a small point of leverage, some point of madness that seemed ridiculous to Billy. He sounded desperate, and Billy knew what desperation could do to a man. He'd been there himself a few times. But this wasn't the Junior Buchanan that he knew. Maybe the deal at the police station had rattled him. If Junior wanted his help, he had come to the wrong place. Billy reminded Junior of his present situation.

"Jess won't listen to me. He's made that pretty clear."

But Junior thought this was simply the adjustments people had to make to live in a small town. If every man wanted to kill a friend for seeing his former girlfriend in small-town America, there wouldn't be many friends left.

"Don't let her get in the way of your friendship. It's not worth it," Junior advised.

Billy stopped him right there.

"BB means a lot to me."

Junior hadn't meant to imply anything different.

"It didn't work out for them," he said, shrugging. "It happens all the time. No big deal." Then after a pause he added, "Good luck," implying that BB was a handful.

Billy could see he was getting nowhere with Junior, a very different animal than Jess. In this battle of brothers, he would bet on Jess any day because Jess was fearless. Abnormally so. His best friend was someone to reckon with in any competition, and in Billy's view, this was nothing but a competition.

Billy promised he would take care of Lieutenant Pederson and his guest.

"Give them the royal treatment," Junior said on his way out.

Billy assured him that something akin to royal is what they would indeed receive.

"Absolutely," said Billy. And then under his breath he added, "Fatso."

Marie entered Buck's study after she knocked on the door like a mouse at midnight. Following behind was a man Buck hadn't seen in a while. He got up from behind his desk and shook hands with Shorty Dewitt. Marie excused herself.

"Sit," said Buck, motioning to a leather chair in front of the large cherry desk.

Shorty held his cap in his hands and smelled like axle grease. Buck missed that smell and this man. He was pleased that Shorty had come to see him, but why?

His old friend sat on the edge of the chair as if at any moment he might dash out the door. Shorty didn't feel comfortable in Buck's house. Shorty looked concerned, and it bothered Buck to see him look like that. If Junior was giving Shorty a hard time, then Buck would have a talk with his son. Shorty was a good man and a good mechanic. A good mechanic was an invaluable member of any ready-mix operation, and Buck realized his son could go hard on his men.

"Buck," Shorty began, and then he fell silent.

There was something Shorty wanted to say but he couldn't find the words, which wasn't unusual for Shorty. He often had difficulty expressing himself. Buck waited patiently for him to continue.

"Jessie's in trouble," he blurted out, finally.

The room fell silent as Shorty sat back in the chair, knowing he didn't have to spell it out. Buck was a fearless man himself, so he asked the most fearless of questions.

' Is his life in danger?"

Shorty was quick to answer, "Yes. And you can't blame just Melvin."

Buck had dealt with Melvin's father, Eugene Banks, for years. Eugene was tough, but he was also a fair man who had served the Brotherhood well under his stewardship. But his son Melvin was a man with a brutal reputation. Buck had heard the stories.

"Junior can't stop them now," said Shorty.

Shorty spoke elliptically, the words punching the air. Buck looked out the window. Had he known it would come to this . . .

"I had to come," Shorty said, again reinforcing the fact that time had run out on Jess.

Shorty recognized the fear in a father's heart when Buck remained silent, thinking.

"Sometimes they don't consider what they do," Shorty said, stating the case for evil throughout the ages.

Both men understood the gravity of the situation. Under Junior, the Brotherhood had gained a reputation for ruthlessness, and Buck took the threat seriously. He knew these men.

Buck shook Shorty's hand and walked him out to the foyer.

"You were the best of them. It's good to know you still are," he said, patting Shorty on the back.

Buck hugged his old friend in a way that made Shorty turn red. People like Shorty don't linger in the homes of others—they come, settle their business, and go. Shorty grinned, relieved that the visit had been well received. He hustled out, leaving Buck to think about what to do next. It took great courage for Shorty to come forward.

The Brotherhood would severely punish him if they ever found out that he had talked to Buck.

Marie stopped Shorty just before he walked away and asked him to come again.

"It's good for him. Be good for you too, you old devil."

Marie sent Shorty off with a hug and tried not to embarrass him, even though she always did. Shorty was shy around Buck and Marie because he respected them so much. And it showed.

In the front-page article in this week's *Island News Times*, it was reported that Junior had gone to the police station to inquire about a missing dog, one that belonged to his brother. If the whereabouts of the dog wasn't known, Melvin thought a well-placed note could deliver a message of intimidation.

The picture on the front page of the *News Times* depicting his boss as a big crybaby didn't sit well with Melvin. If Junior couldn't negotiate from a position of strength, then he would see fit to educate Jess on one very important point—that strength could come from places other than the top. Jess would have to realize that new rules had just gone into effect—the Banks rules.

It was much too early for someone to be knocking on his door. Jess looked at his watch, 5:45 a.m. Whoever was banging on the door was doing a good job of it. He put on his jeans and opened it. There stood his father with his fishing pole and his hat drooped over his eyes like a bum on the street.

"Let's go fishing," Buck boomed brightly.

"Shhh," said Jess. "You'll scare the fish."

His father laughed as he came in. Buck knocked the dirt off his boots before he entered since he knew this son was the fastidious one. Jess looked in the refrigerator for coffee and realized he was out of milk. He put two mugs in the microwave, then went to the back and slipped on a sweatshirt.

Buck sat at the table and looked at the *Island News Times* with the picture of Junior on the front page wiping his eyes. It wasn't a flattering photo, and he was going to tell Wallie, the publisher of the paper, that he wasn't pleased. He understood the emotions of his eldest to be quite spontaneous, erupting any time, and it wasn't the kind of responsible reporting that he would like to see from his hometown newspaper. Jess sat down at the table across from his dad and noticed the look on his face.

"Did you read the story?" he asked.

"Somebody's gonna hear about it."

"I'm not surprised. How did Mom take it?"

"She cried."

He studied his father as he waited for the mugs to heat. He had obviously lost weight and his face was ashen. The blood thinning pills stole the color from his cheeks, but there was still vitality in him. His eyes sparkled with the energy that most people could only wish for. His father slept five hours a night, worked sixteen-hour days routinely, drank for two men, and had suffered the big one. The notion of him being retired was a joke.

'How's the heart?" he asked.

'Still ticking," answered Buck. "May not be here tomorrow. You just never know."

Buck liked to talk that way, as if life was a precious commodity not to be wasted. The microwave bell rang, and Jess scooped up a couple of heaping teaspoons of frozen coffee for each mug. Buck watched his youngest son, a slim figure compared to his brother. Jess looked troubled. He looked like a man when pressed by life. Buck was here to offer his son some advice. Jess set the steaming mugs on the table with a bowl of sugar and a spoon.

"Out of milk, sorry."

Buck put in two spoons of sugar and swirled the hot water. Then he took a sip from the mug and shouted, "Christ almighty!" and pressed his tongue to the roof of his mouth.

Jess felt bad. He felt his own mug. It was hotter than hell.

"Sorry."

Jess got up and added cold water to both mugs. He'd have to get used to the amenities. Microwaves had been out of reach ever since his financial state had taken a severe nosedive.

Buck looked around the trailer. He'd never been inside it.

"This is a nice trailer. If nothing else, you got a nice place to live,"

Jess hadn't talked to his father about the fire. He didn't know why. With his dad, Jess had a way of walking around subjects rather than addressing them head-on.

"It's a beauty," Jess agreed.

"Get your ass in gear. Fish are biting."

It was a ritual they had shared since before Jess could walk. Buck had spent years casting his fly onto the glassy surface of the pond. It was where Jess had learned to fly fish, and it's where his father had passed down all kinds of knowledge to his sons, expounding on things as they waited for the fish to bite. The pond held a lifetime of memories.

The misty morning was not to be missed and Buck felt young again. He took one last sip from the mug.

"I'm going up. You comin'?"

"I'll catch up," said Jess.

He held the door open as his father stepped out into the crisp island air.

"Smell those trees!" roared Buck.

He grabbed the fishing rod and measured the gravel bank. It was a Buchanan tradition to hit the slope running.

Jess watched his father scramble up the gravel bank like an old grizzly bear, his short strides eating up the loose gravel by leaps and bounds. At the top, his father looked down at him, an image Jess would never forget. His dad winded, but snorting with defiance, looking down at him with his arms raised in triumph knowing that he could climb the ridge again. Jess closed the door, pleased to know that his father still had plenty of life in him.

The mist hung low over the water as Buck made his way down to the pond's edge. He thought about his next conversation with his high-minded son. He tossed a fly onto the water and let it rest for a second as he watched the ripples grow larger. As the circles grew, it was clear to him what Big Al, his father, had done. The gravel beneath the pond had remained a secret because it had to come to this. He looked to the ripples all played out. *It's the beauty of living that makes life interesting,* he was fond of saying. *Because you just never know.*

He was here to remind his youngest son of that. He flicked the rod again. A moment later came the strike of a lifetime. In that moment perhaps all things became clear to Buck, as his lifeless body lay slumped next to the pond, waiting to be discovered.

Chapter 12

To all of us who knew him, it came as a shock to hear that Buck Buchanan had passed away. Apparently he dropped dead as he fished in the pond at the old gravel pit. If you've never seen the place, you should drop by. Why, just on the other side of that large gravel bank is the prettiest pond you'll ever see. It's been said that Buck's father, Big Al Buchanan, dumped a mess of lime in that pond and turned the water from blue to green. It's true, because if you have a look, you'll see water as clear as emeralds.

It must have come over Buck like a bolt of lightning because it was a massive heart attack that killed him. His son Jess found him lying alongside the water as peaceful as could be. It's good Buck didn't linger after something like that. Sometimes they can bring you out of it and it just leaves you a vegetable. Buck wouldn't have wanted that. He'd had a major heart attack a few years before, so he shouldn't have been climbing up that gravel slope anyways. But that was Buck, go, go, go.

You know, if anyone was to have money, you'd want them to be like Buck. He did a lot for this town. They'll lay him to rest tomorrow at 7:30 in the morning. It was his favorite time of day. The funeral procession will stop at Bob's coffee shop in honor of the men who had gathered there every morning in his twenty-four years of running Buchanan Construction. They were quite an outfit, laying most every road, every sidewalk, and pouring damn near every slab and foundation on the island dating back to the Depression.

Big Al started it all back in '29 when Emerald and the rest of the island needed something other than dirt roads to drive on. And Big Al was big alright. He was probably six foot four and well over 300 pounds, and with a smile to match. You should have seen him with Buck when they walked down Main Street *on Saturday mornings after ballgames. Buck was quite an athlete and his father was so proud, like a father should have been with a son like Buck.*

But Big Al died young. A heart attack at fifty-two. A man carrying that much weight had to put a load on his heart. Then it was up to Buck to take over and run the company when he was still a young man. He had his doubters too. Eugene Banks wanted to buy him out, but Buck earned the respect of the men when the company didn't miss a beat under him. In fact, some said Buck inspired his men where Big Al just drove them.

Eugene Banks was the first organizer. He got the Buchanan crew to hold meetings and discuss wages and benefits. They decided not to join the Teamsters because they got most of what they wanted anyways. Big Al and Buck were fair men. And remember, this was a time when Dave Beck was running the country out of the back of a laundromat in Seattle. There was some mighty pressure for them to join the Teamsters, but Big Al's crew were bound and determined not to give their hard-earned money to guys who drove Buicks.

A while later, Eugene came up with the name "the Brotherhood," and that's what it's been all along. You can find them down at Bob's every morning at seven-thirty. Some will be wearing those gold and green baseball jackets with the picture of a black knight on the back. Eugene's son, Melvin, is the shop steward now, which is like saying he's the union president.

Why, the fights Eugene and Buck had over the years were legendary. Eugene was a tough man and he liked to bully people, but he couldn't bully Buck. No, sir. Buck was a generous man, but he was also as tough as any businessman, and Eugene respected him for it. In fact, when Buck gets laid to rest tomorrow, Eugene will be holding the front rung of the casket. And he'll probably be wiping his ol' bugger eyes out because he loved Buck too. We all did. Buck was a good man.

Amen.

Jess was at rock bottom. Life could be brutal in its suddenness, and there was no greater grief than to recognize death as lost love, the stunning nature of what might have been. In that moment, Jess turned to writing music again.

The gravity of his father's passing came in waves. The goodness, the indecent, the specific moments of his father's life he would carry perpetually in remembrance, for Jess would mourn a lifetime. He was certain of one thing. He would celebrate the spirit of his father's living each and every day, and feel as if his father was always watching him, a feeling that as he walked through life and its uncertainties there was a proud legacy to uphold.

But Buck's true legacy couldn't be measured in the accumulations that he left behind. It was in the testament of the souls he touched. Words of love were rarely exchanged between them, at least outright. But now distanced from any words, it was an exercise in futility. For Jess, the pain of losing a father was to know that it would never go away.

Marie checked the rib roast, and the meat thermometer read a few degrees shy of the way Buck liked his prime rib. In a restaurant he would order his meat and say, "Just let it hit the fire." She remembered one time down at the Dockside when Billy came out and presented Buck his steak. It was completely frozen. Billy sat down and waited for him to take a bite. Buck didn't dare send it back because he always complained to Billy that when he asked for rare, he meant rare. Billy would laugh and slap him on the back then insult him about being retired, for which he took a good ribbing. Buck loved Billy. He had loaned him a large sum of money to buy the restaurant and Billy paid him back in less than five years. Marie recalled the scene now as Buck looked down at the frozen steak. He was careful not to let Billy know that he'd gotten the best of him. So Buck ate the steak and when he finished, he smiled and said, "Now, that's the way to cook a steak." Billy just shook his head.

Marie said a prayer for Billy but she didn't have time to stand still. People would begin arriving soon. It was 5:30 in the morning and she expected a crowd to stop by the house before church. She checked the rib again and decided not to worry about it for another fifteen minutes. She hadn't slept, worrying about all the things that had to be done in order for it to be the type of gathering that Buck would have wanted.

BB said she would be over at six to help. Marie thought about Jess and BB. They had known each other all their lives, and maybe that was the problem. They had always been together. Marie hoped it would be just a matter of time before they both realized that true love couldn't be denied.

Billy had promised to bring some appetizers from the restaurant after the reception. She wondered if there would be enough to eat. She looked around the house. It was neat and tidy, presentable by even her standards since her husband had passed away the day after she had given the house a good spring cleaning.

Good timing, old boy, she thought.

Marie went about her business with extreme efficiency. The routine gave her something to do. She didn't know if life could be fun anymore without Buck. Maybe she would just grow old and look forward to her first grandchild. She reflected on her two sons. She wouldn't hold out hope for Junior to find a second wife in the next few years, not with the business going so well. He would complain that he didn't have time to see his mother and father, let alone have enough time for a girlfriend.

Marie knew that Junior was afraid to love again. The divorce had been hard on him. Junior wasn't like his father, who loved openly and without reservation. Junior didn't love people. He often said he hated them. It was hard for her not to be critical of her son about that, but Junior *did* love his mother and father, this she knew. His father's death would be hard on him.

Of her two sons, she felt Jess was more resilient because he didn't expect so much from life. Her youngest had inherited his father's ways. It was Jess who would compliment her on a new dress or dance with her on a whim. Marie once dyed her hair a different color, and Buck didn't say a word until Jess came over for dinner a week later and complimented Marie on her new look. Buck swore up and down that he hadn't noticed.

She wondered about that now. Buck was always kidding her. Maybe he *did* notice but pretended like he didn't, just to give her the business. It would have been just like him to do that.

Marie began to cry and promised it would be the last one before BB arrived. Buck wouldn't have wanted a blubbering wife on his funeral day, so she would tend to the gathering with her grief placed where respectable people carried it: in their hearts and not on their sleeves. There would be a time and place for her private tears, and she would reserve those moments for later, when thoughts were not of gatherings, but of a man who filled her heart with sadness because he couldn't be there to hold her hand.

Junior had taken care of the details, and there were many before his dad could be laid to rest. It disgusted him to realize that funerals were, in the end, just another business. What really galled him was the fee the church wanted to charge for rental on the parish hall. After all his mother and father had donated, they still wanted a deposit? Leave it to the Catholics.

Junior had been at odds with his faith ever since his divorce. He'd been married for less than six months when he came home one day and found a note on the kitchen counter saying his wife had moved back to Albuquerque, where she thought she belonged. Why she belonged there and not by her husband remained a mystery to him. His annulment was still pending. Until then, he couldn't take the sacraments.

In the parish hall after mass, Junior listened to stories about his father, particularly the ones of how he was such a good practical joker. Eugene Banks told a story about the time when Buck and Marie had taken their first vacation together. When they got back from the trip, they discovered a company dump truck parked sideways in their two-car garage. Eugene said they had to take the roof off the garage to get it in there, but he fibbed about that too. He said they took the company boom truck and lowered the dump truck down into the garage, leaving it to where there was no way a guy could drive out. Then they simply buttoned up the roof.

But then Buck got the idea to put each of the truck tires on dollies, and they simply turned the truck around ever so slowly, inch by inch, foot by foot. Junior remembered the pictures and there wasn't but a foot on either end of the truck as it sat parked in the garage.

Eugene never owned up to it. But the next time he went on

vacation, he found a large tree stump placed on his doorstep, making it impossible to get in or out of the house through the front door. The stump was twice the width of the door and it still had dirt and mud clinging to its roots, making it look even bigger. The picture made the front page of the newspaper. Everyone knew Buck was responsible, but nobody would own up to it. After he finished telling the story, Eugene dabbed his eyes with a handkerchief. He kept it handy all day long.

Junior divided his time between the gathering and his mother. He felt it was his responsibility to watch over her. He didn't want her to do anything, but Marie couldn't sit still with so many people in her home. BB was a big help. She greeted everyone at the door and took their coats, made sure the buffet table was clean and replenished, all the little things that made for a respectable gathering.

Junior could see it was hard for Jess to have BB tend to the gathering like family, which she was, at least to Buck and Marie. Junior noticed they had stayed apart the entire day. He wondered who would make the first move. Billy was there, so he expected Jess to leave her alone. But it must have been hard for him not to go over and punch Billy right in the mouth. Then again, it was a funeral, and people didn't go punching people at funerals, especially when it's your dad who's dead.

Junior looked at Jess from across the room. He was all dressed up in a coat and tie and he looked nice. He had done a great job with the song he had written for the service. Jess handed Junior a copy of the words to "Here and There" and it was the only communication they had between them all afternoon. Apparently, the trailer and the pickup hadn't done much to ease the tension. But they did share the grief of losing their dad, and now they were on their own to shoulder what it meant to be without him.

Junior felt like the spectator. Half of his attention was on the gathering and the other half was on his dad, his friend and mentor. He took out the words to the song Jessie had written and read the words again. He cried and did so unabashedly. Other men patted him on the back because to cry over the memory of your father is what a good man should do. This time, Melvin Banks put his arm around Junior's shoulder and led him to a corner.

"That's it," said Melvin. "Let's cry for Buck."

HERE AND THERE

Three hundred strong gather in the chapel hall
Three hundred strong gather in the pews
Preacher, he gave an ordinary testament
About a man he never knew

I'm not talking out loud when I say about this man
He set his heart on making a dream
And he was still dreaming at the end of it
The American Dream, he called it his own

Hold on I'm crying
Hold on I'm scared
Hold on I'm crying
A little here and there

I'm having a tough time with all this talking
Can't say a word without thinking of him
A better man I have never known
I've got something to do
I've got to sing him my song

Hold on I'm crying
Hold on I'm scared
Hold on I'm crying
A little here and there

Later that night, in his bed, and BB next door in one of the guest rooms, Jess wanted to creep into her bedroom and share his grief with her. But he couldn't work up the nerve to do it. He would feel really embarrassed if BB turned him down. And he was tired, so tired.

He dreamt that **BB** came into his room, took off her clothes, and slipped into bed with him. He could smell her skin as they enjoyed the push-pull of life. The dream was so real, the next morning he asked **BB** if she had come into his room.

She looked at him strangely, smiled, and climbed the stairs to the kitchen to make more coffee for the people who arrived with the flowers.

There were so many flowers.

Chapter 13

Afiter two days of steady rain, the skies opened up and revealed the heavens in all its brilliant glory. It signaled the end of mourning in the Marie Buchanan household and she chased BB and Jess out the door by telling them that they had lives of their own to lead.

In the driveway, they said goodbye on better terms now. BB was going back to Billy's, and he was going home to the trailer. But first, he wanted to drop by the marina to see if Amanda was there. He hadn't seen or spoken to her in nearly a week because he felt it was inappropriate to drag her into personal family matters.

He gunned the pickup down Swantown Road headed for Sunset Bay with a bit of joy skipping in his heart. Alliances of the intimate kind could make him giddy with happiness. He was but two days removed from burying his father and all he wanted to do was screw Amanda. He didn't know what to make of that. He figured a Freudian would have the answer, but he didn't care. He wanted Amanda and he knew she would be just as willing. If she was still there.

Amanda thought it would be a good day to cruise back home, bright and warm. She gazed off into the distance, and just beneath the slip's roofline she could see Mt. Baker. It was a good fifty miles away but she could see its snowcapped peak clear as a bell. For good measure, she rang the captain's bell that her father had given her and called her mother. She left a message.

It was largely left up to Amanda to check up on her mother while her father, US Senator Anderson Hunt, was away in Washington, DC. She would call her at least once a day. But it seemed Anna May Hunt needed no checking up on since her import business was booming. Her father thought it might give her mother something to do. And now that she had expanded Anna May's to Oregon and California, her mother was doing quite well independent of her father. Amanda was delighted that her father now had to ask for her mother's time and attention.

It was her mother who would make a great senator and not her father. If it wasn't for his inheritance, she doubted whether Anderson Hunt could make it anywhere. Amanda had witnessed her father's management style firsthand when she worked for him during the summers, but truth be told, he could turn a soup kitchen into a slop house. Her father was a private man consumed by his public self, consumed by what he could do for others without looking in his own backyard at a young girl who was left to swing alone.

Amanda had made up her mind to leave Emerald in the next hour. She would catch up on her business in Seattle, then take a few days to see her mother and a few friends, and then be back in Emerald by the weekend. She hadn't seen or heard from Jess in a week and there was no way to reach him. She'd heard that Buck Buchanan had passed away and she figured Jess and Junior were busy burying their father.

But time had become an issue. If they were to pressure Junior, the next couple of weeks would be the time to do it. She wrote a note for Jess telling him when she would be back, and she left his name off it in case Junior dropped by. She tacked it to slip 143's bulletin board.

Amanda brought out the charts and programmed the computer. Once out in the shipping lanes, she would lock in her destination and then go about cleaning the living quarters, a routine she had kept for months while she was seeing Junior. Before then, it was a rare occasion when she had time to get out on the water, but on a whim she had come to Emerald on a weekend getaway when friends told her about a charming island village up north. It was only a three-hour cruise up through Puget Sound and the Rosario Straits to the San Juan Islands. It was like a chapter out of a book when she landed in one of the most beautiful places she had ever seen. It was a place where her soul seemed settled, and it wasn't but a hundred miles from where she had grown up.

She remembered meeting Junior when she docked the yacht at the marina and walked into downtown Emerald. Junior was sitting alone in the next table over at the Pioneer Restaurant and he asked if he could sit with her. He was not her style physically. He was big and morose-looking, but there was something about his manner, so confident of himself, that she admired right from the beginning. Later she learned that he was from a family that had essentially built the town. Whenever she came back to Emerald, her emotions were overwhelming. The joy of unexpected love brought her senses to the edge, where everything became acute—sight, smell, touch, taste. In Emerald, she led a different life separate from her Seattle life, a place where she could become who she really was.

She felt her relationship with Junior could have worked if only he had wanted it to. But now she had another reason to come to Emerald. Although the circumstance seemed a bit wonky at best, she would rise above it, as she was sure Jess could too. But she would have to tell Jess about Junior. Soon.

Amanda's play would be to prey upon Junior's vulnerabilities. He was an emotional man and she would take advantage of it. Plus, the element of surprise would be on their side. Junior wouldn't see it coming. The echo of his gall still rang in her ears. *Leave town*? She would give Junior an excellent reason for why she wouldn't leave town.

As she sat on the bridge with her engines idling, suddenly a familiar face appeared below. Her plans changed in an instant. Amanda turned the engines off because she needed to talk to her client. She might even get a little in the process.

Lt. Carl Pederson seated his date Connie Miller at the table and sat in the chair the waitress had pulled out for him. It was a perfect evening in Emerald. The sunset was brilliant, and they were seated at the center window table in full view of the marina. The waitress brought a bottle of wine to the table and presented it.

' Mr. Buchanan and the Dockside would like to make your evening a special one," she announced.

It was an expensive bottle of chardonnay picked especially for the lady by Billy Wilson himself. He had notified the hostess to alert him when they arrived. He had taken one look at Pederson's date and ordered the chardonnay because Billy knew what Connie Miller liked. The lieutenant could not have known that Connie and Billy were once intimately familiar, and Connie was not the type to broadcast her business—a smart move since she was still married. Her husband was away on cruise. This ought to be fun, thought Billy.

Connie had accepted Lieutenant Pederson's dinner date at the Dockside because she knew it was an opportunity to see Billy again. Connie was an exceptionally pretty woman who liked a good time. Pederson was surprised and happy when she accepted his invitation.

Billy walked over and extended his hand.

' Lieutenant? Hi, I'm Billy Wilson. This is my house. Welcome."

Billy liked to call the Dockside his "house" for the sound of it. He smiled at the lieutenant, but the man's reaction gave him a chill. He hadn't seen that look in quite some time, the one that had left his forefathers hanging from trees. Carl had mistaken the black guy at the bar for a drug dealer or a pimp, and not the owner of this fine restaurant.

' Hello," said Carl, ignoring his hand.

He neglected to introduce his date and Billy managed the oversight with finesse.

' Hello," he said as he reached across the table to shake hands with the lady.

Connie was relieved that Billy knew enough not to let on. She offered her hand.

' Connie," she said, pretending to introduce herself.

' Pleased to meet you," he said, smiling as he shook her hand.

Billy could spot a bigot a mile away and this Lieutenant Pederson was pegging the bigot meter. He placed his accent somewhere from the Midwest, from one of those notorious pockets of white supremacy that grew like the corn in the fields.

"I hope you enjoy your evening," he said, and walked on to greet other tables.

Pederson watched Billy walk away, then turned to Connie and said, "That's one smooth nigger."

Connie decided right then that she would enjoy her dinner and then have the lieutenant take her home. He would probably want something for having spent so much money on her, but Connie wanted the man across the room, a man who greeted another table of guests, a man worth a ferry ride back to Emerald before closing time. She had it all planned by the time the appetizers arrived.

But Connie had to let Billy know what she was planning since he might be otherwise engaged that evening. He always had girls on the side, usually young girls, way too young to mess with a guy like Billy.

Connie caught his eye a few minutes later and *I need to talk to you* was what that look meant. Billy thought it was awfully bold of her to give him the nod right in front of her date. Later, he received a note, *I'll be back on the 10:20.*

Billy decided that he wouldn't discourage it. He felt it was only fitting to give this Lieutenant Pederson his comeuppance.

BB wanted to go down to the Dockside because she was feeling lonely. For days she had been busy helping Marie and now she felt uncomfortable being alone with her emotions. Buck was a special man in her life and she didn't want to grieve anymore. She wanted some action, but Billy didn't like her hanging out at the Dockside. He said it didn't look good.

The events of the past week had left her emotions raw. BB thought about the summation of her life and decided it hadn't amounted to much. She wanted to have a good time, to get her mind off it. It was ladies night at the Kingdom Come, but did she want to sit on a barstool in that meat market? Not much.

What she wanted she couldn't get, not now, not here inside this beautiful house. She tried to think of ways she could balance love, lust, security, companionship, excitement, duty—the list continued on and on in one compartment of her brain while her first mind made the decision to go down to the Dockside despite Billy's objections. She could be ready in a half hour, about eleven, about the time the night people came out to celebrate the darkness.

What she was doing here had become a moral struggle for Billy. Connie sat at his desk and took a gram of cocaine from her purse along with a gold straw. She emptied part of the packet on his desk and drew out two thick lines. She offered him the straw.

Billy hesitated. It was his policy never to drink or drug on the job because the reputation could kill a respectable business. But this was a sexy woman who could keep a secret, dressed in a short black leather skirt, the one he liked so much. It was as much a statement of her intentions as anything short of a sign hanging from her nipples that might say *Come Fuck Me*.

Billy took a line, half for each nostril, and Connie took the other. He asked her to put it away since one of his staff could come walking in at any moment. Connie put it away and then sat back in the hard leather chair and crossed her legs.

"So which little bitch are you screwing now?" she asked in typical Connie fashion.

He laughed. Connie had a bold attitude about her that he couldn't resist. A Southern girl with a southern fried edge. He told her the truth.

"BB Gunderson."

Hmmm, Connie was slightly amused that Billy had ended up with his best friend's girl.

"She's living with me now," Billy finished, letting Connie know his situation.

It must have looked suspicious, the two of them sitting there, with Billy behind the desk and Connie in the chair facing him in a short black skirt that had to reveal crotch if she unfolded her legs. Then she did another very Connie like thing. She unfolded her legs.

If there was to be any action, Connie knew it had to be now, not back at his place like she had planned. Billy was telling her how it stood, but even so, Connie considered marriage and fidelity a lousy reason for behaving in like fashion. There was a gorgeous black man sitting in front of her and why shouldn't she want to screw him? Especially when that line was making her hornier than hell?

Connie was good at this sort of thing, this sex-on-the-spot thing, and Billy was a sucker for a blow job. She lied and said it was all she wanted but Connie knew she could get what she wanted eventually. They ended up against the wall, her naked butt suspended in the air as he held her by the back of her thighs. His business license fell off the wall as it shook.

As things happen, as we move forward at an earth speed of several hundred miles an hour, this is how quickly things change. As lives intertwine in this kneading and venting and grunting of our primal needs, in this flux is created the flow of life, the river of souls, the dams of happenstance. For it was at this moment that Beatrice Bernadette Gunderson chose to walk into Billy's office unannounced and found him with his slacks to his knees and a familiar woman pressed up against the wall. The two of them appeared to be joined at the waist and it was obvious what they were trying to accomplish.

It took BB a moment to recognize the situation for what it was, and then she ran downstairs, and out the door in a brokenhearted hurry. The restaurant staff assumed there must have been a scene because a few minutes later Billy came down wiping his forehead with a handkerchief. He straightened his tie as he walked through the door to the parking lot. He didn't see the red Mustang, so he concluded, rightfully so, that BB was gone.

BB felt burned by love. The cuckold feels cheated and scorned, a place where time stretches out, where everything becomes focused on the pitch of deception. Her soul plummeted into the depths of hindsight. For a slight moment she hadn't realized the situation for what it clearly was, but in the next moment her innocence was lost forever. She would never love blindly again. She wondered why she had taken up with Billy. Why treat her dad with scorn when he only meant well; *why, why, why?*

BB was crying and driving in the rain like a wounded dove. She thought of all the people in the world who loved her and thanked them. She thought of all the people who had mistreated her and cried even harder. Maybe it was her place in life to perpetually do the wrong thing. Maybe her mom had passed on a DNA splice of madness, of always not knowing what to do, and always being confused.

She had thought moving in with Billy was a good idea. Wrong. She was tired of moving, picking up, and leaving. She wanted a place to call home. But first she needed a place to stay, at least until she could get her proverbial shit together. She knew such a place existed, but she didn't want her dad controlling her life anymore. For an instant she saw an avenue of possibility where father and daughter could coexist, a sort of mutual independent dependency.

But did she dare drop in on Jess?

BB was tired and needed to sleep. She found herself parked at the old pit, headlights shining onto the Silverstream. The pickup was not there. She left the Mustang running while she tiptoed to his door. Why she tiptoed she didn't have a clue. She knocked lightly. No answer. She put her ear to the door and didn't hear anyone moving around inside. She knocked again, louder this time. Still no answer. She tried the door and it was locked. Jess slept elsewhere and it elicited another sharp pain in her stomach. He was seeing another. She ran back to the Mustang and locked the doors. It had narrowed her choices to one.

Maybe it was time.

BB believed in fate. So if Jess wasn't there, then it probably meant it was time for her to go home again. She drove the two miles to the turnoff, then down the familiar driveway overgrown with fir branches and blackberry vines, and parked the car in the clearing just beside the double-wide mobile home. She gathered up what was left of her emotions and walked softly to the front door, careful not to wake up Beals. She looked under the large rock next to the steps, but the key wasn't there.

It was late and Pop Gunderson had been sound asleep when he heard the doorbell ring. Beals barked loudly and he looked at the clock. It was nearly three in the morning. As he put on some sweats, the doorbell rang two more times. He wasn't prepared emotionally for what was in store when he finally opened the door.

"Hi, Dad," BB said.

She stood there waiting to be asked in. Finally, he spoke up.

"Well, come in."

Pop had the sniffles from a weeklong bout with the flu. He closed the door and blew his nose. He wondered why BB was here. Had she come back for Buck's funeral? Pop had missed it because he was flat on his back, too sick to be seen in public. He had heard there were a thousand people who showed up at the church. But this was no time for thoughts of funerals. Or maybe it was. Perhaps his daughter's presence signified the death of something. But first he had to apologize for the way they had parted six months ago.

"I'm so sorry," he said through clogged sinus membrane.

"Me too," she said, hugging him.

Suddenly she felt whole again. In her mind she knew it was over, the period when daughter had to reject papa. As confusion congealed, forgiveness was overflowing, and Pop needed a break.

"I'll go make some coffee," he said, and shuffled off to the kitchen.

The last thing BB wanted was a cup of coffee at three in the morning. She lay on the couch and she could hear him whistling in the kitchen. It all seemed too cozy as she drifted off to sleep.

Pop shuffled back from the kitchen in his slippers and saw that BB was asleep. He covered his daughter with a warm blanket and turned off the lights.

"Sweet dreams, daughter of mine," he whispered under his breath.

Chapter 14

One phone call had pretty much summed up his stance on the subject. Junior told the prissy reporter what she could do with her picture and article. She replied that she had simply reported the facts and the facts had told the story.

"You made me look like a big crybaby. What kind of reporting is that?" he bellowed.

Fresh out of Washington State University and not yet sure of herself, Natalie Robinson didn't want to hear this, not with her reputation at stake within the *Island News Times* office. The entire newsroom listened to her conversation since the other reporters were all well aware of Junior Buchanan's reputation. They wanted to know the true mettle of their young reporter and watched as Natalie held the receiver away from her ear. They could hear Junior shouting over the phone.

"Listen, Mr. Buchanan," she interrupted, "we'll have to continue this conversation at another time. I have a deadline to meet. Goodbye."

With that, Natalie simply hung up.

She turned to find the newsroom staring back at her. The editor, Michael Horton, spoke for the rest of them when he said, "Welcome to the world of news, Ms. Robinson."

The others applauded and rose to their feet. Natalie wasn't a perky cub reporter anymore. She had taken the best of what Junior Buchanan had to offer and she had put him off like a pro. The other reporters thought Natalie was a lucky girl since it was rare to have such a pronounced rite of passage in the news business.

"Perky no more," proclaimed Michael, as he ceremoniously taped a Post-It note to her sweater.

The note read *Pro*, and Natalie had to laugh. Then she thought: *Maybe this town isn't such a dump after all.*

Jess felt encumbered by the spirit of his dead father. He wanted to do the right thing, the greatest good, and perhaps it meant he should sell the rock. But someone had to pay for his camper and everything in it. The Guild alone was worth a thousand dollars. He filed a report with the sheriff's office but he didn't hold out much hope. Their preliminary findings had attributed the fire to a lightning strike, an accident of nature.

Right. He asked the deputy investigating the scene whether lightning bolts had suddenly developed the ability for penmanship. Sell? The deputy and the fire marshal attributed the message scrawled on the side of the camper to someone taking advantage of an unfortunate circumstance.

Okay, he thought, but what about this?

He reached into his pocket and took out the note that he found stapled to the tree stump. It said, *We have your dog. Sell or else.*

At the very least it had given Jess hope that Legs was still alive.

The deputy was sure it was someone bluffing, but he took the note to show the sheriff.

But the note did say *We*, and in Jess' mind it pointed to a collection of souls hell-bent on trying to intimidate him. If it was the Brotherhood, then he must honor the "*or else*" since they could easily shoot a dog and justify it. Only a stupid man would consider them bluffers.

A knock on the door interrupted his thoughts. He opened it and Shorty stood there with his hat in his hands looking like an uncomfortable angel of mercy. Jess hopped outside and the old mechanic was quick to make his point, not unusual since he was a man of few words. He was also Buck's old friend. They had grown up together, both in the same class.

"Jessie, I know who did it."

Shorty glanced at the soot-stained camper, or what was left of it.

"Yeah, I do too," Jess said, smiling. Then he shrugged and added, "But what'cha gonna do?"

The older man spun his hat in his hands and looked at the ground. Jess had a specific question for him.

"Do you know who has my dog?"

Shorty looked up and shook his head.

"No, but be careful. I told your dad I'd look out for you. But I can only do so much."

Jess needed some inside information on a thought he knew the answer to. At least, he hoped so.

"Does Junior know what's going on?"

"No," Shorty said, emphatically. "He's your brother. They're careful about that."

Shorty slipped a white pamphlet in his hands and Jess glanced at the heading, *Awake to God!* If ever there was a god-fearing man, Shorty was him.

"Jessie, I got to go."

Jess looked into Shorty's eyes.

"Don't get your butt in a sling over me."

The older man hesitated.

"I loved your pa."

"I know you did," Jess said, patting Shorty on the back as he turned to go.

The old mechanic walked back to his pickup looking this way and that for somebody who might be spying on him. Once he peeled away from the pit entrance, it left Jess with a musing. He raised his eyes to the heavens and said, *"Thanks, Dad."*

What Jess needed most was a phone. The old job shack still had the wires running in from the street, but they hadn't been used in years. It would be a matter of getting a line from the shack to the trailer, simple enough. He knew a man who could help him, but he hadn't talked to Pop since before Buck's death. Pop left a message with Marie to say he couldn't make it to the funeral because he was sick. Jess thought it was a lie since he knew how Pop felt about funerals. He just didn't go to them.

Jess drove to the mini mart to call Pop. On the second ring, a familiar voice answered. He was surprised to hear BB's voice. There was a long pause between them. Finally, Jess mustered up some genuine moxie and said, "Is Pop there?"

"No," she said. "He's at practice. It's baseball season, remember?"

Another pause while he gathered up some more moxie.

"Does he know you're back?"

"I'm in his house, aren't I?" she said.

Jess felt like an idiot. He had called Pop and instead got her wise-ass comments.

"Tell him I called," he said, and hung up.

BB was about to say something more, but Jess cut her off. She knew she deserved the cold treatment. She had the blahs and blamed it on her period.

She thought about her mom. Was she still alive? Should she go try to find her? BB remembered the day her mom left, when she found her father in the kitchen with a note in his hand, crying. Would it be like that again, daughter as mother? She realized that living with her father was only temporary, a hesitation on her journey to some other place.

She got out a pan to fry an egg. Should she go talk to Jess and apologize? She tried to imagine him with his new girlfriend. She was probably a little bimbo with big boobs because he liked them that way. She put on a Patty Loveless tape and began to cry. She understood if he had to be with another woman. And could she blame this other girl, his bimbo girlfriend? Jess was terminally handsome, he came from a rich family, and he could sing and play the guitar with the best of them. What was there not to like?

At the kitchen table with her coffee and a slice of dry toast, BB listened to "The Trouble with the Truth," one of her favorite songs, on the boom box. Jess certainly had the talent to become a star, so was it bad luck, or maybe no luck at all? She couldn't figure out his complacency, not wanting or needing much to be happy. But was he happy? He didn't laugh anymore. He had practically removed himself from society by living out in the old pit. She understood him to be writing something, but he was always writing something.

"We've Been Lonely Too Long" came on and she turned it up. She wondered if his new girlfriend had ever heard him sing and play the guitar, and wondered if it made her cry like BB was doing now, where the tears rolled down her cheeks onto the egg yolk, a yolk that she didn't want anymore.

The Brotherhood had convened at the cabin just outside of Winthrop in the northeast part of the state. Their days were normally filled with stalking deer and elk or birds during the daylight hours, then at night they would fire up the old potbelly stove and play cards and drink until one by one they would stagger off to their bunks, happy with the anticipation of tomorrow, for these men were born to hunt.

But this weekend was different. No hunting. Instead, it was a methodical plotting of strategy to establish all the details of how things would be carried out. Young Buchanan couldn't imagine what they were capable of, and after the meeting they all took an oath of silence. They had nearly a month to get their message across. The date of the bid opening was circled on the calendar, and a series of smaller circles preceded the bid date. Bid day was marked in blue, blue for what they felt they must do.

All members were accounted for except for one—Shorty Dewitt. Nobody had told him about the meeting because it was clear he couldn't be trusted. Some guys thought it was funny to think that a decorated Vietnam veteran and expert marksman—a proven killer—was opposed to violence like some candy ass from the city.

Jess drove into town on a mission to find Legs. If the Brotherhood had him, he was sure he could sense it. He would call a meeting and ask them directly, look into each pair of eyes and decide whether they were telling the truth. Of course, he wouldn't expect anyone to raise his hand and say, *"Yeah, I got him."* But if someone had Legs, he was confident he could guess who it was.

He would also call the meeting to assure the Brotherhood that he was willing to bargain, that he simply needed to know a price. Apparently Junior hadn't decided on a number because he hadn't received an offer. He would put the ball squarely back in Junior's court and let him squirm.

The Albert Buchanan Memorial Library was his grandpa's legacy to Emerald. It was an impressive concrete structure that Big Al had built just before he died. The memorial part was something he hadn't planned since Big Al died unexpectedly, just days after the dedication. Big Al never would have let anybody put his name on the building, it was not his grandpa's style, so they renamed the structure after him once he was gone. Jess parked outside and admired the building. It certainly was the most impressive structure on the island. It said a lot about the man.

Jess entered with his head down and walked directly to the card catalogue. He wasn't too popular with the townsfolk these days, so he kept his eyes lowered, unwilling to meet anyone's gaze. He understood human nature enough to know that their rancor was rooted in the responsibility of making a living and providing for a family. So he would endure the stares without finding fault with it.

Margaret Atkins noticed Jess as he walked in. She hadn't seen him since the Fourth of July parade when her husband had caught her staring at him. She had been a sophomore when he was a senior and she had a major crush on him. He still had that wild unruly dark brown hair and he was dressed in a tight T-shirt and blue jeans. Even up close she thought he had the looks of a movie star.

Jess looked under "mining" in the subject section of the card catalogue. He removed the M's drawer and put it on one of the kid's tables and sat down in a tiny chair. His knees practically hit his chest. Someone from behind tapped him on the shoulder and said his name out loud. He looked up to find Margaret smiling down at him.

"Hi, Margaret," he said.

She was flattered that he'd even remembered her name. She hadn't been one of the most popular girls in school.

"Can I help you find something?" she asked. She pointed to the badge on her blouse and smiled. "It's my job."

Jess was getting nowhere as he flipped through the card catalogue because he really didn't know what he was looking for exactly. Answers, he hoped.

"I need information on methods of excavation," he said.

As she stood next to him, he noticed that Margaret had turned into a very pretty woman, much better looking now than she was in high school.

"What are you trying to excavate?" she asked innocently, knowing the answer.

"Doesn't matter," he said. "I'm just looking for techniques."

Margaret could have drawn all kinds of corny sexual innuendo from his response, but she refrained since librarians were not to flirt with the patrons.

"Let's go to the computer. It'll be faster."

"Maybe for you," he laughed.

He had nearly flunked computer class in college and it had left a lasting impression on him. He could barely turn one on for fear of screwing something up.

As they crossed the room, he admired the way Margaret's loose red curls fell neatly down her back, framed by her white sweater, which he noticed she filled out nicely now. He remembered that she had married Mark Atkins, and it was too bad. He couldn't understand why sweet girls married such assholes. Jess only had to look at Robin Banks, Melvin's wife, for that. Growing up, Robin had been his favorite babysitter. Now he heard stories of how Melvin brutalized her.

Margaret spent nearly an hour finding reference materials for him. He ended up with a stack of books on the table a couple of feet high. By the time he had skimmed a few, he realized he was the wrong guy to research this topic. Many of the texts were filled with jargon he couldn't understand. He was on a mission to find a way to excavate the rock from below the pond without disturbing what was above it. He knew the technology had to exist.

He decided to ask Pop, since Pop was not only a great baseball coach, he was also good at figuring out how things worked. That, of course, excluded the inner machinations of one BB Gunderson, a mystery they had both yet to figure out.

Jess left the library in search of a private public phone to call Pop. It seemed he was perpetually in need of a phone. Maybe it was time to do something about it.

Chapter 15

The proverbial shit hit the fan when the naked pictures of BB made it to the *Playday* subscriber mailboxes. BB had been practicing the ritual of denial, hoping her lawyer could prevent the photographs from going to print, but a contract had been signed. Her last phone call to LA left her with a decision to make. Another phone call made to Pop's house had put her in a vulnerable position. Mr. Johnson cleared his throat.

"Umm, Ms. Gunderson?"

Immediately she recognized the voice. The ooze slithered over the telephone like goo on a stick.

"Yes."

"Do you know who this is?"

"Yes."

The wheels were spinning, about to fall off.

"I've seen your pictures. They're quite nice. Does your father know about this?"

Her dad was an awfully proud man and Johnson had it in for him. She could lie and tell Johnson that her father knew, but it would be taking a big risk.

"No," she said.

He cleared his throat again.

"I didn't think so. They're quite revealing. Personally, I like the thing you did with the ax."

"What do you want?" BB asked, annoyed by his cute rhetoric.

She could only imagine.

"We can keep this our little secret," he said, suggesting a litany of possibilities, "If you treat me nice."

"If you're talking money, I don't have any," she said bluntly.

But she knew what he wanted.

"I'm not talking about money. I have enough of that," Johnson said

She was angry at a circumstance for which she was entirely to blame. What she feared most was a scene in the teacher's lounge in front of all the others. She pictured Johnson with the open magazine at lunchtime, and her father with a look of hurt and disbelief on his face. Whether she told her dad or not, Johnson would still try to embarrass him, and the pictures would certainly do that. She had to prevent it from happening.

'What do you want? Spell it out," she said.

Johnson paused and asked himself the same question. He held the magazine in front of him and pictured that pose.

'Let me be your lumberjack," he said.

Sicko. But until she had time to think it through, she relented.

"Okay, under one condition. Nothing is said to nobody about this Not my father, not your friends, nobody—understand? And it's a onetime deal."

BB Gunderson in bed? Johnson would agree to anything that might get her into bed with him.

"Understood," he said.

It had become a question of where and when, and Johnson was good at pressing his advantage.

"Tonight, seven o'clock. The Hideaway Motel. I'll be in room ten."

"I'm busy tonight," she lied.

She needed time.

"Then get un-busy," he said, firmly. "I'll be looking forward to it."

He hung up, leaving BB with no choice but to plan what she wanted to do to the teacher. Johnson was notorious for his sleaziness even when he'd been teaching and she wasn't the first girl to be threatened by him. But she would be the first to nail him on it. BB thought of all the girls who wouldn't have to suffer his corny sexual innuendos or his threats any longer. She had an opportunity to end it all. But she needed help. And a camera.

Jess walked into the mini mart to call Pop and two pimply faced teenaged boys behind the counter stashed the adult magazine they were looking at back in the cupboard below the register. Jess had seen them looking at it through the front window and he smiled at their boyishness. He could hear them talking as he walked back to the cooler.

"She's his girlfriend," said the tallest boy.

Jess' ears perked up.

"I know it's her," the taller boy said to the smaller boy.

Jess looked up to find them looking back at him. Girlfriend? Jess waited for the tallest boy to elaborate and pretended to look at the potato chips after grabbing a can of pop.

"She used to come in here all the time."

He could only assume they were talking about BB. He took the pop and the bag of potato chips to the counter.

"Hey," said the taller boy as he rung him up nervously.

Jess had put two and two together and the sum was BB had made a boo-boo in LA.

"Do you want a bag?" the taller kid asked.

Jess didn't want a bag. In fact, he didn't want the potato chips. But he asked for the bag in the hopes that the kid might say something more. The boy reached under the counter for the bag and laid the magazine on the counter, opened to the beginning of a nude photo layout titled "Northern Exposure."

"Do you know her?" the taller boy asked.

Boy did he. As Jess looked at the pictures, anger welled up in his throat making his tongue numb. If BB had the indecency to do this, what else had she done? Billy had visited her when he was in LA on business and said everything was fine. The possibilities churned inside him.

Meanwhile, the other boy, the smaller incredulous one, now realized that his taller friend was not shitting him. *Wow.*

Jess dug into the secret compartment in his wallet and placed a hundred-dollar bill on the counter.

"Give me every one of those magazines. Every single one."

The kid was apologetic.

"They don't go on sale until the first. Sorry. Nobody can buy them until then."

Jess stared him straight in the eye.

"The hundred will cover the magazines and then some. You keep the rest. This is nothing but a business transaction."

The tallest boy nodded in agreement because he didn't have the courage to say no to Jess Buchanan. He handed him all seven of the magazines and then cashed out the hundred. He put the remainder in his pocket with his back turned to the camera.

"Nobody needs to know about this, right?" Jess said, stopping at the door. "And that includes your partner over there."

The smaller kid's head snapped up.

"Yeah, you," said Jess.

The kid nodded and saluted him.

Jess went outside to the gas pumps. When he glanced back inside the store windows, he saw the two boys arguing. He laughed. Nothing like a little money to spice up a relationship.

Jess peeled away after filling up his tank. As he rolled down the highway picking up speed, he thought about a woman who had no concern for the consequences of her actions. He was equally angry at himself because he was about to buy every goddamn magazine on the island when he knew he shouldn't care.

The words rumbled around in Jess' brain. And even when he tried to mix and match, none were connecting, nothing made sense. BB sat at the trailer table and told him what she was planning to do to nail Johnson. To Jess it sounded like a plot from a bad B-movie. So Johnson wanted sex from her, so what? There were a hundred men, maybe a thousand, and now with these pictures, maybe a million men who wanted to have sex with her. So why did that qualify Johnson for a special audience?

She was sure that Johnson would make it a point to embarrass her father somehow at school and she needed to stop it from happening.

"Why would he do that?" asked Jess. "What's he gonna do, let all the other teachers know that he reads the magazine?"

To further his point, Jess kicked one of a couple of dozen he had piled up on the trailer floor, waiting to be burned.

"Why not?" she asked.

"They'd think he was a perv."

She laughed.

"They know he's a perv. He's got nothing to lose there."

She would do anything to keep her dad from being humiliated. And she also wanted to humiliate Johnson in the process.

"Look," he said. "Pop's going to find out sooner or later, so don't go to Johnson, go to Pop. He'll understand."

"He won't understand. I know Dad."

"Doesn't matter. You still have to tell him."

"You don't understand. Johnson . . . I could tell you stories."

BB felt responsible for any girl who had to go through what she did, and Jess didn't know what to make of it. What was she asking him to do, watch?

"Just be there in the general vicinity in case there's trouble," she said.

"Where?" he said. "In the next room? In the closet? Where?"

"In the truck," she said. "If I get into trouble, I can always run out and we can drive away. Or you come in. Let me have twenty minutes in the room with him and then you knock on the door. I'll have some of my clothes off and you come in with a camera."

Jess kicked the magazines again.

"Who needs a camera? The pictures are right there. And who's to say it's not consensual?"

The thought made her sick.

"Right."

He got up from the table and walked to the sink. Something was eating at him. He had entertained a thought, an inconceivable one, but a thought nonetheless. While he drove around and bought up all the magazines, it had crossed his mind that if she had no respect for her body, what else had she done for money in LA? He saw an opportunity to feel her out without directly asking the question.

' Jess?"

' I'm thinking."

'About what?"

' Your fucked-up plan."

' It can work."

He took a deep breath and exhaled slowly.

"Okay, so what does a picture get you?"

"Proof."

"Proof of what?"

"He's trying to blackmail me for sex."

"Says who?"

"Me."

"You mean the girl in the pictures?"

She gave him a hard stare.

"Yeah, the girl in the pictures."

"Do you see my point?"

"No."

"Did you make money off of those pictures?"

"Yes."

"So . . .," he said, trying not to say it.

"It's not a big deal," she said.

"No, it *is* a big deal. You sold your body. That's what people will think."

JB was hurt by his insult.

"Fuck you!" she shouted.

He paused, and then spoke calmly.

"In the eyes of others, if you sold your body for pictures, you'd sell it for something else. It's more trouble than it's worth. You don't need that kind of notoriety."

Another long pause ensued while she thought about what he might be thinking.

"Is that what you think?" she asked finally.

"What I think doesn't matter."

"To me it does. Do you think I was some call girl in LA?"

"I hope not."

"I made a poor decision but that doesn't mean I'm a prostitute."

To him, this was getting worse than a bad movie. This was getting to be like television. He sat down at the table. There were holes in her plan, and if she was going to do it right, it needed a little tightening. He would have to make it look like it was her idea, but he'd had a lifetime of doing just that. Anybody who knew BB knew that she was a magnet for bad shit, so in his mind it was not possible to overthink the plan.

If BB wanted proof, Jess thought there might be a chance she could get it, but it would be risky. If she could somehow record Johnson's lechery, get his voice recorded, perhaps she stood an outside chance. Jess went into the bedroom and came back with a small voice recorder. He used it for writing music. Or used to.

"Keep it in your purse. I put the microphone on maximum sensitivity, so you'll be able to hear voices from across the room. Let's try it."

She put the recorder in her purse and set it on the counter. They talked for a few seconds and he replayed it. Their voices were clear and distinct. He realized this was a good time to protest the plan that he had just planned for her.

"You're crazy for doing this," he said. "You don't have to be the hero all the time. Sooner or later the pictures won't matter anymore."

The island community was a forgiving bunch. When it came to scandals, they'd had their fair share. He'd hate to become a member of the scandal society, but he was giving in to BB once more, so he was certainly a candidate for induction if things went wrong.

"Alright, let's do it," he said.

BB was surprised to hear him say it.

"I didn't think you'd go for it," she said.

This signaled a change of heart for BB. Maybe things *had* changed. Jess was giving in to her, for once. It was definitely progress.

They discussed the details of her plan as she got ready. She wore the same blouse and skirt that she had worn for the magazine shoot and the clothes fit her remarkably well. It was time to go. She gathered up her purse, checked her makeup, adjusted her tight skirt, and stepped out onto the trailer steps with three-inch heels on, a feat unto itself.

BB rehearsed the scene in her mind as she drove to the motel, how she would control the situation. She needed to collect the evidence fast because she wasn't about to spend more than twenty minutes in the same room with Johnson. Jess followed behind in his truck. She could see his headlights in her rearview mirror. The recorder fit snugly in her clutch.

She turned into the motel and noticed the creepy orange lights illuminating the room doors. She slowed and waited for Jess to park alongside the road as planned. She turned on the recorder and got out of the Mustang.

"You can do this," she assured herself, out loud.

She knocked on the door of room ten. Johnson opened it with a glass of red wine in his hand. He was dressed in a light blue running suit and wore white leather loafers to compliment his outfit. He looked like one of those guys who sold fried chicken on TV.

"I was afraid you weren't coming," he said. "You're late."

Johnson couldn't believe his luck. BB had worn that same outfit that she had worn in the magazine. He held his breath as she walked by. Her smell was intoxicating.

Before he closed the door, Johnson scanned the parking lot. It was nearly empty, and he took note of the two vehicles parked outside—BB's red Mustang and his black truck. He closed the door and admired BB's beauty from a few feet away.

"Would you like a drink?" he asked.

He stood next to his makeshift bar on the dresser. He had liquor for all occasions. He poured a glass of red wine and offered it to her.

"No thanks," she said, adjusting her skirt.

BB had no desire to start the evening with a drink. And she certainly wasn't going to give him the opportunity to drug her drink.

"Let me take your wrap," he said, extending his hand to take it.

She draped her shawl over his forearm and placed her purse on the desk, positioning it so the recorder was pointed right at them just a few feet away. The plan hadn't accounted for much foreplay, so she sat on the edge of the bed and unbuttoned another button on her blouse, revealing even more cleavage.

Johnson hung her wrap in the closet and turned to find BB looking entirely too provocative. It was too soon. Hell, they barely even knew each other. She had unbuttoned her blouse and it was faster than he wanted to go.

"What are you doing?" he asked, with a hint of menace in his voice.

"Isn't this what you want?" BB asked.

She spread her legs, revealing no panties—a choice she had to make because she didn't have any. She didn't wear them around Jess because they were always coming off.

The events were proceeding faster than he imagined. Johnson sat down next to BB and traced an imaginary line with his forefinger from her knee to her thigh and stopped at the hem of her skirt.

"What's the rush?" he said, eyeing her for a kiss.

His voice made her shudder. She stood up.

"Let's get one thing straight. You want to have sex with me but I don't want to have sex with you. You would be the last man on earth that I'd wanna screw. You're sick, but I'm going to do this. Otherwise, you'll tell my father, right?"

Johnson remained silent. She needed to get his voice on the recorder, so she continued.

"If I go through with this, you'll say nothing to nobody about this, right?"

He wouldn't respond and it was becoming a problem. She was running out of things to say. There were only so many ways she could call him a perverted scumbag.

"I want you to promise me that you'll never bother any girl like this again, okay?"

"I don't bother anybody," he said, looking up at her innocently.

Then the smile left his face.

' But you're bothering me now."

She was wrong in assuming that she was in control, and Johnson felt he needed to set the situation straight. He reached inside his leather bag and took out a jockey's horsewhip.

"You're not going to use that whip on me?" she asked, not quite sure if he was kidding or not.

He smiled a sick smile.

"Not if you're a good girl."

BB couldn't believe what she was witnessing. Johnson had transformed right before her eyes into a person that made her feel like she was not safe. Johnson was not Johnson anymore.

"So if I'm bad, then you whip me. Is that it?" she asked, getting all the details on the recording.

"No. If you're bad . . ."

His words trailed off as he snatched the purse from the desk and looked inside. Johnson found the tape recorder, turned it off, and threw it against the wall for emphasis.

"Do I look stupid?" he asked, continuing in that voice.

In fact, how he looked was of great concern to her now. The man in front of her now suggested nothing but danger. She wasn't sure if she could get herself out of this when she had assured Jess that she could. Johnson flicked the whip and she stood up, not amused.

'Come here, little girl," he said, and pushed BB back down on the bed.

He struck the top of her head with the handle of the whip and it dazed her. BB struggled with all her might but she couldn't push him off. Johnson was a tall man and pressed his legs into her crotch, spreading her thighs with his legs. His hands worked at her skirt, and it was evident he was good at this because he had her skirt pushed up in no time. He pressed her blouse and bra against her throat, cutting off her windpipe. BB couldn't cry out. In the back of her mind, she asked herself, *is this rape?*

How quickly she had been exposed. And she could do nothing about it. She tried to fight back but her strength gave way to a lack of oxygen. She wavered on the brink of consciousness, feeling his hands move over her, tugging here, tugging there, working the skirt up her hips. He admired her breasts as he pressed his forearm harder against her throat. These were the same breasts he had admired in the magazine.

Outside in the truck, after thinking about it, Jess decided that he didn't like the thought of BB inside the motel room with Johnson any longer. Johnson was a tall, wiry man, and if he wanted to hurt her, Jess was sure he could do it. The fear of the unknown was something he wasn't comfortable with any longer, so he started up the truck and drove to room ten and parked it next to her red Mustang, just outside the window. He got out and knocked on the door.

There was no answer. A small alarm went off in his head. He knocked again, louder and longer this time. Still no answer. He checked the room number. It was number ten. He yelled out.

"BB?"

Nothing.

Jess wasted no time. He took the tire iron out of his truck and bashed the motel window in, sending glass flying everywhere. Johnson looked up, startled. The glass had barely hit the floor when Jess climbed through. He spotted Johnson on top of BB and pulled him off, pushing him up against the wall. Jess had every intention of killing him right there but for the gurgling noise that came from BB, who lay on the bed gasping for air.

Jess let Johnson go and pulled her blouse and bra away from her throat so BB could breathe. He cleared her mouth with his fingers and he was startled by the coolness of her lips. He tilted her head back and he was ready to give her mouth-to-mouth when she began to breathe normally on her own.

Meanwhile, Johnson had run out the door and by the night clerk to his truck. The clerk wanted to stop him but Johnson was a regular. The manager would fire him if he ever offended a regular.

But there was also a shattered window and two other people inside room ten. They looked to be average people, not like all the others who came around the motel at midnight. The pretty girl looked like she was having trouble breathing, so the night clerk called 911. He also asked if the police could stop by because there had been a disturbance in room ten and there was evidence of damage.

The clerk didn't know why it was always room ten. Maybe because it was Mr. Johnson's favorite room. He saw lots of girls coming and going, girls he knew from school. He even knew a few of their names, but he had sense enough *not* to call them by their name. It would have been bad for business.

Later, Jess sat in the trailer and thought about how evil had a way of slipping into one's life without notice. It was present, even in a small town like Emerald, if only to remind people that goodness required constant vigilance. It was bad luck how things turned out at the motel, but it was also a bad idea, and bad ideas created bad luck.

When the police arrived, BB was reluctant to tell the truth about what had happened. She was careful with what she told the police and asked Jess to do the same. He felt she shouldn't hide anything, but she said she had to think about it.

Later, back in the trailer, Jess wrote this thought down in his spiral notebook.

As long as evil remains unannounced in the hearts of its victims, their souls must bear the song of darkness.

Chapter 16

There was a knock on the trailer door as Jess sat at the table eating dinner. He thought it might be BB but he wanted it to be Amanda. But Amanda was away, and once more, Amanda didn't know where he lived.

It was neither. Jess opened the door and found Billy standing in the rain with a case of beer under his arm and a shit-eating grin on his face.

"Aren't you gonna ask me in?"

It was raining hard and the beer was getting wet.

"Sure, but it'll cost you," Jess said.

Billy brought the most expensive beer, and along with it, he brought a new attitude and a heartfelt apology. Let bygones be bygones is what Billy had to say, and Jess felt the same way. They hugged in remembrance of all they had been through over the years, and it was quite a lot.

They drank beer well into the wee hours, toasting life and their pursuit of happiness—a boyhood pact that they had shared despite their different paths. After six beers apiece things began to really make sense.

Billy had come for a specific reason, a reason of opportunity for Jess to avenge the wrongs of wrongdoers, to seek justice in a world where there seemed to be little. Billy asked if he would play ball, Docksiders vs. the Brotherhood, for the hardball championship of the island—at the stadium, under the lights, Friday night. It would be just like old times, and Billy needed a pitcher, a great pitcher. And after six beers apiece, an invincible pitcher.

"I'll be there," said Jess, slamming his fist on the table.

There was one problem though. His glove had gone up in the fire.

"I need a glove."

"Got'cha, a glove," said Billy.

"Need some cleats."

"Pair of tens," said Billy.

"Need a bat."

"We got bats," said Billy.

"Need some balls."

"Got plenty of them," Billy said, grabbing his own for emphasis.

"You got yourself a pitcher."

'Got the best in town," Billy said, giving him a hard fist bump and a hug.

Well, he used to be. It had been a while and Jess wondered if he still had it in him. In the back of his drunken mind he thought, well, *he'd better.*

From her office in downtown Seattle, Amanda placed a call to Junior. She wanted to catch him off guard at that hour of the morning, and she did, as he could barely believe what he was hearing. His ex-girlfriend representing his brother?

"That's insane," he said.

"That's life," she reminded him.

"How the hell do you know Jess?" he asked suspiciously.

Amanda explained, leaving out the private details and leaving in the element of chance.

"We met at the Dockside. Jess said he needed a lawyer and I volunteered."

"Knowing you'd be dealing with me," Junior said.

He was more than a little upset at this turn of events.

"Absolutely," she replied.

Her tone suggested it was the bitter pill that he must swallow, and Junior couldn't believe that his brother would do something like this. He realized Jess was still upset about the fire, but even in the heat of anger, one doesn't forget the boundaries of morality. A brother's ex-girlfriend? No fair.

"Does he know about us?" Junior asked.

His question was met with a moment's hesitation and signaled a chink in the proverbial armor. He wanted no part of a lawyer like Amanda Hunt, and if his brother didn't know about the true nature of their former relationship, he was about to.

"Does it matter?" she asked.

Amanda realized it did. She had made a mistake by not telling Jess and now she had placed herself and her client in a jam, one thing a lawyer should never do.

"We'll see about that," he said, and hung up.

Amanda sat in her office overlooking the Seattle Ferry Terminal. Below, homeless men hung out on the corner of First Avenue begging for money to buy a bottle. She watched the Bremerton ferry sail off into the distance and wished she could get a hold of her client. Damn, she wished he had a phone.

Jess awoke with a dry throat. They had drunk the whole case of beer plus whatever else Jess had in the fridge, and the trailer smelled like most of it ended up on the floor. Through the morning light Jess could barely make out a figure sitting at the trailer table. He couldn't remember if Billy had left the night before. He hoped not. Nobody should have been driving in their condition.

"You okay?" asked Junior.

Jess wiped the sleep from his eyes, somewhat surprised to hear his brother's voice. But then again, he figured no other three-hundred-pound man could walk into his trailer unannounced and him not know it. Junior was light on his feet, especially for a big man.

"Sorta," said Jess, between gulps of water.

He stood at the open fridge in his boxer shorts. At least he had remembered to take his clothes off.

"I saw Billy on his way out. He looked as bad as you. You guys bury the hatchet?"

Honestly, Jess couldn't remember if they had or not. The subject may have come up. But they certainly didn't dwell on it.

Out of habit, even though the trailer had a nice bathroom, Jess went outside to the job shack to piss while Junior read more of the sports page. When Jess came back, he grabbed the water jug and brought it to the table with him. He felt like puking, but he did his best not to do it right there in front of Junior.

"So what's up?" he asked, sitting down at the table across from his big brother.

Junior got right to the point.

"Amanda Hunt was my girlfriend."

The announcement lay on the table like bad roast beef and Jess farted.

"But not anymore?" he asked.

"No," Junior said, somewhat painfully. "We broke up a few weeks ago."

"Then what's your point?" Jess asked.

Junior was astonished.

"She can't be your lawyer," he said.

"Why not?"

"It's immoral."

Jess let that one sit just for irony's sake. *Immoral?* He could cite about ten good reasons for why it was absolutely *not* immoral to have Amanda represent him. He cracked the door for a little fresh air after another bad beer fart.

"I thought it would change things," Junior admitted.

His brother's tone had softened, evidence of an advantage Jess didn't know he had. It was apparent that Junior wanted no part of Amanda Hunt. *Immoral?* Perhaps their intimate lawyer-client relationship was a little dicey, but if Amanda could elicit a response from Junior like this, wasn't it exactly what he needed?

"Amanda is a good lawyer. I need a good lawyer. You said so yourself."

Jess felt he was doing a good job of holding it together while making earth-shattering decisions on the fly. But he still wanted to puke.

Junior shook his head.

"C'mon, man, it ain't right."

Jess realized that to discuss it any further was of no use, so he changed the subject.

"I got another note. Somebody said they've got Legs. Look at this."

Jess dug the note out of his notebook and handed it to Junior.

"Know anything about it?" he asked.

Angry at all this finger-pointing, Junior snapped back.

"Forget about the dog. He's gone."

Junior meant it to hurt. Legs meant everything to Jess, and Junior knew it.

"If one of my guys had him, I'd know it. Those things get around."

True. It was hard to keep a secret in Emerald.

"Then I'm going back to bed," Jess said.

He trudged off to the trailer bedroom and closed the door, leaving Junior to read the rest of the sports page. When he finished, Junior took out his wallet and left a hundred-dollar bill on the trailer table. On the back of one of his business cards, he wrote, *Get a phone*.

Chapter 17

The parking lot was full outside Memorial Stadium, and inside, it was the top of the third inning. The pitcher had finished his warm-up tosses and stood off to the side of the mound, rubbing the ball.

The Docksiders held a one-run lead on two hits and an error. Jess had struck out four batters with the hard slider. He didn't have a good feel for his change-up, so he stuck with the hard stuff. He looked off into the distance and admired the sunset. The sky to the west was lit up magnificently. He stood there for a few seconds and the ump got pissed.

"C'mon, pitcher, throw the damn ball."

On the way home from dinner, BB and Pop noticed all the cars parked outside the stadium. Pop was never one to miss a good ballgame, so he asked if they could stop in for a minute.

Much to their surprise, they recognized the pitcher on the mound as soon as they walked in. BB thought Jess looked good up there; he was about the same weight as he was in high school, though he had lost probably ten pounds recently. Billy was at second base and wiggled his ass for all the girls in the stands, BB noticed.

The stands were packed, and people stood three deep on the third base line when they couldn't fit into the stands—just like it was when Jess and Billy were seniors, the year they won the state championship. They had a helluva team, and as BB searched the diamond for familiar faces, she realized that over half the guys out there were from that team.

Jess threw a couple of pitches and Pop spotted a flaw in his mot on. He wasn't striding out and bending enough at the waist. Pop yelled out, "Drive your chest to your knee, Jess."

Jess heard a familiar voice and he looked for Pop on the sidelines. Pop was right. He wasn't driving to his left knee. He let the next one fly and found another three miles an hour on his fastball. The batter swung under it when the ball seemed to rise as it crossed the plate.

Jess shouted at Pop, "Get in the dugout."

He needn't say more. Pop walked inside the Docksiders' dugout, took the scorebook from Dennis Henderson, and shouted to his team on the field, "Okay, boys, let's play some baseball."

It may not have sounded like much to an unwary bystander, but to all the boys who had played ball for Pop Gunderson at Emerald High School, they knew this to be his famous rallying cry. A cheer went up from the Docksider dugout as Pop took his customary place on the outside of the dugout steps, balancing on his left foot while he tucked his right foot behind him against the dugout post.

Was this enough to think that they had a chance? The Brotherhood hadn't been beaten in five years, but with Pop at the helm, BB on the sidelines, Jess on the mound, and Billy at second, some celestial benevolence united a spirit of mutual dependence, that unique force behind all grand upsets.

In the stands, Junior took a ribbing from his buddies because he had big money bet on his boys. But Junior had to give it to him, Jess was shutting them down. He knew that his brother hadn't thrown a pitch in seriousness for five or six years, so his performance up to that point was pretty admirable. The Brotherhood was an intimidating assemblage of brute power, and Junior felt it would be just a matter of time before Jess would wear down. He offered to double the bet that the Brotherhood would win. No one took him up on it.

"Figured," he said, quieting the bunch.

It was the bottom of the ninth, two away, and the score was tied at three. It was the final at bat for the home team, and the Docksiders had Billy Wilson on third, the result of a bunt, a stolen base, and a sacrifice fly to right. One more hit was all they needed, and Jess strolled to the plate with a chance to rectify past wrongs, to seek vindication against a team he wanted to beat more than any team in the world. Of course, most of the people in the stands wanted him to strike out. Looking, no less.

Pop glanced at the scorebook. He saw that Jess had gone oh for three, a sickly collar with two strikeouts and a feeble grounder back to the mound. The old coach took a look down his bench and found three guys with determined looks on their faces but not one was worth a shit. Besides, Pop couldn't pinch-hit for Jess in that situation, Jess would never forgive him for it. Dickie Vandebeak was on the mound for the Brotherhood and he was throwing peas, fastballs that looked like BBs to a hitter.

Pop called timeout. He motioned for Billy and Jess to meet him halfway up the third baseline to discuss their strategy, even though their strategy was pretty simple: Jess had to get a hit.

"How do you feel?" Pop asked Jess.

Jess hadn't faced live pitching in years, and it showed in his bat speed. Dickie had been humming it by him all night.

"Dickie's throwing hard," Jess admitted.

Billy looked to the bench to see who was available to pinch-hit. He saw what Pop knew already—three guys and a grimace. Jess was their best bet, maybe their only bet. The Docksiders needed a hit, and Billy believed Jess was the guy to get it, the perfect guy.

"For Legs, Bro," Billy said.

He put up his hand for a high-five and Jess left him hanging, lost in his swing thoughts. Pop was calm in the face of an overflow crowd stirring with anticipation, knowing that the next few seconds would decide the outcome.

"Okay, wait for your pitch," Pop said. "Let him get a strike up. The next one, he'll follow with the hard one, low and away. Just put your bat out there, Dickie will provide the power. Drive it to right, nothing big, just get some wood on it."

Pop turned to Billy.

"He'll get you in. Don't worry."

In fact, Billy wasn't worried at all. If there was one guy he wanted in that situation, it was his best friend.

"Let's go, Bro. Little bingo."

Billy trotted back to third base while Jess walked to the plate with the bat on his shoulder and his mind set in swing preparation—the zone. He envisioned the first strike, then the outside slider or fastball, then the smooth stroke to right, a line drive between first and second.

Off to the third base side of the field, BB watched the men in her life. She had forgiven each one of them because men were men, she decided. But she also knew what they needed from her now. She sent her spirit out to them, willing them to win—for Jess to get a hit, for Billy to score, and for Pop to be a proud winning coach again. BB followed her father with her gaze as he strolled back to the dugout. He spat out sunflower seeds all along the way, focused on the moment when games become the source of town lore.

Pop put his leg up on the dugout post, adjusted the scorebook in his hands, and shouted to the two Docksiders out on the diamond, "Okay, boys, let's play some baseball."

Jess dug in at the plate and Dickie took the sign from the catcher. He threw a hard fastball—outside, ball one. Jess recognized the spin on the next pitch and told himself not to bite. The slider exploded at the plate going from belt high to his knees in a millisecond. There was no way he could have hit that pitch.

"Stee-rike," said the umpire.

Jess backed out of the box and adjusted his golf glove—his personal fashion statement. The catcher noticed.

"Pussy."

The comment was made to throw Jess off his concentration, but he envisioned the next pitch low and away, just like Pop had said.

Jess dug in and Dickie delivered. Jess kept his head down on the fastball—low and away, just as Pop had predicted, just as Pop had taught Dickie to throw it—and reality was a little bingo between first and second, bringing Billy home with the winning run. Billy jumped in the air as he went down the third base line, pumping his fist in glee. It was a tremendous upset that was definitely etched into town lore. The rock star was the hero.

Naturally the Brotherhood were poor losers. They refused to shake hands, and many of them stomped around the diamond swearing and pointing fingers at Jess, some at Billy. They called Jess a scab, and Billy a motherfucker for bringing in a ringer who really wasn't a member of the team. They even threatened to protest the game, but since Billy was the league commissioner, their protest probably wasn't going to get too far.

The Docksiders celebrated into the wee hours at the Kingdom Come, and Jess got drunk for the third night in a row. He drove home with one eye closed because he was seeing two of everything. He knew he shouldn't have been driving but he had no choice. Nobody was going his way when the bar closed down. Plus, all told, he was going less than a mile down an old dirt road.

Jess arrived at the pit entrance and saw the thick cable on the ground. Then his headlights caught something in the distance. Raccoons were chewing on pieces of garbage and a steady stream of it led to the pond. Jess's heart raced as he ran up the gravel bank. At the top he looked down. In the moonlight he could see the pond filled to the brim with garbage. Dumpsters full of it. The water couldn't be seen for all the waste floating on top.

Jess collapsed in a drunken heap and sobbed. It wasn't a selfish cry, it was more a cry for mother earth and those who didn't understand her beauty. An echo of violation that emanated from deep within his soul.

Paper

Chapter 18

The ticket to paradise requires the price of admission.

Jess wrote this down in his spiral notebook, then leaned back against the trailer table cushions and thought about the last three days. It had taken twelve trips to the dump to clean up the pond, and at five bucks a pop it had put a severe dent in his monthly allowance. He had to dip into Junior's phone loan to pull it off. He was sad because he couldn't buy beer for the rest of the month. The price of admission?

Images floated past his mind's eye once again. He was at a crossroads where community and family affixed themselves like some bulwark to his brain, no passing Go, no pretending that 500 bucks a month could soothe his poverty-stricken soul.

It was cold outside like it had been for days and he couldn't shake the chill from his bones. The frigid pond water had left him practically numb. He wanted to rent a wet suit but he couldn't afford one.

He put on his jacket and left the alcove light on to beam down upon a spiral notebook on the kitchen table, opened to a page where he had scrawled Chapter 18: *The ticket to Paradise*. He didn't mean to capitalize "Paradise" but he left it that way as he walked out of the trailer to do something that few men had the nerve to do, because breaking up is hard to do.

Jess turned into the marina, drove past the bait shop and the Dockside, past the dry-dock storage and down to the ferry landing, where he parked the pickup and gathered his thoughts. He could see the tip of the island and beyond, across the strait to Bisset Island, the next island over. He wondered what life was like over there. He had lived on Clay Island his whole life and yet he hadn't traveled every road, seen every cove, explored every mystery of this jewel in the San Juan archipelago, the second largest of the 173 dots in the great Pacific pool. It was a place where to the west the Canadian boundary extended *south* of where he sat.

He considered the history.

Clay Island was aptly named because the glacier till that made up the soil contained very little rock, something his grandfather, Big Al Buchanan, had discovered when he landed in Emerald with his family. It was before roads and curbs and sidewalks and septic tanks and foundations were needed. Island lore speculated that Clay Island was a pile of brown fudge and years later, as Emerald grew in population, the ground below became a constant source of cruelty to the fortunes of many, where buildings sank in a minute and houses tilted, where the largest building—the old Pioneer building— disappeared one morning, lost in a sink hole as large as a small lake. It was an amazing feat of nature that had everybody thinking, *Who's next?*

Big Al spent what little money he had to look for gravel and he found two major rock deposits, the only sizeable deposits on Clay Island. He bought the land and the mineral rights to the old pit, and a few years later bought the property where Buchanan Construction is located now, on the south side of town. Some in Emerald argued that Big Al held a virtual monopoly and that it was unfair. Others argued that if Big Al was the only one who could excavate the gravel and deliver the concrete and asphalt at a reasonable price, why shouldn't he be the one to own the pits? Sooner or later they would have to go to him, so why not sooner, and save everybody on the markup?

Jess considered the ways of mankind—of grandfathers and fathers, of sons and daughters, of grandmothers and mothers and daughters and wives and girlfriends, and how it all figured into one grand scheme. Jess wasn't the smartest guy in the world but he recognized that greed and ignorance and lack of aforethought would provide no answer to the problems inherent to progress. Was the inevitable step forward. . . destruction?

A song ran through his head along with the idea that he must remember to handle what he was about to do with heart and tact. Amanda was a friend and ally, someone he liked and admired. It was a difficult thing to say, that he loved another, and he would try to handle it with compassion and empathy. The chorus of a new song, "What'cha Gonna Do?," kept running in his head, that melody in the back of the brain that never went away for a songwriter, no matter how hard he tried to block it out.

Deception was a dangerous game and Amanda realized the truth of it now. She had truly meant to tell Jess about her former relationship with Junior but the opportunity had never presented itself. At least to her liking.

"But it's no excuse," she said.

Jess replayed the events in his mind—their meeting, the escalation of passion, their shared moments of intimacy—moments that wouldn't have provided an opportunity for this kind of truth telling.

"I can see how it happened," he said.

Amanda ached inside, but she wasn't willing to show it. He was telling her how he loved another and she was happy for him. True love was something she had known once, long ago. But that boy had taken his life on a bleak morning before finals in their second year of law school. Jess had some of Keith's mannerisms, like the stutter shake in his left leg in times of anxiousness. She put her hands on his knee to quiet the shake.

"I still want to counsel you," she said, and Jess was relieved to hear it. "If you decide not to sell, it'll take a lot of courage, and I admire that," she added. She walked to the kitchen side of the stateroom and said, "People who believe in something besides what it might do for their pocketbook are few and far between. Believe me, I know. I'm proud of you." Then Amanda added, "Besides, you need me. You just don't care enough about money."

True, he cared for some, but not a lot. But this was not about money, at least to his way of thinking.

"I won't let Junior take advantage of you. He can't bullshit me," she said.

Jess recognized in Amanda the proverbial eye of the tiger, just the thing he wanted to see from his lawyer, because she was going to need it.

Then he felt a calm drop over his senses. It was the movie guy again.

The movie guy looked serious, like he had pressing things to consider.

" I've been reading up on methods of excavation. I believe we can save the pond," the movie guy said, like a man who knew something that others didn't.

Jess watched the movie guy from across the room. He said something more and Amanda turned her head slightly, like the way Meryl Streep looked over her shoulder in *The French Lieutenant's Woman*. The camera eye framed Amanda's features perfectly. Her expensive earrings dangled from her petal soft earlobes, throwing a brilliant hue about her cheeks. The movie guy drew her in.

"One last time?" he whispered.

Before Amanda could reply, they were down on the stateroom carpet again. Jess watched as the series of love motions progressed, blue jeans and panties pulled off to plunder, to take, to push Amanda's sweet butt cheeks to the floor.

"Do me," she said huskily to the movie guy.

Other than a few expressions of primal lust, no audible words were spoken between them. They were scat singing that famous song—"One Last Fuck"—and the movie guy handled himself pretty well. He had good rhythm, and with one last thrust, Amanda met the movie guy halfway in the ultimate shock of gratification, the bedrock for all last fucks.

Not bad, Jess observed.

The movie guy and Amanda were both out of breath. Lying there together on the floor, Amanda looked over at him and laughed, saying, "I guess we got that out of our system."

To begin his engagement to BB on a note of deception was not the best way to start off, Jess thought. Yet how could he ever explain to BB that it was the movie guy and not him who had screwed Amanda?

It was inevitable, that thing between them. As children, BB and Jess were best friends. As teenagers, they explored what it was like to be infatuated with one another. Now, as adults, their love had become a responsibility to each other, beyond just giving comfort and joy. They had spent a lifetime together playing at love rather than being *in love*. It was a distinction they had to fix. Love had come too easy for them. There had been no mystery, no discovery. He knew her secrets as she knew his. They had known no reason to search, or to lie in bed at night and wonder who it might be, their one true love.

Jess and BB shared a gift and took turns being irresponsible with it. But it was their natural inclination to test the boundaries, to find out what it meant to be *in love*. For them, their emotional bond couldn't be measured. There was no dipstick to show this is how much I love you, nor was there a description in a book or a poem worthy of an explanation. It simply had been there. Always.

BB was confused by Jess' tone over the phone. He had asked her to come over and it sounded like the Jess of old, that private voice she hoped he reserved only for her. Did it signal a change of heart? Would she be willing to confess to loving him now more than ever? Or would he admit, finally, what she had suspected all along: that he was in love with someone else. But his tone had the tenderness of old in it. Could it be, after all they had been through? They had been hurt, but hurt could be brushed aside, uncertainty dispelled, with one long kiss.

All her questions were answered once she arrived at the trailer. Jess confessed his love for her, how he wanted to marry her, and she did the same for him.

BB also gave him her answer in standard BB gusto. She took his hand and marched him back to the bedroom. Over the radio, George Jones and Tammy Wynette sang "Together Again," certainly an appropriate backing track.

But there was one more thing. Jess was glad that he had taken the time to wash.

Jess sat in the director's chair once again, 7:17 and counting. Not everyone had arrived. Many of the Brotherhood milled about, leaning on their pickups while Jess sat alone on his side of the cable. They were all waiting on Junior.

"To hell with it, let's get started," announced Melvin.

"Sounds good to me," said Jess. "Who dumped that shit in my pond?"

He tossed a pebble over the cable separating them from him. It landed with an audible *plink*. Silence. Nobody answered.

"Don't know what you're talking about," Melvin said.

"Game night, somebody came in here and dumped garbage all over the pit. Most of it ended up in the pond. It took me three days to clean it up. Hell, you can still smell it."

He could smell other things too. Forty-two pieces of shit staring back at him blankly.

"Couldn't have been any of us," said Melvin. "We were all at the game."

The men laughed.

"All of us except Shorty."

The men grumbled.

Jess laughed, mocking them.

"Right. It must've been Shorty."

"If you want to blame us, he's the only one who could've done it, cuz we were all at the game. . . all of us except for him," Melvin said.

The men seconded his explanation. Collectively, it sounded like an urge from the primal gutbucket.

"*Aaarrrrgh.*"

Jess had taken his best shot, realizing that he probably wasn't going to get very far. But still, he had to take it.

"Anymore *incidents* like that and we don't meet, understand?" Jess said.

He emphasized the word "incidents" because it was clearly

something more to him. One of the men shouted, "Quit yer belly achin' and sign that contract."

The other men grumbled in agreement.

"*Aaarrrrgh.*"

Jess was beginning to understand their language, but their vocabulary left something to be desired. A contract? He wasn't to blame for that one.

"Junior hasn't offered me anything. How can I sell something without even knowing a price? You got a number, Melvin?"

"You know I don't," Melvin said, staring him in the eye.

"That's right. So you should be talking to Junior, not me. A man has to know a price before he sells. That's pretty basic, isn't it?"

The men considered this. In Jess' mind, they must have agreed because he heard another collective grumble.

"*Aaarrrgh.*"

"We'll talk to Junior," Melvin said.

Then Melvin followed with an outright lie.

"We're on your side, Jess. We want to see you get a fair price for your land."

"That's all I'm asking," Jess replied, smiling back at them with all insincerity.

But there was another point to this meeting, the most important point.

"I got a note the other day. Whoever wrote it said they have my dog." He looked into each of their faces. "Do any of you have Legs?"

Some men looked down to check and everybody laughed.

"We've all got legs," Melvin said, smartly.

It was the gavel hitting the block. The men dispersed quickly, laughing and joking among themselves as they walked back to their pickups.

It left Jess alone in the director's chair. He created a scene in his mind and barked orders to an imaginary movie crew. He sat in a tower seat like some big-shot movie director. In the reenactment, Jess imagined the scene in an action movie where the movie guy wipes the smile off Melvin's face with a Dirty Harry bazooka blast to the forehead—*bah-boom.*

Jess folded up the chair and walked back to the trailer. Inside, he took out the Martin and wrote, "What'cha Gonna Do?"

What'cha gonna do, What'cha gonna do?
When there's no timber in the forest
And we rip the jungle by the roots
What'cha gonna do?

When we build our castles so high in the sky
And we cry, Progress! That's what we need
When we rape a place with dust in our eyes
And we cry, Progress! That's what we need

When there's no air to breathe
No sunlight to see
No clean water to drink
Dust to dust you see
Dust to dust
For me and you
What'cha gonna do?
What'cha gonna do?

Junior didn't like Melvin's insinuations. He stared back at him from behind the desk and leaned back to present a broader angle—the body language of intimidation. He chose his words carefully and explained to Melvin that indeed he had decided on a number and when he wanted to discuss it with Jess was entirely their business, not the business of Melvin Banks or the Brotherhood.

Melvin faced the irony of the world, two different viewpoints interpreting the same events.

"Then what's the number?" asked Melvin, testing Junior.

"It's none of your business," Junior answered.

Melvin disagreed, but he was in no position to argue.

"Okay," said Melvin. "But that number better be good."

Melvin stood in the doorway because he had another question. Junior looked up from his paperwork.

"Last week you said you'd give a bonus to whoever had the dog. Where's that at?" asked Melvin.

Junior bristled.

"Who's got the dog?"

"What's the bonus?"

"Keep your job, for one. Because if somebody has that dog, and they don't give him up, they're done. Gone. Forever."

"Nobody's got the dog," Melvin laughed. "I just wanted to know the bonus is all."

"Get a handle on these guys or I'll fire every damn one of them," said Junior. "That garbage deal was bullshit."

"I thought it was pretty slick," Melvin said. "Give the boy something to think about."

"Get a handle on it, or I'll take care of it."

Melvin stared Junior down.

"You give us a good number. I'll take care of the rest."

Junior growled, "Get outta here," and went back to his paperwork.

Melvin lingered in the doorway a while longer, looking out of the windows to Sunset Bay and the ferry gliding into the ferry landing. Junior looked up.

"Now what?"

"What a view," Melvin mused.

Junior took this to mean something very different than a poetic musing.

"Get back to work!"

Melvin took this as his cue to leave. He meandered back to his truck thinking of a number himself. On the drive back to the south pit office he sang along with the radio. It was his favorite Beatles song.

"That's what I want . . ."

Marie came to the door after the first ring, a bundle of nervous energy. She looked strangely at her son, a little flustered that he felt compelled to ring the doorbell. Jess had noticed a familiar vehicle parked outside and thought it might be BB driving Pop's pickup. But he wasn't sure.

"You're so funny," said his mother, as she kissed him on the lips.

Pop stood up when Jess entered the living room. He looked all done up. His hair was combed back nicely and he had on a nice western shirt with a bolo tie. He shook Jess' hand, more out of a show of respect to Marie since they never shook hands. Some bonds didn't require hand shaking.

His mother talked a mile a minute. Sure, he would have a cup of coffee. A piece of pie too. Marie went into the kitchen, leaving the two men alone.

He looked at Pop.

"What's going on?"

Pop sat back on the couch and folded his arms.

" I've come to see your mother. People get lonely sometimes."

He noticed the sincerity in Pop's voice. Jess wanted to give him the business for coming to see his mother, but he refrained, knowing it would have been in poor taste. Marie came back holding a silver tray. On it sat her most favorite possession in the world, an antique milk pitcher. She had enough milk in that pitcher to serve coffee for a year. She served the two men and then sat down after pouring a cup for herself.

"Pop tells me you pitched a good game against Junior's team."

"We won. That's what matters," he said evenly.

Jess hated talking about games. He could remember his dad waiting up on Friday nights just to talk about the game, and more often than not, Jess would go to bed without saying more than a goodnight. He felt bad about that now.

"What did Junior have to say about the game?" his mother asked.

"Nothing."

His mother couldn't understand that defeats were nothing to discuss, especially ones that were elevated to town lore.

"Funny Junior didn't mention it when he came over this afternoon," she said, innocently.

"He got beat, Mother. He doesn't want to talk about it."

The point didn't connect with Marie.

"He was rooting for you. I know Junior. Family comes first."

She smiled and looked at Pop for a reaction.

"It certainly does," Pop seconded, knowing it wasn't true.

She freshened all their cups of coffee, then dished the pie.

"Don't be hard on your brother. He loves you very much. He gave you his truck and trailer, doesn't that prove something?"

"It proves that he feels guilty about torching my camper," Jess said sharply.

Marie pooh-poohed him.

"He had nothing to do with it and you know it. Your brother loves you very much."

Jess didn't want to have this conversation in front of Pop. He was embarrassed by the way his mother always felt she needed to instruct him in the ways of love.

"Okay," he said, and then added under his breath, "asshole."

Marie took this to mean that her youngest was finished with the subject. She wouldn't press. But in her mind, it was a discussion they would have to have at some point. She wanted peace among her children, even if it meant that she had to referee. Such was a mother's right.

Pop watched them interact. Mothers and sons had a different way of relating to each other, nothing like fathers and daughters. Pop had come to pay his respects to Marie since he hadn't attended Buck's funeral. He saw an opportunity to say what he had come to say to both. He cleared his throat.

"I need to say something here."

Pop had rehearsed the words but they were failing him now.

"I can't say how sorry I am for you both. I know how you feel because it was my loss too. Buck was my best friend. All our lives . . ." His voice trailed off, crackling with emotion.

"We know," Jess said, hoping this wouldn't set his mother off.

Pop wiped his eyes with the napkin and continued.

"But I think of him every day. We had a lot of fun together. If I had a brother, I guess it was Buck. I know he loved his wife, and both his sons. Families aren't perfect, hell no. And Buck knew that. I'll miss his laugh and his funny comebacks and his . . . well . . ."

Pop's top lip quivered. He wanted to say something more, but he couldn't. He sat back in the couch and dabbed his eyes with a hankie. It moved Jess to go over and put his hand on his shoulder. Marie began to cry and left the room. Pop felt responsible for making her cry.

"She does this a lot," Jess said, patting Pop on the back. "She'll be okay."

They could hear Marie in the guest bathroom wailing the sound of widowhood, of love and love lost. Pop claimed he had something to do and got up from his seat. Jess knew it was a lie but he couldn't blame him. His mother was really going at it.

"Tell Marie I said goodbye," Pop said, putting on his derby hat.

They walked downstairs to the landing and stood at the threshold with the door open.

"Do you think there's a way to get to the gravel without hurting the pond?" Jess asked Pop, getting right to his problem.

It was a good question, thought Pop. He would have to ask around, make some calls to his friends, old college buddies who were high-powered engineers in Seattle.

"When do you need to know?" Pop asked.

"Tomorrow?"

"I'll see," Pop said. "I'll have to make a few phone calls."

There was one other thing Jess wanted to talk to Pop about, but this was not the time or place.

"Why don't you come over tomorrow and I'll show you what I'm thinking?" Jess said. "I'll barbecue some salmon."

"Just me?" asked Pop.

"BB doesn't need to be there," Jess said, and Pop understood what he meant.

"Then I'll see you tomorrow," Pop said.

Jess closed the door behind and went back upstairs to wait for his mother to finish crying. She was taking her sweet time in the bathroom, so he went into the master bedroom to find something he could keep in remembrance of his father. His mother found him going through his father's closet. She didn't have the nerve to get to it. Not yet.

Marie said she had just the thing for Jess to remember his father by. She took down an old shoebox from the top shelf and inside was Buck's floppy fishing hat with the flies still attached. It was a memento she had been saving specifically for this son.

"Try it on," she said.

He did, and just as Marie suspected, it fit.

Jess had come to see his mother for another reason, a specific reason, and he waited until they had walked back upstairs to announce it.

"Mom . . . BB and I are getting married."

Marie hesitated, not quite sure if she heard him correctly. Then, as the whole of it sank in, she started to cry again, tears of joy. She excused herself and went back downstairs to the master bathroom. Jess figured it was a good time to leave since these things could go on forever.

Chapter 19

Jess climbed the gravel ridge to bathe in the pond and stopped at the top. Below, he spotted a lazy-headed white swan swimming aimlessly on the water.

The albatross?

If it was a sign, he surely didn't know what it meant. He slipped into the water, careful not to disturb her. The water was cold and he washed himself quickly, rubbing his skin with a bar of soap and a washcloth.

When he finished, he slipped on his robe and sat down on the bank and watched her. She floated effortlessly across the pond, seemingly undisturbed by his presence. Her whiteness shone in deep contrast to the clear emerald water and there was a look of serenity about her. Jess wanted that look. As he sat there, he thought about people he knew and wished they could understand the way of the swan.

Detective Harris parked the unmarked police car at the old pit entrance and sat for a moment, looking at the scene before him. He took it all in. Huge white lettering faded with the years was stenciled on the ancient ready-mix loading chute. It was a large green barrel, shaped like an ice cream cone, that stood thirty feet high. The letters read in bold type, "Buchanan Construction Co., est. 1929."

It was definitely a good time to start a business, thought Harris, during the Great Depression when labor was cheap. He tried to imagine what the pit must have looked like back then. Old mixer trucks like the ones he'd seen in the movies ran in and out of the pit, pulling under the freshly painted chute, then gunning their engines, straining to make their way down Old Pit Road, the road that would take them to the highway and back to town. People could hear the Buchanan mixer trucks groaning under the weight of their loads, out to pour another foundation or sidewalk or curb.

Harris knew the history. Buchanan Construction had played a significant role in the building of Emerald, and the family had amassed a fortune from it. It was something one had to understand in order to assess the situation. He looked at the burned remnants of an old camper to gauge the sentiment of the town—the awful bitterness that was directed Jess' way. Harris wondered why Jess hadn't hauled the burned camper away. He heard he was strange but that was definitely a little crazy, having the sight and the smell right there in his proverbial front yard.

Ed knocked on the trailer door hoping he wasn't disturbing anybody. Jess opened it and recognized him, the little towheaded cop from the station.

"Hello, Jess," said Harris.

Jess took stock of his recent actions, trying to recall something that may have warranted this visit from the police, especially so early in the morning. It was eight o'clock.

"Hello, officer," Jess said, shaking his hand.

"Actually, it's detective. But do you have a minute?"

Harris nodded toward the heap of burned metal, not more than ten feet away, making the surrounding air smell like charcoal. The sheriff's office had investigated the fire, but since Jess lived two miles outside of the town limits, this was beyond the jurisdiction of the Emerald Police. Jess glanced at the camper and then at Harris, questioning why was he there?

"Sure, come in."

Detective Harris hadn't expected to find an immaculately clean trailer inside. He had pegged Jess for a slob musician type. Jess motioned for him to have a seat.

"Want a cup of coffee?"

"Swell," said Harris.

Harris realized his reply sounded vintage detective. He looked around the trailer, impressed. He had heard that Silverstreams were nice.

"Nice trailer."

"Thanks. It's my brother's," said Jess, warming the mugs in the microwave.

This didn't add up in Harris' mind. Brothers at odds didn't lend Silverstream trailers to one another. They were expensive, and they looked it. Everything was trimmed in red mahogany and cherry, and the wood gleamed with polish in the sunlight. It was a helluva lot nicer than his apartment.

Jess knew what the detective might be thinking.

"Junior didn't know anything about the fire. I'm pretty sure of that," he said as he put the coffee mugs in the microwave.

Of this, the detective wasn't so sure. But he knew enough to let it go for now.

"You certainly made out in the deal," Harris cracked, with an inflection in his voice that sounded more like George Segal in *King Rat*.

Harris had meant for the comment to be taken lightly, but Jess was still smarting from their disagreement at the police station.

"I lost most everything I owned," he said coolly.

Well then, the guy had recouped magnificently, thought Harris. A Martin guitar case leaned against the wall and it didn't appear to be a cheap one. Harris had seen Jess' band at the Seattle Pier and thought they were pretty good; in fact, *real* good. He had all their tapes and played them all the time. But Harris couldn't let his admiration for Jess as a singer-songwriter interfere with his judgment. He was a cop first. Not a groupie.

"I saw your band at the Pier in Seattle."

"That was a long time ago."

"Not really. Three years."

Harris always wanted to learn how to play the guitar but instead he had to work for a living, which he set out to do right now.

"I've got the sheriff's report on the fire. The investigating officer concluded that it was lightning hitting the camper and igniting the propane tank, causing an explosion."

Harris paused.

"Is that what you believe?"

Jess smiled.

"Does a duck have balls?" Jess asked.

It was a strange question, and Harris didn't have an answer since he had never really thought about it.

"Okay, then what happened in your version?" Harris asked, moving on.

' Who was the investigating officer?" asked Jess.

Harris looked in the file.

' Lawson Banks."

' I rest my case," said Jess.

' Then you think it was intentional?"

' I'm not very popular these days."

' Then who did it in your opinion?"

Jess set the mugs on the table.

' Isn't that your job?"

The detective couldn't understand why Jess was being so uncooperative. He sipped the coffee. It was terrible. Worse than the stuff they had down at the station.

"There was lightning over the area that night. It may have hit the camper," Harris said.

"Then why are you here?" asked Jess.

Good point, thought Harris. He couldn't tell Jess that a little birdie had told him differently. Jess trusted no one and suspected everybody and Harris couldn't blame him. He adopted the good cop attitude, trying to get on the same side.

"If you're in danger, I can help."

If Harris thought the Emerald Police could protect him, he was seriously mistaken, thought Jess. The Brotherhood were hunters of the highest order. If they wanted to kill him, they could. And would.

"If they want me dead, I'm dead."

"They?" Harris asked.

Jess had to be careful here. He didn't want to point fingers since he still had some investigating to do.

"Whoever wants to hurt me . . .," he said, letting the thought trail off.

"I can have a car watch the area. It might help," offered Harris.

It might, thought Jess. But he didn't need the police to guard him like some prince, showing he was afraid.

"I don't think it would do much good," Jess said.

"Leave the thinking to me," said Harris, getting up from the table. "Thanks for the coffee."

Harris had a few other questions for young Buchanan, but it was apparent that Jess didn't want his help. However, there was one last question he felt he needed to ask since it mattered a great deal.

"Are you gonna sell?" Harris asked. "It would help if I knew."

Act and consequence rummaged through Jess' mind along with trust and suspicion. He had nothing to hide, so he answered the question truthfully.

"I don't know yet."

The detective knew the airfield bid was a month away. Time was not on Jess' side.

"I'll stay in touch," Harris said.

The detective stopped at the door and glanced at the guitar leaning against the wall in the corner.

"Can you play 'Stairway to Heaven'?" he asked, looking at Jess in mock seriousness.

It was a little inside humor, guitar-player humor, since it was the question asked of every guy with a guitar the world over. Jess smiled and thought maybe Harris wasn't so bad after all.

Harris stepped out onto the trailer steps and looked up at the immense wall of gravel that rimmed the pond. He decided to climb the bank to have an up-close-and-personal look at this pond he had heard so much about.

Once he scaled the gravel ridge, he stood at the top and looked down at a white swan swimming leisurely on the surface of an emerald-green-colored pond, the water as clear as any Hollywood pool. Harris imagined a house where the trailer was now, one with concrete arches and a sun deck in back. A waterfall ran down the bank into another pool below, a private swimming area where Hollywood starlets sunned themselves in the light of a hot day. *Who'd want to trash this?* he thought to himself. Harris vowed to find out because . . . well . . that's what good cops do.

Junior punched in the numbers once again just to make sure. By now he had them memorized. He looked at the final numbers and knew he had a winning bid if only he owned the rock.

Junior picked up the phone and dialed Amanda. It rang four times and then Amanda's voice instructed the caller to leave a message. He listened to her voice, very different from the one he knew in more intimate circumstances. He missed her. But now he had to deal with her business side, and she was someone to reckon with in that respect. She was tough, and Junior admired that about her. He was fully prepared to give them what they wanted, as long as it was in the ballpark of what he thought the mineral rights were worth. The message ended and he heard the beep.

"One point eight million, Amanda. It's more than fair. Let's sign the papers," he said, and hung up.

She listened to the message again that night. Junior was right, it *was* fair. But these were hardly fair conditions, so it was only fair that Jess realize the full benefits of the American Way. In her view, Junior had enjoyed an unrealistic business environment for too long and she had an old friend who might be interested in bidding on that airfield too. Sim Caggiano was a man who had the resources to make Junior look like a boy playing in a sandbox, and Sim owed her one. When she went into the private sector after her time in the King County Prosecutor's Office, she was a much sought-after lawyer in Seattle because of her connections. Yes, being the daughter of a senator certainly had its perks.

If Junior had counted on community sentiment to pressure Jess into selling, then Jess was going to fight fire with fire. It was something he had wanted to do for quite some time, and now seemed like the perfect opportunity. He would invite the children of Emerald out to swim in one of the best swimming holes in the state.

Jess placed an ad in that week's *Island News-Times* announcing the Saturday Swims, an event he intended to hold all summer. Marie had donated the money to pay for the advertisement and BB offered to help lifeguard. The ad encouraged parents to come and help watch because his greatest fear was of an accidental drowning. He would have a hundred eyes making sure that every kid was accounted for at all times.

Also, Jess felt enlisting the help of everybody was building a sense of community, something Jess felt had been lost once Emerald and the island became such a popular destination for tourists. Of course, the old pit was still private property, so ultimately he'd bear the responsibility of ownership and all the liability that came with it. But if it would create great memories for kids, Jess was more than willing to share the burden. And maybe unload a bit of guilt in the process.

Pop arrived at six with a case of Bud. He stepped inside the trailer and looked around. He dreamt he might own something like this someday. The inside of the trailer was trimmed in mahogany and red cherry, and the space didn't feel cramped at all—an easy, livable home. It was something he could tow to his lot on the peninsula and live in for months at a time, a place where his Scandinavian predecessors had landed years ago with the wind in their eyes and the salt brine in their noses. He imagined their first steps on the rocky shoreline, with the sight of the majestic Olympic Mountains in full view.

Retirement life wouldn't be so bad with a trailer like this, Pop thought.

"You're stepping up in the world," he said, with obvious envy. "I'll trade my home for this trailer straight across."

Jess couldn't tell if he was serious.

"It's not mine to trade," Jess said, putting the beer in the fridge.

Pop would have never guessed the refrigerator was located right across from him. It was built into the wall so neatly, hidden from plain view.

Jess went outside with two spuds wrapped in foil and placed them in the fire. The kings were running and everyone in Emerald had salmon. He found this fillet on his doorstep wrapped in foil. He wondered if it was poisoned since anybody who put salmon on his doorstep knew he would eat it, poison or no.

He had to laugh at his own paranoia. Had it evolved to this. He couldn't accept an act of charity anymore? It was freshly caught salmon and he would barbecue it as his father had taught him years ago, a recipe guarded by decades of family tradition.

"Hey, Pop. C'mere."

Jess could tell that Pop really admired Junior's trailer. Pop stepped out onto the steps and Jess directed his attention to the phone wires that ran from the road to the old job shack.

"Do you think they're still good?"

Jess pointed to the wires.

"I don't see why not," Pop answered.

"So how do we get the wires from the shack to the trailer?" Jess asked.

"We don't. The line will have to end at the shack," Pop said. "The trailer isn't stationary."

"But I'd like to have a phone in the trailer," Jess said. "I don't plan on moving it anywhere."

He couldn't imagine getting up and picking his way barefoot to the shack every time the phone would ring.

"Then get one of those new cell phones and get current, boy," Pop said, smiling at his word pun. "Landlines will be passé in a few years."

Jess didn't like the idea of carrying a phone around with him. If people had access to him 24/7 it could create all kinds of trouble. Besides, they were extremely expensive. The only people he knew who had cell phones were Amanda and Junior and Billy, and they all needed and could well afford them.

"That's all I need, people calling me in the dead of night to tell me I'm an asshole."

"Your number wouldn't be published," Pop said.

Simple enough, but in Emerald everybody knew everybody's number, or at least how to get it. The likelihood of someone finding out his number was about a hundred percent. Besides, Jess couldn't imagine a phone going off at three in the morning just for somebody to tell him he was gonna die if he didn't sell.

"I don't have that kind of money," Jess said.

"Put one in the shack. Christ, you gotta have a phone," Pop said.

Jess knew his friend was right. *Friend*? What was Pop to him now, former baseball coach? BB's father? His dad's best friend? His father-in-law? Whatever he was, and obviously he was all of them, Jess had to concentrate on one of those relationships now as he asked for BB's hand in marriage.

"Pop, I'm gonna marry BB. Even if you say no," Jess said.

Jess thought he would use the smart-ass approach since the solemn one didn't quite fit their relationship.

Pop hesitated for a moment, as any father might when told that his daughter would marry. It took him a second to consider the gravity of it, one that he had always felt was a given. In one fell swoop it cemented the blood-tie that he had with this young man. The one he could now call his son.

Jess stirred the fire, waiting for Pop's response.

"It's about time," Pop said finally.

Pop stood up and hugged Jess, then turned away, happy to know that the kids had finally come to their senses. It was something he and Buck had known all along, and Pop thought of his old friend now in the form of a specific remembrance. It was a time when BB and Jessie were very young, and they were playing on top of one of the mountains of sand. The men kept an eye on them as they drank beer and fished, a little prince and princess building castles in the sand.

Time and memories rushed through Pop, of his daughter and her fiancée, and of Buck, his closest friend. Privately, Pop swore that his only duty in life now was to protect the kids and their kids. Buck would have wanted it that way.

Over dinner they discussed the possibility of extracting the rock from below the pond without disturbing the pond above. It would require bulwarks, tunnels, and extra machinery, but Pop's question to him was what any businessman would ask, "How much would it cost?"

Jess' look suggested that it didn't matter.

"This is gravel you're after, not gold," Pop pointed out.

"But what's it worth?" asked Jess.

"I suppose anything less than the cost of having it shipped here," said Pop, taking another bite of salmon.

Jess grabbed another beer from the cooler.

"If that airfield goes in, the noise will be unbearable. I've had a few fly-bys already, enough to know that we couldn't live here."

Pop thought he was kidding. The navy wouldn't be that callous.

"I'm not shitting you. They come flying in here just above the treetops. You know how loud they can be."

Anyone who had spent time hiking in the North Cascade Mountains knew what he was talking about. The jets from Whidbey Island would use the mountain terrain for training, and sometimes an unaware fisherman or hiker would be jolted out of his serene surroundings by a jet flying at more than the speed of sound, a hundred feet above the treetops. It was heart pounding.

Pop went to his truck and came back with the *Island News-Times*. He showed Jess the front-page article with the headline, *Budget Cap Threatens Airfield Installation*.

In the article, Junior admitted that he didn't have enough gravel to complete the job. There was also mention of a budget cap, a control number issued by the federal government. If the bids failed to fall under that number, the navy could choose to build the airfield elsewhere, or scuttle the project entirely.

On the surface the article didn't bode well for Jess. He imagined his next trip into town, where his likeness would be posted everywhere on Emerald community bulletin boards with the inscription *Wanted,*

Dead or Alive. The *News-Times* article also underscored an avenue of chance, a small possibility filled with control numbers and budget caps. The wheels in his head were spinning.

"You haven't seen her, have you?" Jess asked, changing the subject.

Pop looked up, puzzled.

"Who?"

"Dierdre," said Jess.

"Who?"

"Come here."

Jess led him up the gravel bank. From the top of the ridge, the white swan looked magnificent as she floated on top of the water.

"Dierdre, huh?" Pop asked.

"Dierdre," said Jess, smiling. "She's elegant."

Together they marveled at her, and in the years to come, Pop would remember this night and its importance. It was truly a postcard for the heart.

After Pop left, Jess sat by the fire and finished off the rest of the beers. He sat so close to the fire, he could feel the warmth through the soles of his boots. His heart wouldn't stop pounding. He thought that the airfield was a done deal, but here it was on the front page of the *News Times* in simple enough terms. If he didn't sell, he might stop the airfield from going in. If the cost of shipping the rock to the island was too high, and the bids were too high, the airfield would have to be built elsewhere, far from this property.

Jess couldn't tell anybody what he was thinking. Secrecy was his best and only ally because if he didn't sell, no telling what would become of him. Jess looked to the heavens. It was stupid to think that his father had a hand in all this, but had he known all along? The reasonable answer was no, his father couldn't have foreseen this series of events years ago. But the way it was playing out, Jess wondered about that now.

"Who's got a plan?" he asked the gravel animals, loud enough for all to hear.

Jess took another long pull off his last beer and listened for the answer as earth sounds hummed inside his brain, reciting over and over the incantation of life in the immense river of things. To Jess, it sounded more like the beginning of a question asked the world over: *What the fuck? What the fuck? What the fuck?*, that inexplicable note of confusion that grew more persistent as life wore on, as the world turned a darker shade of gray. Jess prayed that his campfire might shine like a brilliant beacon, a communication to the heavens and to the all-knowing minds who could instruct him in the ways of the greater good by simply telling him *sell* or *don't sell*.

Damn, it was times like this that he missed his dog.

Chapter 20

Amanda had done her homework and concluded that time was still on their side. She wanted to beat Junior Buchanan at his own game, so she made one phone call on this, the third day after receiving Junior's offer. She left a message.

"We've received another offer. Will you counter? I'm in Emerald and I can meet."

Amanda hung up just as Billy Wilson knocked on her door. She was ready to pick Billy's brain for all the details, the colors of the personalities involved, or more importantly, the history behind this decision as a member of the Buchanan family and their relationship to Emerald.

What would it mean for Jess if he didn't sell? Would he be banished from Emerald? Would public sentiment force him to leave? These were questions that needed answers since it would affect the rest of Jess' life. No stone should be left unturned, and it was Amanda's job to make sure that Jess understood all the consequences of his decision.

But there was something else on her mind and Amanda thought that Friday afternoon was a good time to share a few cocktails with Billy. And if something else should occur . . . well, she knew how to handle that as well.

After returning to the yacht later that evening, Amanda heard this message in her voicemail.

"Fuck you. Call me."

She wondered, who could that be?

It was the beginning of the Memorial Day weekend and it was

also her father's birthday. She called and hoped he wouldn't answer. Luckily, she only got the voice message.

"Happy birthday, Dad. Sorry I missed the bash. Couldn't make it down because of work. You remember that don't you? Work?"

She giggled and hung up, thinking of the reaction she might get when her father heard the message. It wasn't far from the truth.

Amanda poured another drink. She was already drunk, but she sat on the sofa in the dark and thought about Keith. He had been dead twenty years now. She remembered losing her virginity to him on this same Memorial Day weekend at a rock concert at the Gorge. She remembered how they had pitched the tent out in the open alongside a thousand other tents, the cacophony of lovemaking filling the air once the music stopped. The tents were pitched side by side so the moans and groans were shared by everyone as each couple took a turn wailing the ecstasy of life, when love could be as carefree as a coupling after a first meeting. . . "Yes, you. I want you tonight."

Keith had taken his own life and it haunted Amanda how she had missed the signals. He was always such a sweet guy. She finished the brandy, turned out the lights, and concluded that yes, it was a good day for memorials.

BB arrived early. Jess had been locking his door at night and he regretted it now. He got up and stumbled to the door. She greeted him brightly in her yellow outfit. BB was built for swimwear.

"Time to get up," she said.

He could tell she was excited. They kissed and her full lips felt cool against his. When she entered the trailer, he could smell the suntan lotion mixed with her perfume—her classic summer scent. He loved the smell of this woman. She could wear dog shit and make it smell like flowers.

He got a hard-on and his dick poked out his boxers. BB had her back to him as she made the coffee, and he sat down at the table to hide his lack of control. He watched her putter around in the swimsuit that barely covered her breasts. When she leaned down to take the milk from the refrigerator, he wanted to take her right there, but something told him it wouldn't be right, not with all the children about to arrive.

"Did you tell Pop?" he asked.

BB was bold but not with her father. She had spent a lifetime trying to please him, and the pictures would only hurt.

"No."

"Are you waiting for someone to bring it to his attention?"

BB knew Jess was right. She didn't have a good explanation for why she hadn't told Pop.

"I don't know what I'm waiting for."

She turned away and Jess felt a fierce need to protect her.

"Let's go to the police. Tell the whole story. They'll do something. They've got to."

Of that he couldn't be sure. But if the memory of Johnson at the Hideaway Motel still bothered him, what was it doing to her?

"They'll never believe me, not after the pictures. You said so yourself."

"Fuck the pictures," Jess said hotly. "Tell the truth. You have me as your witness."

"I don't want everybody knowing my business."

"You mean, Pop."

"Fine, whatever you say."

He saw an opportunity to interject some humor.

"They're pretty good pictures. Who knows, Pop might like 'em."

BB laughed. Her father would get embarrassed when he saw her in her underwear, let alone the buff.

Jess reached up and stroked her face. Her face had healed nicely, just a small white line circled her chin. He thought it might not leave a scar since her skin was so soft and clear.

"You're going to have to tell Pop," he said.

"I know. I just haven't found the right time."

He looked her in the eye.

"Look, whatever you decide is alright with me. All I want to do is help. I can handle people like Johnson, but can you? Do you need to go talk to someone?"

EB couldn't look up at him. This was a discussion for later.

"I love you, Jess."

She broke his heart with that one. Philosophically, Jess had worked marriage into his heart because if he didn't marry BB, who was going to take care of her?

It was to be a record-high ninety-two degrees in the shade, and people were sweating and cussing the heat. The kids loved it. They began arriving at nine in the morning by the carloads.

Jess had built a wooden raft the year before and stuck it into the woods for winter. Some guys helped him carry it down the bank and they set it afloat in the middle of the pond. Dierdre got up on it and sat there like the queen of the lake. Jess warned the kids not to pet her, and for the most part they stayed away. A few times he caught Dierdre snapping at a child who wanted to touch her. But she meant no harm. She just wanted to be left alone.

Many from the Emerald community came, including a good number of adults, because nobody had air conditioners in their homes. A ninety-degree day in the month of May was a miracle. Cars jammed the roads all day long with people who drove around aimlessly with their air conditioners on full blast, trying to keep cool.

Here, Jess found the sense of community that had been lacking in his life. He was feeling robbed by the strict drunk-driving laws and all the other reasons for why people stayed home and didn't go out anymore. He sat on the western rim of the pond observing the parents who were watching the children.

The parents were a great help. A spirit of "*let's do something for the kids*" pervaded the entire day, and Jess and BB were all smiles. Robin Barks, Melvin's wife and Jess' former babysitter, dropped off a van full of children and kept going back to town for more. She drove the streets picking up any child who stood by the road with a suit and a towel.

Melvin Banks owned a maxi van about the size of a small bus, and he also had a wife who was about the nicest person alive. In the world of babysitters, Robin had been Jess' favorite. He could remember dragging the gut with her, listening to the Stones, honking at everyone who passed by. Robin had a boyfriend named Space who rode a Norton chopper. Sometimes he would give Jess a ride. Space hated Junior for some reason. Maybe because Junior always called him Spike just to piss him off.

Jess couldn't imagine Melvin and Robin together. They were rarely seen in public. Perhaps there were people on this earth, angels sent down to balance the eternal pairing of light and dark. He got up and told the girls he was going to take a walk, leaving Robin and BB on the blanket. He thought it might give them a chance to talk.

The two watched as he walked off. Jess was a well-built man but now he looked gaunt, and they could see it in his chest and through his arms. He was going through hell, thinking too much, worrying and losing weight. BB made a promise to have him over for dinner more often, or invite herself over to the trailer more often since he was a much better cook than she was.

Robin spoke up.

"I hear you two are getting married."

BB pawed the rocks with the toe of her sneaker.

"It's supposed to be a secret."

Robin laughed.

"One thing's for sure, nothing's a secret around here. If you've got secrets, we'll hear about 'em."

Robin spoke from wisdom gained through experience. She had been the object of town gossip when she got pregnant out of wedlock while she was still in high school. But when she and Melvin—who was ten years older—got married, the whispers died down.

Robin liked BB when most other women were mistrusting of her, jealous of her beauty. Robin was no slouch in the looks department either, so at least they had that in common.

"Look out for him, will you?" Robin said.

She looked to BB in confidence, concern etched in her face.

"People are mad. They'll do almost anything when they're mad."

As if to punctuate her point, a giant shadow caught their eye, moving over the water like a dark cloud. Robin and BB looked up.

On the eastern rim of the pond, the Brotherhood gathered and stood arm in arm, suggesting that no one gets out of here alive. Jess looked up when the shouts and the screams of the kids stopped, all of them frightened by the men. Jess spotted Melvin staring down at him with the menace of the ages.

"Robin!" he bellowed.

Melvin's voice rang from rim to rim.

"Get over here!" he shouted.

BB felt her stiffen, and she put her hand on Robin's hand.

"Don't go," BB whispered.

But Robin couldn't take it anymore, this embarrassment. She got up from the blanket and marched toward her husband. She intended to give all the men a piece of her mind. As she approached her husband, he flicked a backhand to her cheek and knocked her down. She got back up and stood a few feet below her husband, wiping the hair from her eyes. Robin spoke loud enough for everyone to hear.

"You men get out of here. You embarrass yourselves. Look at the children. They're scared to death. You ought to be ashamed of yourselves. Now git!"

When she finished, Melvin took a few steps forward and flicked another backhand across her other cheek. This time she didn't go down. Sheer determination left her standing.

"Melvin!" Jess shouted.

He came running toward them.

"You stay out of this," Melvin warned.

From the opposite end of the pond, BB could see Jess' anger. It was the kind of anger that she had witnessed only a few times from him in all the years they'd been together. The last time she had seen it, he had almost killed a man in a barroom brawl after the guy had intentionally felt her up as they were standing next to the jukebox at the Kingdom Come.

"I'm not gonna stand here and watch you beat her," Jess shouted back at him. "I don't care how many men you've got. I'll stop it in a damn hurry. Now get off my property."

A collective note of disapproval rumbled through the Brotherhood.

"Aaarrrrgh."

Melvin paused, filling the air with a sickly tension. Some of the children cried. Jess and Melvin held their ground, measuring each other. Finally, Melvin laughed the laugh of torment and threat.

"She's gonna get it twice as bad at home."

His words cut to the truth of it.

"You can stay here," Jess said to Robin.

Melvin's laughter rang through the trees, a vile chuckle that grew louder once the others chimed in. He held his hand up and the area suddenly became quiet once more.

"Watch yourself," he said to Jess. "Don't go poking your nose into somebody else's business."

Then he glared at Robin.

"Need pretty boy's protection?"

Melvin chewed on a toothpick like a movie tough grading out poorly in the role.

"Pretty boy can't protect you. He can't even protect himself."

Melvin delivered a parting shot to Jess.

"Watch your step, boy."

The Brotherhood peeled away in groups, proud of their act of solidarity. But what happened between Melvin and Robin left the other parents with a sick feeling. The Brotherhood had cast a bad light upon their cause. In the parents eyes, the real hero was Robin Banks.

Later that night, Jess awoke when he heard a gun blast from outside. He jumped out of bed and ran to the door. In the full moonlight, he saw a pickup speed away.

A feeling of dread came over him as he raced up the gravel bank naked in his bare feet. He looked down at the pond and spotted Dierdre crumpled up on the raft. Even from that far away, he could tell she was dead.

Chapter 21

Naturally it was John B Kidd who knocked on the door of the trailer. John B was the leader of the Forever Group and heard of Jess' plight through a mutual friend. He saw in it a damn good cause. The Forever Group would save this pond as a poetic footnote, and perhaps grab a little attention in the process.

Or, at least, that's the way Amanda had pitched it to John B. Since they were childhood friends, John B didn't hesitate. He led the expedition to Clay Island and brought KSEA 11's Wanda Nichols along with him. Wanda was the eco reporter for the only independently owned TV station in Seattle, which John B thought was okay since it wasn't controlled by the corporate reach of *the Man*. Wanda had dark hair and an ample cleavage, which she took to showing on-screen, much to the chagrin of her fellow reporters.

Wanda thought John B was the most charismatic man alive. A mountaineering stud of the highest order. She would often accompany him on his Forever Group expeditions throughout the Great Northwest. The faceoff over the gravel pit and the pond, tied in with the navy's intention to build the airfield on Clay Island, sounded like a good eco story to her. It would also give her a couple of nights with John B too. Getting banged in the woods had become an exciting part of her weekends.

Jess opened the trailer door and recognized him immediately. John B had a ruddy complexion and a warrior look about him, a man who could pack the mule himself. John B stuck out his hand. Behind him stood fifty of his followers, acolytes of the Forever Way, the constant monitor of our earth. Man vs. Man vs. Earth is how

John B described their mission, and their logo was M v M v E. The followers pasted it everywhere. On recycled paper, of course.

"Hello, Jess."

"Hello, John B."

They looked into each other's eyes solemnly, and it marked an occasion of special kinship. Wanda witnessed the event and related it back to John B that night, the way it seemed so natural, as if the two had met before. "Brothers in arms" was the way the Forever Group wanted to interpret it, because whatever John B Kidd did had special meaning in their eyes.

' We've come to help you," he announced.

The others clapped in perfect unison, one time, and then stopped. Jess didn't see a signal or anything to cue them in, yet it was perfect, like the sound of one man clapping.

Jess stepped down from the trailer in his stocking feet and looked at John B at eye level, or about an inch above him, which was surprising since John B looked much taller on television. In the passing of a moment, Jess had the answer to the terror game. The Forever Group had a reputation for doing whatever was necessary to accomplish their goal—true modern-day warriors. In fact, in Jess' mind, the Brotherhood vs. the Forever Group was about an even match.

After lunch, Junior headed out to the batch plant. He found the geologist there sampling the soil and the rock when he arrived. Junior soon found out what he had suspected all along. He was getting only 60 percent rock per yard of material now, where years earlier it had been closer to 90 percent. The geologist told him it was a guess as to how much good material was left, certainly not the amount they had projected initially.

Junior's rocks were getting smaller and there was nothing he could do about it. His eyes swept the pit and the plant, an enormous production of machinery and manpower. His sand piles were huge, his stockpiles of pea gravel were prodigious. But when he looked to the other side of the pit, the piles of crushed rock were much smaller by comparison.

Junior was in a helluva bind and he had a brother who wouldn't provide him with the very thing that could save his ass. He cussed Jess for being selfish. Maybe the trailer and the truck had been a mistake. Hell, if the other side wanted to play hardball, Junior could do the same. He had given Jess a place to live, a truck to drive, and to this day his younger brother hadn't dropped by the office to thank him. Of course, if he were in Jess' shoes, Junior would have stayed away too. Just to keep everybody guessing.

It was beginning to smell like a joint venture, but Junior couldn't assume anything with Jess and Amanda. He wanted to take the personalities out of the deal, but the trouble was, his problem was all about the personalities. If it wasn't for Jess and Amanda haunting his senses, Junior was confident he could railroad them into taking a number far below what he had in mind as a fair number.

But then Junior did a very uncharacteristic thing. As he drove back to the office, he took a step back from it all, and looked at this multifaceted jewel of complexity that his father had created. The issue essentially concerned everybody in the kingdom. Junior smiled as he turned into the office parking lot. It was just like his father to do something like that.

Jess sat on the top step of the trailer while John B and the rest sat cross-legged in the dirt before him. He told his story, and they were moved by his testimony. When Jess finished, they all clasped hands and vowed to guard the property until the bid opening and beyond if necessary. Some in the group openly relished the opportunity to have it out with such men who would steal Jess' dog, burn down his camper, trash his pond, and shoot the swan. The Forever Group understood these men, having developed their tactics with the loggers on the peninsula, who were no day at the beach either. Some even had the scars to show for it. They sat around the fire, eating nuts and vegetables and berries while reciting tales of heroism, and rolling up their wool sweaters to show the scars.

The Forever Group chose not to go to the bathroom inside the old job shack. Instead, they pooped in the woods. Even the women. Jess tried to imagine all the turds laying down on the ground and got a little concerned. He walked those woods often.

But John B put his mind at ease. He took Jess into the woods and showed him how they did it. John B cleared away the soil with his hands and left a hole about the size of a small mixing bowl. When he finished crapping on the ground he covered it up, leaving the ground exactly as he had found it. It amazed Jess how the Forever Group could live in the old pit and not have a shit to show for it.

Later that night, with BB beside him in bed, and thirty tents mounted outside the door in a show of protection, Jess told her about his experience with John B in the woods. BB couldn't believe it. It was even harder for her to believe that Jess had witnessed it.

"So you watched?" she asked.

Jess admitted that he had.

"It was like a ritual," he said.

BB laughed so hard she nearly fell out of bed.

"These people are fucking crazy!" she said, a little too loudly for his tastes.

She may have had a point. But Jess wasn't laughing. These people were there to protect them, and at least she needed to show some respect.

"Shhhh . . .," he whispered, muffling her face with a pillow. "They'll hear you."

BB slugged him in the gut a little too hard. His ribs were tender for days.

Junior stared at the numbers on his small computer screen. The totals were shocking, even to him. The difference between buying and shipping the rock to the island was enormous. Barges were not cheap. Tugs cost even more. Plus, he would have to unload the rock from the barge, and truck it to the plant, adding another huge expense. If the navy's budget cap reflected what they felt were true market costs, judging by the control number, somebody was seriously misinformed.

One last payday was all Junior wanted, but the gravy days seemed to be over. Margins were tight. He crunched the numbers again, allowing for less time unloading the gravel at the old seaplane dock, and the numbers held steady. He glanced at the calendar. It was Memorial Day, so he faced a short business week ahead. He would have to make more phone calls and try to whittle down some of the costs.

Junior dialed Amanda's number. He wasn't prepared to hear her answer.

"Hello?" she said.

"Hi," he said feebly, caught off guard.

Amanda upbraided him for his last phone call.

"Thanks for your last message, you prick," she said.

Amanda had a way with words and Junior admired the way she could cut through the crap.

"Sorry," he said. "I was mad."

He meant it. At least the sorry part.

"Thank you," she replied.

Amanda could sense a man on the ropes. Time had become her ally and she was going to take full advantage of it.

"As I said in my message, we have another offer. Will you counter?"

"Who is it?" Junior asked.

She knew a lot of heavyweights. But he also thought she might bring in a ringer just to bid up the price, an outfit that really had no intention of bidding. Junior could either bite on the bluff or not.

"That's my client's business. If you'd like to counter, I'm listening."

"Will Jess sell?" asked Junior.

First they needed to establish the endgame. If Jess wasn't going to budge, Junior felt there was no use discussing the matter.

"For the right price. My client isn't stupid. But it's going to take a lot to move him off his position. He's a man of conviction."

She didn't know the half of it, thought Junior. If only she could imagine what he'd gone through in a lifetime with Jess. His brother was an immovable force once he landed on something.

"I need to talk to Jess in person," he said.

Without hesitation, Amanda agreed.

"Then I suggest you get off your ass and go see him. This is ridiculous. The man holds your future in his hands and you can't even talk to him like a fucking grownup?"

Junior interjected.

"I gave him the truck and told him to come see me. It's the least he could do."

That really pissed her off.

"He doesn't have to hunt you down," she said. "In fact, he doesn't have to do anything. And that's the world you live in right now, buddy," she said heatedly. "If you want to talk to Jess, try knocking on your trailer door. That's where I'd start."

Junior appreciated that Amanda always had the answers, even when she didn't. That Jess was willing to talk numbers without Amanda being around was news to him.

' Got'cha," he replied, and hung up.

Amanda knew Junior would be surprised to find her old school chum camped out at the old pit. Later that afternoon she would have to take a drive out there to see what John B had become. She remembered him in the ninth grade, already a Spartan, an eco-zealot of his mother's making. Amanda figured Jess wouldn't mind the company since men didn't admit terror. Fear maybe, but not terror.

It had been a beautiful spring in Emerald. The rain shadow from the Olympic Mountains had provided ample protection from the wind and rain blowing in from the Pacific Ocean. Emerald normally received only about a third of the annual rainfall that other communities to the north and south received because of where Clay Island was positioned next to the mountains.

But that year, June more than made up for the lack of rainfall in the spring, filling the water tanks to overflowing. The children would climb the steel cyclone fences and stand under the cascading water from the overflow of the sixty-foot metal tanks. Every so often a child would get knocked flat by the force of the water and the older ones would have to wade in and drag them out before they drowned.

The kids didn't mind the rain. Except for the little leaguers who were disappointed with all the rainouts. But the rain also kept them out of the strawberry patches that year, and despite the fact that they didn't make any money, the kids were glad it got them out of the hard work. Plus, waking up at five in the morning in the summertime was no picnic either. The strawberries were awful that season. It was just that kind of year.

Jess had a legitimate concern and he decided to take it straight to the source. It was times like this when he really needed a phone. He called the *Island News-Times* office and asked for Natalie Robinson, but she was out. He left a message that he would call her later that day.

Twenty guys followed him wherever he went now, including here at the mini mart telephone. Darrel Ivie gave Jess a hard look when he rang him up for a bag of nacho chips. The Forever Group guys were all dressed in leather, some carried bows and arrows slung behind their backs. And really, if a guy didn't know who they were, if he hadn't seen them on TV, Darrel thought somebody walking into the store without any forewarning would have thought that these guys had just stepped out of a Davy Crockett movie. Jess walked in the middle of the entourage like some rock star surrounded by security. To Darrel, the bodyguards were over the top.

"Where did you find your friends?" Darrel sniffed.

Jess took the comment in stride. But he did let Darrel know that he didn't appreciate it.

"Under a log," Jess said smartly.

The Forever guys honked like geese on the way out.

When they pushed through the door, Darrel shouted after them, "They can't protect you forever."

Jess stopped cold. He turned and looked into Darrel's eyes and saw before him a man that didn't know any better. So he left it alone. This time.

One by one they loaded into the van. On the ride back to the old pit it was raining hard. In the back of the van, the Forever Group guys smelled like musty buckskin. Jess thought it smelled like the essence of dead animal and he could barely breathe. To distract himself from the smell, he thought about what he needed to do next. He really needed to talk to his mother because he had a question for her. It was something that had been bugging him.

Did Dad want him to sell?

The swoop attack maneuvers came regularly now. Whidbey Island Naval Air Station posted their training schedule in the *News-Times* and Jess noticed an increased amount of flight activity around the north end of Clay Island. The navy said it would simulate the air traffic once the training facility was operational. The jets flew over the trailer every hour on the hour, just above the treetops. It made life miserable for him.

The ticket to paradise?

In the parking lot, Junior got out of his car and felt like he needed a hall pass to see his brother. Vans painted green and black lined the old pit entrance and big guys milled about the old pit like something out of a movie set. Junior figured it had it to be John B Kidd since Daniel Boone was dead.

Amanda claimed to have known John B from their childhood, but the proof was in the pudding. Junior looked over the entire scene before him. The Forever Group was in full plumage. They wore leathers with M v M v E written across the back of their jackets in bold lettering. Collectively they looked like they shopped at the Hudson Bay Fur Company. Junior was stopped at the steel cable by a guy with a headband and a bow slung across his shoulder.

"I want to see my brother."

"Are you Junior?" the Forever Group guy asked.

It was raining hard and Junior didn't have time for this.

"I'm the only brother he has."

"Wait here," he said.

The Forever Group guy walked to the trailer. He knocked on the door and someone inside opened it. There was a short conversation and then he walked back and told Junior he could go in.

Junior caught his foot on the thick cable as he tried to step over it and fell down hard on his knees. The rain drops on his coat trickled up around his neck. It was not a good day for him and the Forever Group guy offered to help him up. Junior's jeans were muddy and when he wiped off his knees, it only made matters worse. Now his hands were caked in mud.

Junior walked to the trailer thinking if Jess was going to play like that, then he would too. Plain and simple, his brother would have to find another place to live. Junior had given Jess a hundred bucks to get a phone, but here he was having to ask his brother for an audience like he was the goddamn pope. What kind of gratitude was that? Junior rapped on the door, leaving mud all over it. Jess opened the door and immediately recognized that his brother was pissed.

"What the hell's going on here?" Junior fumed.

Junior barged in and Jess looked down at the mud on his shoes. He wanted to tell Junior to take his shoes off, but he realized it might get him hurt, since Junior was obviously really mad.

"Are you fucking crazy?" Junior said, taking off his coat and throwing it on the kitchen countertop.

There was mud on Junior's coat too, the kind that was nearly liquefied from the steady downpour outside. It was smeared all over Junior's sleeves from where he caught himself when he stumbled. Now it was all over the counters. Junior sat down and talked down to Jess without realizing that it was a pattern of a lifetime. They sat at the table across from each other.

"The Brotherhood killed Dierdre," Jess said solemnly.

It didn't register.

"Dierdre?" Junior asked.

"The swan. She lived in the pond. They shot her."

Junior guessed that the bird obviously meant a lot to Jess. But all this Forever Group shit for that?

"I'm sorry about the bird," Junior said, without much comfort in his tone.

"She was a *swan*," Jess said, as if it made a big difference.

Junior recognized fear in his brother's eyes, unusual for Jess. His brother was a tough man, and if Junior had to choose a guy for his proverbial foxhole, Jess would have been his first choice. Nothing bothered him. Jess was good on stage because he was fearless. Junior had watched his brother's band in arenas warming up headliners, and thousands of people watching him didn't faze him one bit. Junior put himself in Jess' shoes for a moment, staring out at twenty thousand people staring back at him. It was a scary thought.

"They broke up the Saturday swim too," Jess added, hoping to get some sort of reaction out of his brother.

But Junior didn't have an answer. The Brotherhood had always been a thorn in his side and if his men were out of control, what could he do about it? Fire every last one of them?

"It's got nothing to do with you anymore," Jess said correctly.

Junior was quick to answer.

"Unless you sold," Junior said. "I've offered you a fair price. I wouldn't buy it from anybody else for that. Take the money and run. What have you got to lose?" he asked, pressing his point.

"About every dream I've ever had for this place," Jess answered.

Junior looked at him, puzzled by what he thought was an obvious choice.

'A couple million dollars can buy you a nice piece of land, something a helluva lot nicer than this."

It was the first numbers Jess had heard. Yes, two million dollars was a lot of money. But just as Jess finished the thought, a roar from above shook the trailer. It was an ungodly noise and Junior hit the floor when the sound caught up to them in full force. Once the jet had passed, Junior looked at Jess, who appeared unbothered by it. He suddenly realized what the US Navy had been putting Jess through for the last month. *Damn*, that jet was *loud*.

If Junior had come for a decision, Jess didn't have one. His second mind told him not to buckle in a moment of indecision. But it would have been so easy to give in right there, to rid himself of this intolerable weight. If the jets were to continue like this, he knew he couldn't live there.

Junior saw that his brother was wracked with indecision. He was caught in the web of a hellacious circumstance and the toll it was taking was etched in his face. Jess looked tired and gaunt, the result of principles born out from a lifetime of idealism. But reality had shaken him to the core. Junior could feel the decision to sell, as palpable as honey to the lips.

Just say it. C'mon.

"I need more time," Jess said.

Junior exhaled loudly. The moment of truth had slipped through his fingers once again, and now, did he have the heart to yank the trailer out from underneath his brother? If he took the trailer and the pickup away, would it do more harm than good?

"I need to know an answer," said Junior. "Time's up."

"I can't think with all this other stuff going on. Hell, I can't even go into town without wondering if someone is going to shoot me," Jess said, admitting the truth of it.

Junior couldn't imagine it happening. But he also couldn't guarantee that it wouldn't happen either. He thought Jess' imagination might be getting the better of him since the likelihood of something like that happening in Emerald was pretty slim. Yet the incident at the police station had taught Junior a lesson. It could happen anywhere.

"You know, they'd stop all this crap if we told them you sold."

Jess looked at his brother like he was crazy.

"But that would be a lie."

Junior had to laugh at his innocence.

"So fucking what."

Those words sounded more like the title track of a head banger's album and not the answer to his problems.

"And if I don't sell, what then?" asked Jess.

"That's called 'we couldn't come to terms,'" Junior said. "In the end you drove a hard bargain and it was too steep for me. People will believe anything you tell them. What matters is that we agree on something. Everything else is just hearsay."

Junior couldn't believe what he was doing. He was outlining the battle strategy for his nemesis. *Nemesis*? Maybe that was it. How could he view his brother as the enemy? Looking at Jess, what he really needed was a haircut and a steak.

"I'm sorry you gotta deal with guys who wanna make your life miserable. I just need that rock. A lotta people need that rock."

Jess stood up from the table and reached into the refrigerator for a beer. He didn't offer Junior one because he knew Junior was still on the clock. Jess uncapped the beer.

"I'm trying to do what's right for everyone," Jess said. "It's not lost on me that I have to still live in this town when it's over."

Junior had to go. He got up from the table.

"Okay, we'll play it your way for now. But *dammit*, I need a decision. I could be making phone calls that I don't need to make."

Junior rubbed his forehead with his hand.

"What a bid, Jesus."

Junior walked out of the trailer and growled at his escorts as they reached for his arms.

"Get the fuck away from me," he said, pushing them away.

Two Forever Group guys escorted him to the cable, and one offered to help him step over the cable after witnessing Junior's entrance. Junior ducked under the cable this time, his gut barely letting him squat down as much as he needed to. He nearly had to get on his hands and knees in the slop. The rain pounded the bill of his cap, and in the forefront of his mind Hawaii was looking better and better every day.

For years the Forever Group battled the loggers over the clear cutting of the old growth national forests in Washington State. The symbol for that fight became the spotted owl, one of many living things that the Forever Group tried to protect in the forests of the Great Northwest.

Unfortunately, it also spawned an increase in the deaths of spotted owls. The loggers and their sympathizers began shooting them on sight.

The skies finally cleared, and Jess played the guitar and sang for the Forever Group gathered around the bonfire. The fire sent smoke billowing up in the still night air and could be seen for miles. Some in the group weren't shy about joining in, and they sang odd harmonies—sometimes on pitch, most of the time not.

John B particularly liked Jess' song "Listen", and asked Jess to teach it to him. Jess simplified the chords since John B wasn't the best of guitar players. In Jess' mind he hadn't climbed Mt. Rainier fourteen times either, so he thought it made them about even.

Naturally, the Emerald Fire Department showed up and asked Jess to put out the fire.

"Why?" he asked. "This is private property."

"Doesn't matter. It's a fire hazard," Trent Banks, deputy fire marshal, explained.

"It's been raining for a month," Jess said pointedly.

John B intervened when he noticed that the fire marshal had recognized him. Deputy Banks listened calmly to his point, but when John B finished, the fire marshal said, "This is a matter for Jess. Nobody else. It's the law."

Once he heard that, Jess went into the job shack and took out a couple of buckets he had stored in a corner for mopping his floors. He told the Forever Group to make a bucket brigade to the pond. It took quite a while to douse the bonfire that way. The fire truck couldn't leave until the fire was out. They had to wait almost three hours. On taxpayers' time, of course.

Listen

Listen to the falling rain tapping lightly on my lid
Listen to the evergreens gently swaying in the wind
Listen to the northern train moaning a cry to watch out
But some folks never hear the sound,
Too busy talking about themselves

Outside the rain is falling, repeating an old refrain

Telling me hush in a word of wisdom
Listen
Listen, she says

Listen to the ebb and flow of the river rolling by
Listen to the eagle wings gently strumming the sky
Listen to the ocean wave finally strung out to the end
But some folks never hear the sound,
They're on the outside looking in

Outside the rain is falling, repeating an old refrain
Telling me hush in a word of wisdom
Listen
Listen, she says

Chapter 22

Pop stood in the kitchen with the magazine opened to the pictures of his daughter without any clothes on. A Post-It note beside the magazine said, *I'm sorry.* He flipped through the pictures and his heart sank. He wondered what his daughter had done for money in LA since she wouldn't take any from him. He hoped this was the worst of it.

He took the magazine out to the burning barrel and lit it on fire. He stood and watched while it burned. Pop would remember that moment as his final separation from BB's mother, Margaret Mary Kincaid, the other spirited woman whom he had loved in his lifetime. Pop counted back the years and realized BB was now the same age as her mother when she left them. In a funny way, it made sense. BB was just like her mother, boobs and all.

John B's girlfriend, Wanda Nichols, had asked if she could bring in the KSEA 11 news crew to cover the story. At first Jess told her yes, thinking it might be good to present his side of the story. But Wanda had asked simply out of politeness. In her opinion, this was everybody's story, whether Jess gave her permission or not. An hour later he apologized and told Wanda that he had decided against it. He would rather not make the Seattle news.

Wanda nodded and told the crew to get ready to shoot anyway. Jess went off on Wanda, shouting at her, and while he was at it he got into John B's face and accused them of using him for their own agendas. John B was mortified to have his friend call him out like that. John B was also furious with Wanda, thinking she had no right to barge into the middle of a situation that he had under control.

But Wanda had Emmys in her eyes. She was sorry to burn the John B bridge, but she wasn't happy with him either. Two days ago she saw him duck into Mountain Lion's tent when he thought she wasn't looking. Wanda put two and two together and felt like she had nothing to lose at that point. Mountain Lion had long dark hair and a cute figure, and she was also ten years younger than Wanda. John B went to Mountain Lion now after walking away from Wanda. He took her by the hand and led her to his tent.

Jess watched it happen and then shouted, "I want you all off my land."

He heard grumblings among the Forever Group.

"It's my battle. It doesn't concern you. I will never forget all you've done. Thank you."

John B heard Jess' announcement and came running out of his tent. He caught Jess just before he entered the trailer and pleaded with him.

"They'll hurt you, Jess. I know these people. I'm sorry. It won't happen again."

He spoke in a whisper, prophetic words if Jess listened. But Jess was in no mood to listen because he couldn't stomach all the drama. He looked into his friend's eyes.

"Thank you. But this is my battle."

"It concerns all of us," John B said.

Jess paused for a moment and put his hand on his friend's shoulder.

"Maybe it's not a battle. Maybe it's a way of life."

John B understood what Jess meant, why they had to go. He hugged Jess, gathering him in his big bear arms. Jess had to catch his breath after the hug, and John B instructed the others to break camp.

Wanda Nichols stood behind Jess' property line and the KSEA 11 film crew videotaped the scene as the Forever Group struck their tents and loaded the vans. It took them all of seventeen minutes to clear out. Even in leaving, they were brutally efficient.

The news crew stayed behind until everyone had left, shooting the before and after videotape of a story that would air that evening. Wanda knew that Seattle was an environmental city, and she knew that Jess' plight might be better received in the city rather than in an island community desperate for work.

The clouds had parted and a brilliant light shined down on the old pit in those hours before sunset when the shading brought out its deepest hues. The place was certainly deserving of its reputation, Amanda thought. Before she stepped out of the car, she took it all in. Hyperbole for once was not enough in this age of hyperbole.

She got out and walked to the trailer. The Forever Group was noticeably absent—no vans, no campsite. She knocked on Jess' door, nervous that she might be interrupting something.

Jess opened it. He was surprised to see her there. Amanda had never seen the old pit and he was happy to show it off. He also noticed her perfume. It mingled nicely with the smell of ripe fir and cedar. He helped her into the trailer.

"Where's John B?" she asked, gathering herself.

Jess left the door ajar just in case BB came back.

"I asked him to leave."

Amanda wore a dark blue business suit, and together with her auburn hair, it was a devastating combination. Her perfume evoked an air of sophistication. And although those days were over, Jess realized he was still a man in the proximity of a beautiful woman. They couldn't stay inside the trailer for long.

"Why did you do that?" she asked, placing her purse on the trailer table.

Amanda had come for answers. It was that time in the negotiations when decisions had to be made, and Junior wasn't the only one waiting on Jess' response. Amanda had brought another number with her, one considerably better than Junior's previous offer. She had done her job. Now it was up to Jess.

"Let's step outside," he suggested.

He looked down at her shoes. The pumps wouldn't do. He found a pair of sneakers in the closet— BB's, size eight. Amanda tried them on, and they fit well enough. The white shoes set off her beautifully tanned legs and Jess tried not to notice.

They went outside and he helped Amanda climb up the gravel bank. At the top, she looked down, and the sight nearly took her breath away. Her eyes landed on the wood raft near the middle of the pond. A sign nailed to it said, *Here Lies Dierdre.* Jess explained to her the way he had buried the swan, filling her gullet with gravel, and sencing her to the bottom.

They sat on the gravel ridge and talked. He was touched by her concern for his safety and he agreed that the Forever Group had been a good idea. But he felt their presence did more harm than good. If his fellow islanders couldn't understand his point of view, then he would have to convince them otherwise. He would have to live among these people long after this issue was settled.

"If you're looking for respect, you're not going to get any," she said.

She was probably right.

"But I can't live in fear," he told her.

He drew in another breath.

"At least, I can't show it."

"Why not?" Amanda asked. "It's only human."

But she sensed it was more than that. Jess lived with the constant threat that his life could end at any moment. The weight of that emotion could drive people to madness.

"Let's look at your options," she said. "I've got a verbal offer from Caggiano. As far as the gravel goes, he'll take what he needs for the pour and that's it. Once the job is done, he's out. But it's all contingent upon him winning the bid."

"If I don't sell to Junior, he'll kill me himself," Jess said.

The thought made them both laugh. His answer didn't surprise her. There were deep family bonds to consider.

"But can Junior be sure of that?" she asked.

"I don't follow," he said.

She smiled at his innocence.

"Simple. I want to put you up for sale. Anybody who wants to bid on the airfield comes to us for an offer."

Ambitious, yes, but . . .

"Why would they? I'm selling to Junior. Not them."

"We'll just keep that our little secret," she said coyly. "If you're going to tear up what I'm looking at right now, we don't really know what that price is. Let's let the market determine that, and to establish a market you need bidders. The more the merrier."

Amanda stopped talking long enough to make sure Jess was following her. She knew he had a penchant for drifting off, but he still looked engaged, so she continued.

"We need to determine a fair market price. Wherever that price lands—and it'll be obvious—that's our number."

Jess played soft toss with a handful of rocks, throwing them in the water one by one. His right shoulder was still sore, but it was the good kind of sore. To throw a complete game after you haven't thrown in years was nothing short of abuse. At one point he let a rock go about as hard as he could throw it and it dropped into the pond about midway. That gave him the idea that he was arm was back to about fifty percent.

"I have a question," Amanda asked.

"Okay," he replied, "but no BB stuff."

Amanda was comfortable with that.

"I think we can safely say that the Emerald community doesn't respect your position."

Amanda was fully functioning on that one. He couldn't even walk into a grocery store without somebody giving him they eye.

"But all they know is what they hear. And what they hear is all coming from the other side, negative stuff, stuff that really doesn't put your position in a great light. So let's change the narrative."

He was up for anything at that point.

"How do we do that?" he asked.

Then he felt a calm drop over his senses.

It was the movie guy again. Jess tried to hold him off since all hell could break loose if he got on a roll. But the movie guy was winning. The movie guy wanted a cigarette, and he knew Amanda carried a pack for emergency situations.

"Gimme a smoke," he said.

Amanda had not heard this kind of bravado in Jess' voice, well, in ever. She liked the attitude.

"Okay," she said, digging out a Camel Light from her suit pocket.

The movie guy took the cigarette from her and acted like a movie tough when he said, "C'mere."

Short for "come here," Jess guessed. The movie guy had to work on his diction.

Amanda stood next to the movie guy after he lit her cigarette. They blew the smoke at the same time, and somewhere about midway across the water, the smoke intertwined and curled into one big swirl.

Not a moment after that, right on cue, a jet came screaming in just above the treetops, unannounced. The noise was terrifying enough, but to someone who had never heard the sound before, it scared the hell out of Amanda. She jumped into the movie guy's arms, her chest heaving with fright. The movie guy noticed her heaving chest and gave her right breast a squeeze.

"Don't worry. I gotcha," he said with a wink.

He said this, inches from her nose. It was an Audrey Hepburn nose, he noted. The movie guy traced it now and said, "You just have to get used to it."

Amanda was indignant.

'Not me, pal."

The jets were an obvious message and Amanda needed to find out who was behind it. Who would give such an order? Those jets weren't flying in here that low for no damn reason.

"I couldn't imagine living with the noise," she said.

"It's the price I have to pay, I guess," said Jess.

"I don't think so," Amanda replied, thinking of what she could do to stop it.

Amanda could see Junior's handiwork in this and some higher-up was going to hear about it. After all, there were perks to knowing the senior US senator from Washington State, so somebody's head was going to roll over this.

Then Amanda felt the movie guy's hips press up against her. The intent was obvious and they lay down in a pile of gravel. The movie guy had her skirt pulled up, and that's when Jess turned to look the other way. BB was due back soon.

After a few monumental thrusts, the movie guy snapped his hips into Amanda one final time and she moaned loudly. Her butt made a nice little indentation in the rocks in a spot where, when Jess walked by later, he got excited from the memory. He waited for them to finish up while he thought about his situation.

At every turn, it seemed Jess discovered a new nuance, a different wrinkle in the big picture. He was caught in a game he had no business playing, while Junior and Amanda were experts at it. Somehow, he felt like the learning curve would have to stop sometime.

Jess felt paralyzed with doubt. He wanted to glimpse into the future to see how act and consequence would finally play out. Jess envisioned himself destitute, begging for mercy in some lonely back alley, hammered into submission by the cruel folly of fate. His hubris had been replaced by self-doubt, and it was taking a toll on his self-esteem.

Jess looked at his ten-dollar watch. It was four o'clock. He would have an hour to prepare the salmon dinner before the five o'clock news. He'd have an additional fifteen minutes before Wanda's story flashed across the screen. The eco segment normally came on about halfway through the broadcast.

"It's getting cold," Jess said. "Let's go inside and I'll make dinner. Will you stay? It'll give you a chance to meet BB."

Amanda admired Jess' resiliency when a moment ago he looked like he was the loneliest man on the planet.

"I've got no plans," she said. "But I've been told to stay away from your coffee."

He laughed.

"You've been talking to either Junior or Billy. My money is on Billy."

"But you don't have any money," she said with an elegant wink.

Did she really have to go there?

At the steps, BB was about to open the trailer door when she heard voices. She watched the two make their way down the steep slope. Jess leading and holding Amanda's hand all the way down. Perhaps in other times she may have assumed something different, but they seemed so comfortable together. BB realized Amanda was good for him. She was older, more secure with herself. And certainly attractive.

Once they were on flat ground, Jess turned to BB and announced, "Guess who's coming to dinner?"

He wouldn't let go of Amanda's hand. He gave it a good squeeze to reassure her that everything was okay in light of what had just happened.

BB laughed.

"The other woman, I presume?"

Amanda smiled and said, "Past tense, girl. Way past."

BB disarmed Amanda with a genuine smile and a handshake.

"I've heard so much about you."

"Some of it good, I hope."

"It's all good," Jess said. "Hell, it better be good."

BB scolded him.

"You leave her alone."

It didn't surprise him that the two would hit it off. He let the women talk among themselves as he prepared dinner. He had a fresh king salmon fillet and he decided to make a mustard dill potato salad along with some baked beans. He would add his own ingredients to the can of beans, which made them taste special, unlike your average can of beans. And he had picked up a loaf of French bread that he would toast in the oven. In total, it was the standard salmon dinner lineup in the Great Northwest.

The women came inside a little later and asked to help, but he would have none of it. Jess opened a bottle of white wine and poured a glass for each. He would stick to beer.

Midway through the newscast, a familiar scene appeared. They all sat down to watch. It was short and to the point. Wanda explained the situation in a way that made Jess feel uncomfortable. It was harmless, but in order to do justice to his side of the story, she needed his comments and footage of the pond. Maybe he was wrong for not letting her do her job.

Watching him onscreen, BB was struck by how handsome Jess looked. She glanced at the guitar case. Not now but later, they would have that talk again. She was positive his music could go places if only she could light a fire beneath him. Besides, it wasn't such a bad way to make a living. It sure beat the hell out of what he was doing now.

And then BB thought of her father. The next time she would see him he would have seen the pictures. She wondered how it might change their relationship. Maybe she would get lucky and he wouldn't even mention it. They both knew she would have to suffer the embarrassment for the rest of her life, so wouldn't that be punishment enough?

But as it turned out, there would be no embarrassment. BB would always be the girl in the magazine to the islanders. And how many girls in this world could actually say they were a real-life *Playday* model? People understood how truly beautiful she was. It was a source of respect and pride, knowing that she was a hometown girl. *Their* hometown girl.

The next morning, Jess found an envelope taped to the trailer door. Inside was a handwritten note that read, *The dog is dead. Your next.*

So much for third-grade grammar. He imagined a scene where he met the guy who was responsible for writing this. It was a dark urban alleyway with only one way out—through him. Then he dismissed the thought because his fighting days were over. After his last brawl, he vowed that he'd never raise his hands in anger again. If Legs was dead, he would have to take it on the chin and man up.

Still, his dad was dead, and didn't that account for something? He cried, thinking of his dad's early departure from this earth. Through the snot and the saliva he repeated over and over, *"Shit! Fuck! Fuckshit!"* the chant rolling off his tongue in a truck of a groove. It was the song of the be-fucked, where his choices gnashed like rocks on the shoreline. In his hunt for wisdom, it was like trying to rope the elusive white elk. Was there such a thing? And if there was, how much did it cost?

The police chief wanted to see Harris. When he closed the door to the chief's office, he found out why.

"I want you to lay off the Buchanan investigation," said the chief.

The chief was fat and always wore black. Ed was a good cop and would do what he was told, but he needed a better reason.

"Why?"

"Because I said so."

A good enough reason in the Emerald Police Department perhaps, but was it good enough for a good cop? Harris seemed to be stymied at every turn. He had a lead source but no proof. Mum was the word on the street and now the chief was asking Harris to do something his instincts told him was dead wrong. Should he defy the order? After all, a man's life hung in the balance.

The chief looked up from his papers.

"That's all."

Harris left without saying a word, his face red with anger. As he walked down the hall, others noticed.

"What's wrong with him?" asked one patrolman to another.

"People on pedestals get knocked down," was the other's reply.

When Harris got back to his desk, he found Jess Buchanan standing there with a piece of paper in his hands.

"Look at this," Jess said to the detective.

He handed Harris the note.

"Can I keep this?" Harris asked.

"I don't want it," Jess said.

Harris put his finger to his lips and led him out back.

"Something's going on. They want me off the case. Can you meet me out on Sleeper Road tomorrow night? You know the turnout?"

"I do."

"Meet me there at ten. Maybe I'll have some answers for you."

"I know who's behind all this," said Jess.

"Way ahead of you, pal," said Harris. "I just can't get anyone to talk. But do me a favor. Go tell your brother to get his head out of his ass. These guys are outta control. They mean business."

To Jess, this meant what it implied. That the web of events had reached far and wide, and now it even had the Emerald Police wrapped up in its grisly web of fugue and subterfuge.

Chapter 23

City hall, the fire department, the police station, and the *Island News-Times* office were all located within a stone's throw of each other at the top of Monkey Hill.

Enough said.

Jess walked through the parking lots of the police station and the fire department and stopped in at the *News-Times* office. He asked for Natalie Robinson or Michael Horton, a former baseball teammate of his at Emerald High School. Together they had won the state championship their senior year, and Mike was their second baseman and lead-off hitter. He was a good baseball player but he had an even better sense of humor. Jess could use a good laugh. He was told that Natalie was out. The receptionist called Michael over the speakerphone.

"Michael, Jess Buchanan is here to see you."

"Who?" asked Michael.

"Jess Buchanan."

"I thought he was dead," he said, with deadpan deeply rooted in his voice.

The young receptionist didn't quite know what to make of Michael's reply.

"Well, he's standing right here," she said, quite genuinely.

"Check his pulse," said Michael.

She paused, not sure if Michael was serious. As the news editor, Michael Horton was an important man in the office. It was only her second day on the job, so she did what she was told. The receptionist put her fingers around Jess' wrist to feel his pulse. He was definitely alive in her opinion.

"His pulse is good," she said.

"Are you sure?" asked Michael.

"I just checked it."

"For real?" he asked.

Jess vouched for her.

"For real, Mike."

"Oh, Ms. Martin, it'll be a pleasure to have you around," Michael said. "Send my friend Jess back to my office please, fourth door on your right.'

"Will do," she said dutifully, and led Jess down the hallway to the fourth door on the right.

Jess knocked and went in. He smiled at the man behind the desk. Michael had kept the weight off through the years and he still looked like a second baseman.

"I guess I'm not dead yet," Jess said, shaking Michael's hand.

Jess noticed that Michael looked a bit older, and he was losing some of his hair.

"How the hell you been, man?" Michael asked. "Long time, no see."

As they shook hands, Mike could tell that Jess was a man out of sorts. His angular face looked drawn; his cheeks lacked color. He still wore his hair to his shoulders when it wasn't the norm. But Michael knew his old friend didn't care about norms. He marched to a different drummer. And it was something Michael always admired about Jess.

"I see Billy down at the Dockside. He's doing well for himself," Michael said, sitting down behind the desk.

"Yeah, he sure turned that place around, didn't he?" Jess replied.

"Do you guys keep in touch?" asked Michael.

"He's a pretty busy guy."

"I saw BB the other day. She's pretty as ever."

Jess had to smile, remembering Michael's affection for her. They had shared a chemistry class together, the three of them having no clue, but having a lot of fun being dumb.

When the reminiscing was over, Michael said, "What can I do you for?"

Michael sensed his old friend was on a mission. He also understood the airfield situation on all sides. BB had brought him up to date on where Jess stood on the sale to Junior. It came as no surprise to Michael, but it was important to hear it from Jess. Third parties tended to color the facts with their own impressions. In the world of reporting, it was necessary to get at the truth.

"How much do you know?" Jess asked.

"BB told me things. Billy thinks you're nuts. Natalie's filled me in on Junior's position and the navy's. It looks to me like you're on the hot seat. From the letters we've received, it's about five to one in favor of the airfield. We get an occasional bitch about the noise, or an opinion on the environmental impact, but nothing as impassioned as what it will do for the island economy. Hell, it's a whole new industry in a place that doesn't have much. Outside of the tourist dollars, Emerald doesn't have anything to offer in the way of jobs."

"But what about the noise?" Jess said. "Can you imagine sitting on the deck at the Dockside with a drink in your hand and having this jet come screaming down on top of you? I know who'll be getting the business. The frickin' clinic from all the fucking heart attacks."

Michael laughed. He envisioned a busload of senior citizens with tubes sticking out of their flowery print summer wear. He pictured the brochure: *Come visit Emerald. Stay a week, maybe two, depending on your condition!*

"From what I understand, the noise won't be that bad. The jets will fly in and out over the water on the north end. Emerald won't be affected much."

"Like hell," Jess said. "I live a couple miles outside of town and I'm getting pounded by jets."

Michael turned his chair around to view a large map of the island tacked to the wall behind him. He took a pointer and pointed where the airfield would be built and the proposed flight patterns. Michael was right. In theory, the Emerald community shouldn't be affected all that much, and certainly not to the degree that Jess had been subjected to over the last couple of months.

Michael looked up from the map.

"Sounds to me like you're—"

"Getting a heavy dose of persuasion?" Jess said.

"You could say that."

"Or how about getting fucked in general?"

"That too."

They both sat back in their chairs. In Michael, Jess had an old friend who was in the know as far as the politics surrounding the issue, but he still didn't have a read on Mike's position. It was understandable since Mike had to remain neutral.

"Can I speak off the record?" Jess asked.

Michael would like nothing better than to have this complex man explain himself.

"Absolutely."

"Jeez, Mike, that sounds like one of those movie answers just before the guy gets blown to bits."

Michael rocked forward in his chair and put his elbows on his desk.

"I'm a news guy and I think that's why you're here. But I realize what your family has done for the community. I went to college on a scholarship funded by your father."

This was news to Jess. He gave a mental *atta boy* to his dad.

"I didn't know that."

"So what I'm trying to say is, if I can be of help, I'll certainly do whatever I can. But I'm also bound by the ethics of my position. Right now, we're just a couple of old friends talking. Right?"

"Okay, where do we start?" asked Jess.

Jess had come to plead his case, but how much information should he offer?

Through his years as a professional reporter, Michael understood the mechanics behind the drawing-out process. He had to make Jess feel comfortable, interject some humor.

"Well, let's begin with. . . I know where you were born and raised, and by whom. I also know you've got a great arm, that your curveball—when it's working—can buckle the knees of any hitter. You play the guitar and sing with the best of them. But what I really want to know is, are BB's boobs for real?"

Michael said this without cracking a smile, and Jess realized that he was, on a certain level, dead serious. Apparently, Michael had not seen the magazine.

"Okay, here's the deal," said Jess, quickly dismissing the thought. "You've been out to the old pit, right?"

"Many times," said Michael. "Most of the time too drunk to remember. I'm surprised nobody ever drowned at one of those keggers."

Jess leaned forward and folded his hands on top of Michael's desk.

"So you know what the pond means to me. Or what it could mean to anybody who's been there?"

"I do," said Michael. "It's a beautiful place. One of a kind."

"I always knew I'd live there," Jess said. "I dreamt about it. And that's the point."

"So the point is, you got your wish?" Michael asked, unsure where this was going.

Jess' next words were spoken in a hoarse whisper, as if it was the most private of secrets.

"It's a place for *dreams,* man."

Michael sat forward in his seat, sensing the heart of the matter.

"Okay, it's a peaceful place. Good for thought."

"No, it's something more than that," Jess whispered.

Did he want to go there? Jess hadn't admitted this to anyone, not to BB, or his father, or Billy, and certainly not to Junior. But something told him that Michael could be one of the few who could understand.

"I'm listening," Michael said.

Jess got up from the chair because the movie guy wanted to take his place. To be honest or not to be honest, that *was* the question. Could Jess hang in there and reveal his innermost secrets without the movie guy's intervention? Would Michael be left with an impression that he was out of his mind? Then again, if he were shot dead tomorrow, nobody would have ever known.

"Jess?"

Jess couldn't look up because he was afraid Mike might not receive this information well.

"Dreams, Mike. It's the stuff of spirits. Remember in history class when we read about the Indians?"

Michael nodded and let him continue.

"Do you remember who the shaman was?" Jess asked.

"Sorta like the medicine man?"

"Okay, for our purposes, we'll leave it at that. Now the shaman had a gift. He could transport his mind or his spirit in many different ways Sometimes it would take on the form of an animal, or a dream, where he gathered all sorts of insights about the world."

"Got'cha," Michael said.

"Now a shaman would go to a certain place to prepare his mind and body and spirit for the journey. It was his holy place. There, anything was possible. It was the door to his dreams."

Jess made sure Michael was following. He seemed to be, so Jess continued.

"Do you still like music? Like we did back in high school?"

The question came at Michael like one of Jess' fastballs.

"Mike?"

"Okay, I *really* like your music. I listen to it all the time. And not because I know you."

Jess smiled.

"Do you know why you like it? Enough to give it a definition. Why it hits a nerve?

"It's hard to explain," Michael said.

"Exactly. It just does something to you, right?"

"Absolutely."

"It connects."

"Like a solid double to center," Michael said.

Jess leaned back in his chair. Here, they were getting to the heart of the matter.

"In high school, did you ever hear me play the guitar, or even know that I could sing?"

"I never saw you lugging one around," Michael said honestly.

Actually, it was news to everybody that Jess had this hidden talent.

"I didn't want anybody to know," Jess admitted. "Until I was ready."

Michael laughed.

"You had a talent that people only dream of having, and you kept it a secret? That's amazingly fucked up."

Michael saw where he could inject some humor into this revelation.

"If a guy could play guitar in high school, that was pretty much a hall pass for pussy. Looked what you missed out on."

Then Michael realized who he was talking to. Jess had the most beautiful girlfriend in the world. Of course he didn't need pussy.

But while they were on the subject, there was one thing he always wanted to ask Jess should he ever run into him again. After Jess had quit the band, he had become a very private person, and Michael felt it was unfortunate. Jess would have been great at the happy hours down at the Dockside. He knew everybody in the crowd that would meet every night after work. Life was fun for a twenty-something in Emerald.

"Why did you quit playing?" Michael asked, hoping he wasn't bringing up a sore subject.

Jess didn't quite know how to answer that. Words failed him whenever he tried to list all the specifics. It was not on a whim. Surely not.

"It seemed like the right thing to do," Jess said.

Michael felt it was a cop-out.

"Man, that's a crazy," he said. "You're one of my all-time favorite artists. When I heard you had quit, it was a sad day in my life, and not because I know you personally. Shit, you could have been from the moon for all I cared. You went out and got us all hooked on your stuff, and then you just quit playing. That's really fucked up."

Jess had no idea Mike felt so strongly about his music. He didn't know what to say except, "Man, I'm sorry."

He felt bad for Mike. Having one of your favorite artists suddenly quit making music must have really sucked. For Jess, it would have been like Clapton getting run over by a truck. *Strike that. Clean slate.* He couldn't even entertain the thought.

But they needed to get back on track. Where was Jess going with this? The shaman, the sacred ground . . . he gathered his thoughts. He had never voiced this belief out loud, this thing he knew about the pond, about what it could do. If it could do it for him, then he was sure it could do it for others, especially the ones who were really gifted. The pond could be a source of inspiration for artists and dream-seekers alike, an endless fountain of inspiration. Someday he wanted to build an artist colony there in the old pit. But first . . .

"I gotta piss," Jess said.

"Second door on your left. Jiggle the handle when you're done," Michael said.

It left Michael to think about what Jess had said, or more to the point, what he was trying to say. If the pond was a spiritual dream machine like Jess thought, if it could work for others like it did Jess, what was it worth? Regardless of whether it was true or not, if the pond could inspire Jess to write the songs that he wrote, well, that was good enough for Michael. Jess could touch people in ways that he obviously hadn't considered, and that was an amazing revelation to Michael—that Jess had no clue how good he was.

In the bathroom, Jess thought if his songs could stir people like Mike to develop such passion for his music, wasn't that a good enough reason to continue on his path to feed his artistic soul? If he could do that with his songs, could he do that with say. . . a novel? Could he ever move people as deeply?

Michael was on the phone when Jess walked in. He sat down in the chair across from Michael and waited patiently for him to finish his phone conversation. He thought about his next move when Michael hung up.

"So where were we?" Michael asked, knowing full well where they had left off.

"I need to ask a favor," Jess said.

"Like I said, anything I can do."

Jess leaned forward and folded his hands on Michael's desk, almost prayer-like.

"I need for people to understand my side of the story. I don't think they know what I'm up against. If I don't sell, what then?"

"You mean after your brother drags your carcass up and down Main Street in a Buchanan dump truck?" Michael asked. "If you survive that, then I suggest you move out of town to a place way the fuck away from here, acquire a phony identity, and pray your brother never finds you. In other words, lay low until the shit blows over."

It was almost the unspeakable truth of it. Michael couldn't see how Jess could live in Emerald if he didn't sell. He would be an outcast in his hometown, where he once was a hero. Michael understood Jess' side of the story, and also, that it really hadn't been told. Ninety percent of the people on the island had never seen the pond. Here, Michael saw an opportunity where the plan could come together and showcase Natalie's skills.

"Let's do this," Michael said. "Natalie Robinson has been following the story."

"I know. I've tried to reach her a number of times."

"Did you leave a number?"

"I don't have a phone."

"That's a problem," Michael said. "How about we set up a meeting between you two? She'll meet you at the pond and bring her camera."

"Can she bring a real photographer?" Jess asked. "I'd really like to showcase the way the pond looks."

Michael smiled.

"She's the best photographer we've got. And she's pretty fucking amazing," he said, seriously.

Jess caught something in Michael's voice as he got up from the chair.

"Are you screwing her?"

Michael smiled.

"Are BB's real?"

"You oughta know," Jess said. "You stared at them all through high school."

He left Michael laughing, knowing it wasn't far from the truth.

Jess drove to the cemetery, got out, and walked to Buck's gravesite, stopping for a moment to pick flowers from the hedge that bordered the property. He dusted the grass cuttings away from the marble tombstone and laid the flowers next to the monument. As he knelt, he said a prayer of forgiveness for every time he had disappointed his father in his lifetime, and it was plenty. He also asked for direction, an answer to the pressing question for which he had no answer. His soul bore the weight of many considerations, and heaviest among them was his love for his family. He read the inscription, the epitaph.

Albert Buckminster Buchanan
A Good Man

They couldn't even call Buck by his name in death. Jess and Junior had gone round and round about it, but Junior finally won out and decided to leave "Buck" off the monument. He figured everybody knew him as Buck anyways.

His mother asked Jess to write the epitaph. He couldn't decide between *gentle* and *good*. He went with *good* because his father was not always gentle. *Good* spoke closer to the truth, and the summation of a life should be truthful, at the very least, he felt.

On his walk back to the truck, Jess read some of the other epitaphs on the tombstones and figured them to be a lie. Humanity was just not that decent.

Jess drove back to the trailer and locked the door. He made a cup of coffee and sat down at the table. He felt like a sitting duck. "*Your next,*" the note said. He had to forgive the grammar since it really bugged him, but there was no mistaking the sentiment.

Fear.

Should he go see Junior and do like Harris suggested, ask him what was going on? Junior said he'd threatened the men with their jobs, so what more could he do? Men were terrorizing him and Jess realized he couldn't do anything about it. Except to sell his soul.

Jess tried to write. He sat with a pen and stared blankly at the spiral notebook, creation lost in his soul's upheaval. Where the imaginary was once a haven for his emotions, the secret garden had been replaced by something unsecured and vulnerable. He noticed his hand shook. The silence spoke doom. Without Legs to stand guard, Jess was left out in the open. There would be no warning.

Jess was supposed to meet Harris the next day. But the detective admitted he had nothing. So what would another day bring, more futility? And Natalie, what could a picture of the pond and a few words do for him?

If he didn't sell, Jess understood that he couldn't live in Emerald anymore. He might as well pack his bags and leave. On the other hand, if he did sell, he would have to make restitution to the gods of creativity once the pond was all torn up. He hoped that creativity was the benevolent sort; the kind of thing that could forgive him.

He sat staring at the spiral notebook unable to bring himself to write. Then it occurred to him that maybe the payments to the gods of creativity had already begun, just because he *might* sell.

He quickly loaded up the truck with his camping gear and took off for the mountains. He wasn't about to serve himself up on a platter if somebody wanted to shoot him dead. They didn't have far to look if they wanted to hunt him down.

He left a note for BB and taped the envelope to the trailer door so she wouldn't worry. He told her where he was going. But not for how long.

Chapter 24

The next day, Natalie drove out to the old pit looking for Jess. She knocked on the trailer door and there was no answer. She glanced at the note taped to the door and wanted to peek at it, but then she decided against it since it wasn't addressed to her.

Michael had talked to her at great length about the background and historical perspective of the Buchanan's. Michael had lived in Emerald all his life and had been in the same grade as Jess. Junior was four years older. He told her a story of gravel pits, of fathers and sons, of their women, of their sometimes hatred among the people of Emerald just for who they were. He told her he had gone to college on a full scholarship funded by Jess' father, Buck.

Michael told the story almost like an enchanted spectator. He explained how time was running out for this generation of Buchanan's. Their fortunes lay in the gravel pits, and now the issue pitted one brother against the other. He told her how, on the surface, there was a simple solution. If Jess sold, there would be no issue. But there was nothing simple about Jess. He was a talented man with a peculiar outlook on life. In Michael's opinion, he wasn't quite sure whether Jess was crazy, or onto something. His approach to living was almost unthinkable.

Natalie climbed the gravel ridge to have a peek at the pond. At the top, she put her photographer's eye to the spectacular beauty, breathtaking in its visual possibilities; the shading, where through the trees the fractured bits of brilliant light hit the emerald green surface in spots of reflective splendor.

Immediately, she felt a source of inspiration. She aimed the camera eye and began to snap frame after frame, a veritable *ménage au naturelle*. She flew about the quarry in a concentrated burst of creative energy, aiming to capture the *feel* of it. After every shot she repeated, "Gorgeous, nice, perfect, uh-huh," and trusted that the lens was seeing what she was seeing. She knew a picture could do more to explain Jess' position, more than any words. She understood now. And Michael was right. The pond *was* worth saving.

Jess sat bivouacked on a spit on Jackman Creek, separated by raging torrents on either side of him. The June rains had excited the flow to where it was nearly impossible to cross without a stronghold, a tie line. There, he felt secure from the outside world. His only concern was for the bears. They could cross the waters in a split second and would too, if he gave them reason enough. He marveled at the way they could anchor down in the flow and pick and choose the trout with relative ease. He hung his food from a tree as far away from the tent as possible. Just in case.

But to say he was afraid of bears wasn't true. He would rather face a bear than a Banks any day. At least with a bear he knew where he stood.

The rain finally stopped and he took out the Martin. It sounded good echoing off the canyon walls. Whoever was within earshot got his best effort. All night long a parade of critters came to check out the dude on the spit, the human who needed answers to some very troubling questions.

The songs probably sounded like an improvisation of gibberish to the animals. Jess could spot the tiny red reflections peering back at him, their eyes in the firelight between the ferns and the bushes and the trees. He wanted to speak their language, to tell them of his choices and their consequences. In the end, it was an equation upon the condition of life, when circumstances demanded probing the soul, pecking at it.

Melvin called a meeting of the council of the Brotherhood. They met in the pit office and discussed the situation. By all reports it looked as if the kid had taken off, so it would make things easier. The biggest question facing them was, did they wait until the eleventh hour?

Melvin proposed they stick to the original timetable. As with most things, the council agreed with him. But they also needed to deliver a message to one of their own. Silence was key, and everyone had to honor that code. Those who didn't would have to suffer the consequences, or what were codes for? It was a known fact that Shorty had talked to the police.

To close the meeting, it was ceremonial to clasp hands over Melvin's desk. The council was doing this as Shorty Dewitt walked into the pit office with an order he didn't understand. One of the guys closed the door behind him. After a short discussion, Melvin gave the signal. Four men gathered around Shorty and instructed him on the ways of the Brotherhood. In short order, they beat him senseless. A steel-toed boot landed flush on his back and sent him to the ER with three fractured ribs.

In the emergency room, the nurse asked Shorty how it happened.

"A horse kicked me," he said, with a blank look on his face.

The nurse couldn't imagine how he managed to drive himself to the clinic. She figured he must have had a tremendous threshold for pain.

But pain and tolerance was something Shorty was running short on. His wife Betty couldn't understand how a horse could hurt him like that, since he was so good with them.

"It was a mule," he admitted, finally.

It was the first Wednesday of the month, men's night at the Emerald Country Club where they were serving ten-buck rib-eyes. TBR night was for the thirty or forty guys who would show up in the men's lounge to play poker or crib or pool. Junior worked until seven and decided there wasn't much more he could do, not without a decision from his brother. He thought if he went out to the club he could unwind. Steaks and poker fit his mood.

Junior made out two bids, one where he owned the rock, and

one where he didn't. He knew his bid without the gravel would be competitive, but he was sure others could beat it. The marine construction guys who already owned the barges and the tugs could easily beat his number. But they were big outfits who probably wouldn't see money enough to stick around Emerald after the airfield was gone. But the airfield would boil down to a pissing match of who wanted it most, like most bids, and the big boys would all come to play. Junior was sure of it.

Junior had countered with a fair number for the old pit gravel to where the margins couldn't justify anything more. He was counting on his brother to come to his senses and for Amanda to steer him straight. Junior knew his brother wasn't built for business; he would just as soon give the concrete away to the people who really needed it. But it would be a lesson in cold hard reality for Jess, this whole ordeal, and Junior felt his brother would become a better man for it, a wiser man.

Junior imagined Clay Island without gravel. He smiled as he turned onto Swantown Road, amused by the thought of the public outcry once people realized the true inflated cost of concrete and asphalt. Finite resources could demand unbelievable prices.

Junior thought about his father. It must have been a helluva decision to walk away from a load like the one under the pond. Hell, the pit they were working in now had about half as much rock to sand. Maybe his father moved the plant to save the pond, but Junior doubted it. There were other factors involved. Buck needed a new facility, a bigger facility, and the south town property had a lot more room.

Junior thought about the bid and who would bid it. Naturally, the marine outfits would be all in because they were all on the same playing field, having to barge the gravel in. The difference would boil down to the trucking. The marine guys would purchase a piece of land close to the airfield to get as close as possible to cut down on the trucking. The old pit was a two-mile run. You couldn't buy a piece of land as close.

Junior turned into the country club parking lot and cruised the lot for an empty space. He ended up parking in the grass out in the north forty, the overflow lot, about a quarter mile away from the clubhouse. He locked the Lincoln and began a brisk walk. He only wore a light nylon jacket for warmth and the winds were whipping off the bay, making it feel even colder.

Junior landed on this final thought to take his mind off the cold.

The original map showed the deposit extending past the boundaries of the pond. It was an area so large that it approached the concrete fence on the east side, and Junior figured there just might be enough gravel to build the entire airfield in that area alone. He might not even *have* to disturb the pond.

But it was something he would keep to himself, because in the end it really didn't matter. Eventually he would need the rock if he was going to stay in business.

As Junior approached the clubhouse, he heard shouts from inside. Guys were having fun and he wanted some of that. Thinking back, he hadn't had any fun since his breakup with Amanda. Then he tried to shake thoughts of her. He missed her smile, her voice, her sense of humor, her beauty . . . and on and on the list went, shoved to the back of his brain, because, Jesus, he really fucked that one up.

On Baker Lake, Jess rowed to the other end because he needed peace and quiet to think. He was the only one on the lake, and he drew in the oars and floated aimlessly to ponder his next move. He would have Amanda draw up a will because he had to think of BB now, what would be in her best interests, should he be shot dead. If he didn't sell, at least she would have something to tide her over in his permanent absence.

He thought of what she might do with the old pit. He knew she would probably sell it to the highest bidder, maybe Junior, but that wasn't a certainty. She hated Junior. But if she did sell the old pit, then everybody could live happily ever after. He amended that. Maybe not happily for him since he was dead. But people would forget soon enough.

But one thing was for sure. He would be responsible for his own epitaph. He had a will and it stated exactly how it should look on the tombstone.

Jessie James Buchanan
"Jess"
He meant well

The descent was now complete. Jess realized he needed to rally but he didn't know how. He was resolved not to let madness rule. He was drowning in something and he needed to surface, to break free of this thing holding him under. Anger wasn't the solution. It just fueled his pity.

He would need to find a job. But what function could he serve in Emerald? He could write a song and he was a good singer. He played the guitar pretty well. He was writing a novel but there was no telling what would come of it since the ending had yet to be determined. And now, staying alive took precedence over everything because his clear and present danger suggested he better concentrate on that part or he was out the rest of one lifetime.

If his pond was as big as a lake, it might resemble Baker Lake, he thought. Jess rowed the green rowboat close to the shore, looking for animals hiding in the forest. The trees, mostly Douglas fir, reached all the way down to the water's edge, much like the tree line of the western rim of the pond. The wake of the rowboat looked substantial in the quiet glassy water. The lake smelled of trout, and altogether it suggested peace and tranquility in him, where images of love and life crystallized in his brain. He was discovering how life could be with BB, and he realized his love for her affected every part of his being. He would die for her. And come to think of it, he might have to.

On the way home from the country club, Junior got pulled over by Officer Skip Nelson of the Emerald Police for suspicion of drunk driving. Nelson made him walk a straight line and then asked Junior to take the breathalyzer. Junior refused. The officer told him to lock his car and took him in.

Junior called Amanda when he got to the station. He had been drinking alright, but he'd also had a steak dinner. He wasn't driving dangerously, he hadn't even crossed the white line, but it didn't matter to Officer Nelson. He was weaving erratically enough to justify stopping him.

Amanda wasn't home or she wasn't answering her cell phone. He got the recording. He left a message and hung up and called his own lawyer, Harry Wolf. He wasn't home either. Junior needed time to think. Officer Nelson led him down the hall to cell B and locked him inside.

Detective Harris heard what was going on with Junior Buchanan and wanted a few minutes with the guy while he was feeling vulnerable. Maybe he could hammer some truth from him on a much larger issue. Harris asked Officer Nelson to put Buchanan in cell D, separate from the drunks, while he waited for his lawyer. Nelson was a young by-the-book policeman and he did what he was told. He respected Harris, the way he went about his business. Nelson wanted to become a detective someday, and in his eyes Harris was a good one to pattern himself after.

Twenty minutes later, Harris went back to cell D and stood outside the bars to chat with his old friend. Junior was happy to see him, after all he was a familiar face.

"You're in trouble again, 'ey, Buchanan?"

Junior laughed.

"Sort of. I'm waiting for my lawyer."

This wasn't funny to Harris. He cut the big man down with his glare. The detective went right up to the cell bars to make sure Junior got the message.

"A DUI is a serious offense, bud. You could have killed somebody out there."

The air in the room became icy silent. There was something behind his words that was fueling this passion. Harris didn't like Junior. It was evident, and Junior wished the little cop would come right out and say why.

"Do you know the danger your brother is in?" asked Harris,

shifting the conversation to the real reason why he wanted to talk to the big man.

There, as he suspected.

"I don't think *danger* is the word for it," answered Junior, a little too smug for Harris' tastes.

The detective handed him the note. Junior looked surprised when he read it.

"He never mentioned it to me," Junior said, handing the note back to the detective. "Personally, I think it's all bullshit."

"Are you willing to take that chance? Do you think it's something I should ignore? Help me here," said the detective.

Junior rubbed his forehead. What did Harris want from him? A confession?

"I don't know. Yeah, there are people who want Jess to do the right thing. I don't think they would hurt him over it. This is Emerald, not New York."

"Who are *they*?"

Junior was in a vulnerable position with the little cop's shadow cast over him while he sat on the bunk. He got up and stretched all six foot two inches right in front of Harris.

"I wouldn't hurt my brother even if my life depended on it. Sure, I want to kill him sometimes because he's just not like the rest of us. But don't take me literally. I love my brother. If you don't believe me, I don't know what else to tell you."

Harris did believe him. To a certain degree.

"Okay, Buchanan, this is the way I see it. The Brotherhood is doing all your bidding for you and you're not trying to stop it. They burn down your brother's camper, they dump garbage in the pond, they shoot at him when he's riding his bike, they shoot the swan, they scare the hell out of the children swimming in the pond, the jets fly over his trailer every hour. . . little annoyances, right? Now I've got a note that says they've killed his dog and he's next if he doesn't sell the gravel *to you*. How convenient is that? Just look the other way. Right?"

Harris patted himself on the back for the delivery. The passion was there.

"I want to talk to my lawyer," Junior said, ending the conversation.

Junior didn't need some little cop telling him how the world went round. He couldn't take this guy seriously. Hell, he never had to make a payroll. The cop probably made thirty thousand a year. Shit, he spent that in *tips*.

Officer Nelson came back and led Junior to the phone. It was late and Amanda still wasn't answering. He left another message and Nelson walked him back to the cell.

Junior sat on the cold steel bench and thought how events in his life just weren't adding up. Maybe it was time to buy that condo in Hawaii, hang out the *Gone Fishing* sign and kick back. Did he have enough money to be secure for the rest of his life? Probably not. But he could always make money. It was one thing he knew how to do. He also faced a night in jail with a headache and the shivers. Didn't anybody turn up the heat?

A half hour later, Amanda came to bail him out. She had been drinking, so she walked up the hill to the police station in the crisp island air. He gave her a big hug when he saw her.

"We'll go back to the boat," she said.

Amanda hated to see such a proud man humbled. Junior didn't appear to be drunk. Of course, it had been a couple of hours since his first phone call, and even then he hadn't been slurring his words. There might be a chance to have the charges dropped or at least reduced. She had seen worse. On the walk back to the marina, she asked him a direct question.

"Were you drunk?"

Junior summed up the pernicious effect of alcohol.

"I don't think so."

The next morning, BB and Marie stopped by the Bayside Bakery on their way to the Emerald Boutique. Marie thought it would be a good idea to shop for a wedding dress, at least to look for a few possibilities. BB was excited. For the first time it hit her what it was like to be a bride.

A bright sunny day in June could get any new bride's heart

pumping in the hopes that her wedding day would be as beautiful. But they hadn't set a date, so BB wasn't gonna get too excited. They hadn't even discussed what type of wedding they wanted. She had a setting in mind, but it made Jess uncomfortable to talk about it. Maybe because he had other things on his mind. She could understand. Their future was very uncertain. Would they be rich or would they be poor? BB thought it really shouldn't matter because they were going to be together. But as for marriages, there was no harm in pricing cakes and looking at dresses. It was Marie's suggestion and BB loved spending time with Marie. The two of them were like mother and daughter.

The bakery was full. It was 10:30 in the morning, time for coffee and doughnuts for the tourists and the Emerald townsfolk. It's a ritual shared across America, where the locals gather for gossip and news about who is doing what, and when. Many of the locals recognized who had just walked in. It was Marie Buchanan and the girl in the magazine. They talked in hushed whispers. *Such a pretty girl.*

One of the younger men whistled. For a moment, Marie thought it was just some young guy giving BB the business, innocent horseplay. But as they stood at the counter and talked to Matilde the owner, BB looked out of the corner of her eye and recognized Barry Lindell, a guy she knew from high school, and he was nothing but trouble. He wore a cap with *Damifino* written across the front and BB thought it summed up his mental capacity pretty well. Barry whistled again and the crowd laughed. Then he stepped over the line, feeling inspired by his newfound celebrity. He was also drunk at ten in the morning.

"Hey, honey, sit on my face!" he shouted.

There were elderly ladies present and one of the good guys shouted, "Hey, watch your mouth!"

Marie turned and searched the room with her eyes, trying to locate the man with the big mouth. People seated next to Barry pointed him out. He sat in the back of the room, near the windows that looked out over Sunset Bay.

"I hope you weren't addressing us ladies, young man," she said. "Because if you were, I'll have you arrested."

The room became stone quiet, not quite sure if Marie Buchanan could do that. But it was Marie Buchanan, so honestly she could do anything. Nobody would question her on it. She was island royalty.

Marie waited patiently for his reply. Barry pretended like he hadn't heard her. It was obvious that he didn't want any part of Mrs. Buchanan, especially when Marie waded through four rows of tables and positioned herself right in front of him. Barry's face was red from drinking. It bordered on crimson now, out of embarrassment.

"Did you say it, young man?" Marie asked, pointedly.

"I don't think so," Barry said, trying to muster up some smart-ass to save face.

"How can you be so sure?" replied Marie.

A woman seated at the next table called him out.

"It was him."

Marie decided a good lecture was what he needed and she waded into Barry with a mother's angry tone.

"Because you're drunk, I won't hold you responsible for your actions, young man, since it's obvious you have *no* manners. Now I don't know whether it's true for you in more sober times, but if not, then I suggest you acquire some manners, because in this town I can assure you it will catch up to you someday. Now, if you will apologize to everybody here in the bakery, I will forget this matter. Stand up."

"No way," Barry said. "I ain't standing for nobody."

BB felt it was a good time to leave. She followed Marie's path back to the table and stood right next to her in case something happened. A couple of big guys walked over to the table, each taking one side of Barry.

Barry made a quick summary of his chances and decided that standing might be his best option. He stood slowly, and when he reached his full height, it was apparent that he was significantly smaller than the two men standing next to him. He'd made a good choice.

Marie raised an eyebrow and presented her chin.

"Well?"

One of the big guys nudged him.

"Mrs. Buchanan is talking to you."

"I'm sorry," Barry blurted out after a slight hesitation.

Marie wasn't convinced.

"What for, young man? Is it something specific or are you just sorry in general? You see, normally an apology is accompanied by a statement for why you're having to make it."

BB placed her hand on Marie's arm. Marie was pressing and BB was proud of her. But she had seen too many barroom brawls in her lifetime and she knew when the shit was about to fly.

Barry shuffled his feet and adopted another pose. He hooked his thumbs in his back pockets, making him look like he was standing in the principal's office.

"I'm sorry for what I said," he muttered with his head down.

BB tugged at Marie's arm and whispered, "Okay, let's go."

But Marie wasn't finished. She looked directly into Barry's eyes and held his gaze.

"All right, young man. I'll accept your apology." And here she looked around the room at the many faces she recognized and said, "For all of us. But if I hear of you acting like this again, I'll personally talk to your mother about it."

Barry was surprised to hear that Marie Buchanan even knew his mother. They weren't the most popular family in town. His brother was in jail for trying to rob the Emerald Bank, which gave them some notoriety. Just not the good kind.

Marie walked to the door and BB followed close behind. A smattering of applause could be heard as they exited. When they got outside, BB realized she was responsible for that scene, and felt she needed to explain it to Marie. BB knew there were more incidents like this to come. But if it was hard for her to talk to her dad about it, it was doubly hard for her to tell Marie.

"Marie, wait a minute," BB said, trying to catch her by the elbow.

"What is it, dear?" Marie said.

Marie kept walking down the sidewalk, using short strides so she wouldn't fall going downhill. BB could barely keep up.

"I have something to tell you."

Marie adjusted her purse on her arm as she walked. She was in a tizzy wondering, *Have all the young men forgotten their manners?*

"No, you don't," Marie replied, and kept walking fast.

"I do. It's something I did in Los Angeles," BB said, finally catching up to her and grabbing her by the elbow.

Marie stopped and turned to face her future daughter-in-law.

"You mean the pictures?"

Her reply nearly knocked BB over. Had Marie known all along, and not bothered to mention it?

Marie was still in a lecturing mood. She thought this might be a good time to address the elephant in the room, even though they were outside in the bright sunlight.

"Personally, I wouldn't have done it for *any* reason. But forget about the pictures and soon enough they will too. Sometimes people just want to knock you down a notch, and believe me, we could all use it."

Marie took BB's hands in her own and said, "God loves you, honey. No matter what you've done, or will do. That's all that matters, okay?"

BB laughed like a giddy schoolgirl suddenly free from a dark secret that she had been harboring for months.

"Okay," she said, giggling in relief.

BB kissed Marie on the cheek right in front of the Emerald Boutique, but she was still hesitant to go in. Inside, she might get the same treatment, the whispers, the glances. Marie noticed her hesitation and gently scolded her.

"You can't let other people run your life," she said. "Let's go."

Then Marie did a very uncharacteristic thing. She waved her Gucci purse in the air, the one that Buck had bought her for her sixtieth birthday, and said to BB, "Besides, money talks!"

Marie was right of course. The ladies in the Emerald Boutique fussed over BB for hours. It wasn't often that they got to fit a real live model for a wedding dress, at least one with such a big budget, courtesy of Marie Buchanan.

That night, Detective Harris waited for nearly an hour on Sleeper Road but Jess didn't show. He got concerned. He drove back through town and out to the old pit. As he turned onto Old Pit Road, he noticed a car parked off to the side, a few hundred yards from the entrance.

He turned into the old pit parking lot and stopped at the thick steel cable. He shut off the motor but kept his headlights on. The trailer was dark. He got out of the unmarked patrol car and looked to see if that sedan was still parked beside the road. It was. He walked to the trailer, looking around to see if there was any physical disturbance. All was quiet. He knocked on the trailer door but there was no answer. He tried the handle and it was locked.

Harris ran up the gravel bank and took a mental note of the area. The moon gleamed off the water as he scanned the quarry walls on the west end. There was no sign of a disturbance. But it was quiet, maybe too quiet. He ran back down the gravel bank and walked briskly to the trailer. He shined his flashlight through a window, through a small opening in the curtains. Everything seemed to be in order.

On the drive back to town, Harris noticed that the sedan was no longer parked on the side of Old Pit Road. He smiled. It was a good thing he remembered that plate number. It was the sort of innocent detail that someone other than a good cop might have overlooked.

Chapter 25

Saturday morning, cloudy, and still no Jess. BB put up a sign at the old pit entrance, No Swimming Today, just in case some of the children were wondering. She called Junior to let him know that Jess wasn't back. They were all wondering when he might return. Amanda too.

Junior needed an answer. A little brotherly courtesy is what he felt Jess lacked. He could forgive him on the professional level because he knew no better. But as a brother, his absence was unforgivable. Junior wondered if he ought to take a drive up to Jackman Creek, where he thought Jess might be camping out.

The bid opening was a couple days away and he needed a decision now. He would try the spit on Jackman Creek first. If he knew his brother like he thought he did, he would probably be there since it was their dad's favorite spot. But then, knowing his brother like he did, he could just as easily not find him there.

Junior drove up the winding logging road and saw campfire at the spit on Jackman creek. He had guessed right. He shouted out to Jess from the other side. The creek split at that point and two torrents of water surrounded the spit. It flowed as fast and hard as a small river.

"Jessie?"

Jess heard a familiar voice call out his name, the one person who would know where he'd go. It was his father's favorite camping place, and every summer Buck would take the boys up in the mountains and camp there for a week, away from the real world and ringing telephones.

But the creek presented a problem. How was Jess going to get Junior across the high water? He wondered if Junior had strength enough to hold on to the rope that stretched across the torrent, in some places chest high.

"Yo!" said Jess, who appeared on the other side. "Come on over."

Junior looked at the rope stretched from one side of the creek to the other in disbelief that he could cross the creek. Jess shouted to him above the roar of the water.

"Grab the rope. Wrap it around your waist and walk across."

Jess pointed to the tree along the bank. Junior shook his head.

"I don't know, man. The water looks pretty ragin' to me."

Jess had to laugh.

"Come on, you can do it."

Junior had a better idea.

"Why don't you come over here?"

A good point thought Jess. Why didn't he?

"Nothing over there interests me," Jess shouted over the roar of the rushing water.

Junior thought for a second. Jessie had been camped for a couple days, so he was probably hungry for something other than trout and baked beans. It might be an opportunity to do like they used to do when they were kids, when Buck finally had had enough of the campfire food.

"If you come over here, I'll take you into Concrete and buy you a steak."

"Don't want to go to Concrete," Jess said, although a steak sounded pretty good after a few days in the wild.

Jess knew that the Cascade Room at the Concrete Café was the place to be on a Wednesday night in Concrete. It was where he had met a few girls in his lifetime. Concrete was to the mountains like Emerald was to the water, the essence of its surroundings.

Junior stood on the bank of the creek and measured his chances of survival, wading into the torrent with a girth nearly twice the size of his brother. Maybe if he was younger he would have stood a chance. He computed the force of the water and the fact that he couldn't swim for shit. The roar of the water rebounded off the canyon walls so loud that he could barely hear himself shout.

"Are you sure I can make it?" Junior shouted.

Jess laughed and shook his head.

"No."

Jess looked at the water rushing through the bottleneck that the spit created. The rains over the last couple of days had excited the flow to where it was as high and as fast as he had ever seen it. No, Junior couldn't make it if he had any doubts. One wrong step and he'd be carried downstream so swiftly that holding the rope would eventually pull him under. Hell, Jess even questioned if he could make it.

"Here," he shouted to Junior.

After tying one end of the rope to a fir on his side, he motioned for Junior to do the same on the other side.

"Tie it up high as you can."

"Where?" asked Junior.

"Anywhere up high."

Junior wrapped the rope around a large fir about halfway up the bank and pulled it tight. He tied it off and looked back at Jess and gave him the thumbs-up.

Jess measured the distance between the middle of the rope and the water. He would try to shinny across upside down like a possum. In the middle he was sure to get wet, but he hoped the rope wouldn't give so much that he'd go under. Jess shouted to his brother.

"If I drown, tell Mom I love her."

Jess meant it as a joke but Junior didn't think it was funny. Junior respected the force of the water. He had watched Jessie nearly drown in that same place when they were kids.

Jessie had gone down to the creek when Junior and Buck heard the cry. Junior had never seen his father look so scared or move so swiftly. Jessie had fallen in and the water carried him downstream, where he was trapped under some tree limbs on the other side of the creek, barely able to keep his head above water. Buck left on a sprint and dove into the water at a spot where the current miraculously carried him right to Jessie. Junior remembered his father shouting, "Keep your head up. I'm here, Jessie. I'm here."

With one hand he held Jessie's head out of the water by grabbing hold of his shirt collar, and with the other he broke off dead limbs one by one. Once Jess was free of the entanglement, Buck carried his son to the opposite bank and laid him out, ready to pump the life back into him. Junior had run down the bank across from them and saw Jessie sputter, the water gushing from his mouth. Jessie finally caught his breath and began to cry in his father's arms. "I'm sorry," he kept saying while his father rubbed his back. Junior remembered his dad's reply.

"That's okay, tiger. I gotcha."

Jess was ready. Junior watched as he kicked his feet up and hung upside down from the rope, his head leading the way. He shinnied across the water in no time, barely getting his back wet in the middle. When he cleared the water on the other side, he jumped down and said, "Filet, medium rare."

Junior squeezed his younger brother's shoulder.

"Anything you say, boss."

At the south town pit office, the message was relayed to Melvin via the telephone. The caller implied that everything was set.

" My driveway needs a sealcoat," said the caller in code.

" I'll have a look at it," replied Melvin.

He hung up without saying goodbye, like they do in the movies after speaking code talk.

Melvin hoped it wouldn't get that far, that the kid would come to his senses and sell the rock before they had to do what they had to do. But the Brotherhood was willing to do anything to protect their interests. Junior was no longer the man to lead the charge. Arm twisting was a thing that Melvin knew something about, and he hoped the kid would get back before the bid opening. Otherwise, he might not have a pond to worry about.

The moment of truth came after the salad, while they waited for the steaks. Junior tried to make it sound like it wasn't any big deal, but he needed to know.

"Are you gonna sell me that rock?"

Jess looked into his water glass. It was the decision of a lifetime. He concluded that all life was a compromise, but somewhere, sometime, someone had to make a stand on principle alone. He hated what it would do to Junior, but in the end he believed in Junior more than he believed in himself. Junior would find a way to make money with or without that rock.

"Yes," and here Jess paused.

Junior exhaled in relief. He had braced himself for the opposite answer, sure that his brother wouldn't sell. His future was secure now.

But there was more, and Jess continued.

"You can have all the gravel around the pond, but you can't touch the pond itself or the west end. The woods, the trees to the west will remain standing. You can take the new growth and everything under it on the southern hillside, but any damage to the pond and I'll shut you down."

A different matter altogether. Junior looked at his brother surprised by his manner, the firmness in his delivery. He had obviously given it a lot of thought and it was something. But was it enough? Had his brother just thrown him a bone?

"I've got my own plans for the property, so the pond's not for sale," Jess added. "You can dismantle the job shack and take the gravel to the east all the way to the rock walls. To the north, the old rock crusher and the chute will remain as is. If you want to use it, be my guest."

Junior was shocked by his wealth of information. It seems Jess knew exactly how the deposit was spread out over the old pit.

"How do you know all this?"

Jess smiled.

"You don't think Dad would leave me hanging, do you?"

Junior made quick calculations, picturing the map of the geological survey in his head. The pond was about dead center to the deposit. Surveys were an inexact science, and by his calculations what

Jess offered would probably provide him with all the rock he needed for the airfield. But it was only an estimate on paper. Once they got into it, the actual density of rock to sand could vary either way. He'd have to dig around the pond and hope the main load wasn't there.

"What else did Dad tell you?" Junior asked, curious.

Suddenly Junior felt he was behind the eight ball. His father and his brother plotting behind his back?

The waitress came with the steaks sizzling on a platter. She put the tray down and cleared the salad plates. She served the steaks and refilled their water glasses without saying a word. Junior appreciated that kind of service, in and out without having to make a big production out of it.

While she tended to the table, Junior's question was left unanswered. What were his options now? Given the parameters, if he fell short of rock, his number for the bid could go sideways in a hurry if he bid it as if he had all the gravel. If he didn't, it would be back to the shipping, and Junior didn't even want to consider that option.

Junior stared at his plate, lost in thought. Jess noticed his brother's inability to pick up a knife and fork.

"Man, I thought you'd be elated."

"I'm thinking."

"Well quit it. Eat the steak."

"I'm not hungry," said Junior, staring off into the distance.

"That's a first."

"You didn't answer my question."

The steak looked so good and he was so hungry, Jess couldn't recall what the question was in the first place. He took another bite, a big one, and reeled his mind backward. Still nothing. Zippo. *El blanko.*

"Remind me."

"What else did Dad tell you?" Junior asked.

Jesus, that was a pretty open question. His dad had told him quite a bit over a lifetime. To catalogue it all right now would take a helluva long time.

Jess swallowed a big bite of beef and asked Junior, "Can you be a little more specific?"

Junior picked up his knife and fork and began sawing at the steak.

"Do you know something I don't?" he asked Jess.

It was another open-ended question that left Jess without an answer, at least a specific one. He knew Junior was feeling a little disappointed by his final answer, but hell, that was life.

"Do I know something you don't? No, I pretty much know what you know. I'm leaving a fortune on the table, we both know that. But I have my reasons. I mean, realistically, it's my land. I can do whatever I want with it, right?"

"If you had no conscience," said Junior.

Jess took another bite and tried his best to understand where Junior was coming from.

"I know you're disappointed. I'm sorry. But at least it's something. Do you know how close I came to not selling? If you weren't involved, I wouldn't sell a damn thing. Do you know what it's gonna do to the place? You might just as well drop a bomb on it. It'll never be the same."

Junior knew this. That's what he was counting on. The place would be so tore up, that Jess would just relent and sell the land.

"What does Amanda think? She's a smart lady. What has she counseled you to do?"

Jess dug into his baked potato and glanced over at Junior's plate. He had barely touched his food.

"It's my decision and she knows that. But you can thank her for this deal between us. I thought it was all or nothing until she found a way. You two have talked, right?"

Junior smiled.

"More than I want to."

Perhaps Jess was right. He should be happy with a deal that would give him a considerable edge on the airfield bid. But the long money was in the maintenance. Once the jets started pounding the runways with their touch-and-goes, it would be a constant source of income, replacing one concrete section after another. But without the rock, it would be back to square one, dealing with the shipping.

"Can I ask a dumb question?" asked Junior.

He wasn't ready to give in, not yet.

"Do you know what this means? You'll have some income over the next two, three years—and that's *if* I get the bid. Then what are you gonna do?"

It was a good question, and Jess didn't know the answer. He knew that this whole airfield thing qualified him as the world's lousiest businessman, so that career was out.

And just as he thought this, the movie crew showed up. The movie guy now sat in the seat across from a guy who looked an awful lot like Junior.

"I'm gonna write a novel," said the movie guy.

Junior considered all that he had to consider when considering his brother.

"I thought you wanted to be a songwriter?"

The movie guy was indignant.

"I *am* a songwriter."

Junior wasn't eating his steak and the movie guy was way ahead of him. The movie guy was hungry as hell, being in the outdoors for days. He even ate all the asparagus.

"You realize you're losing out on a lot of money. Amanda's got me up to two million. The bitch."

Junior said this with all due respect and the movie guy had to laugh.

"I've got a good lawyer."

The movie guy looked in control and Jess appreciated the portrayal, standing on the other side of the room behind the cameras. The movie guy was lean, like he was hungry for something. The two men looked comfortable with each other.

The director shouted for the action to begin and suddenly a fight broke out in the bar, the Cascade Room. It spilled out into the restaurant, tipping tables and sending glass and cheap china flying. Two lumberjacks were really going at it. Women and children were herded out of the way. A few stragglers from the bar wandered into the dining room to watch the action. No one was willing to stop it. Junior got up from the table when he saw the fight headed their way. The movie guy had his back turned to the action while he finished eating.

"Look out!" Junior warned.

A wayward fist caught the movie guy flush on the cheek, a wild punch that happened to connect with the wrong person. The movie guy reacted, not knowing who or what had hit him. He rolled the two lumberjacks off him and singled out the one he thought had delivered the blow, the one who seemed to be winning the fight.

The movie guy rained punches down on his face, five or six blows before the logger could react. Finally, he slumped to the floor in a semiconscious heap.

The logger who was losing the fight welcomed the break. The movie guy had given him a chance to recover, but as he witnessed his buddy getting pummeled, he couldn't decide whether he should help him or not. He took a quick inventory of what he had just seen and decided diplomacy might be the best tactic.

"Thanks," he said, giving a nod to the movie guy.

The logger slung his buddy over his shoulder and carried him back into the bar.

Junior looked around the room, waiting for someone to step out and nail Jess. Loggers were a notoriously tight-knit group and Junior wanted no part of it.

"Let's go," he said, and headed for the door.

The movie guy followed. The people in the restaurant watched him walk out the door. When they got outside, it was another camera angle, another scene.

"What the hell did you do that for?" asked Junior.

The movie guy didn't have an answer. The camera eye caught them from a distance as they stood by an empty storefront. In the window, a sign read, Available for Lease. Most of the Concrete community was out of work.

They piled into the truck and Junior drove back to camp. They crawled up the side of the mountain on a winding logging road full of switchbacks. Jess' cheek sported a mouse under his left eye.

"You'll have to find another place to live," Junior said, after a long silence.

Jess didn't want to think about it. All he wanted to do was look up that logger someday and tell him he was sorry for the way the movie guy had acted.

Chapter 26

The next morning, Jess drove back to the San Juan Islands on Highway 20, the North Cascades Highway, through Concrete and Lymon, pushing westward out of the foothills into the Skagit Valley, through the larger towns of Sedro Woolley and Burlington, still headed west over the Swinomish Slough onto Fidalgo Island and Anacortes, where he boarded the 11:05 ferry to Orcas, San Juan, and Clay islands.

On the boat, he went upstairs to the concessions area and met a girl from Seattle named Kirsten. She was on a bike trip, and he thought it was pretty bold of her to be going it alone. But she looked to be the spunky sort, a real risk taker.

Jess knew that kind of girl and he couldn't wait to see her again. He felt himself getting stiff just thinking about his homecoming with BB. He excused himself and went to the bathroom so Kirsten wouldn't get the wrong idea. He washed his face with cold water and thought about his father so his stiffy would go away. He thought about the time his dad rescued him from the creek and wanted Buck to do the same now. A stall was open and he cried on the toilet. *Jesus, he was getting as bad as his mother.*

Jess arrived at the old pit just before one o'clock and wondered what the hell was going on. People by the dozens mingled in the parking lot like they were at the fair. His first thought was that something terrible had happened. He parked the pickup and got out. He asked a guy, one of the bystanders, what was going on. The man looked to be a good solid citizen.

"Bid opening tomorrow. That navy airfield. People in the trailer are negotiating the deal right now. Gotta support your town. People need work. The sonuvabitch who owns this property won't sell his gravel and he needs to or kids'll go hungry."

Jess asked a question and got a sermon.

"Thanks," he said.

"No problem," the guy replied, looking at Jess like he recognized him from somewhere.

Two cops guarded the property line and stood behind the cable on Jess' property side. With all the people standing around, the concrete wall on either side of the opening made it look like Jess lived in a fortress, the prince under siege. He walked up to one of the cops.

"What's up?"

The cop recognized him.

"Where you been?"

"Why?"

"Junior's in the trailer with your lawyer. They're trying to work out a deal."

Confused, had his decision fallen on deaf ears? Jess walked to the trailer thinking, shit, if he couldn't trust his brother to honor his word then what would the future hold? He would have to trust him with the pond, not to destroy it, and that was a huge level of trust.

Some of the townspeople in the gathering recognized Jess. They shouted at him as he walked to the trailer. A few rocks whizzed by the back of his head. He opened the trailer door to find Junior and Amanda seated at the table. BB stood next to the kitchen sink, doing bar dips.

"Where have you been?" asked Junior.

Did he really have to answer that? Had last night been a figment of his imagination?

BB kissed him on the lips. They felt cool and lush. He wanted to push her down and take her from behind, but he sensed it wasn't the time or place.

"Welcome home," she said.

He could tell by her look that BB wanted him. The air was stuffy inside, so he cracked the door open.

"Shut the door," said Junior.

Jess smiled at Amanda as he pulled the door shut. She looked harried. It suddenly occurred to him that he had never seen them together, Junior and Amanda. It felt kind of funny. BB squeezed his hand, and he knew something was up. She wouldn't leave his side.

"What's the deal?" he asked, looking at both Amanda and Junior.

Junior felt he should answer.

"I told the crew this morning what you had decided. I guess word got out. They want you to sell the whole pit."

Jess went to the refrigerator and took out a jug of cold water. It gave him time to think. They? Who? He drank big gulps from the jug. He was thirsty as hell.

"Who are we talking about?" he asked.

Of course it wasn't a question he needed to ask, but he thought he would give it a try anyways, just to get it straight and out in the open.

"That's the problem," said Amanda. "We don't know who exactly. It could be anybody in town. You see them out there."

Jess tried to imagine Amanda and Junior in a passionate embrace and the picture wouldn't focus.

"Do they think they can change my mind? Hell, they're fortunate that I'm willing to sell anything."

Jess harkened back to his entrance. In the rewind of his mind, the Brotherhood was conspicuously absent. He looked at his watch. By now they were finishing up their lunchbreak.

"They're waiting for an answer, Jess. It's either all of it, or none of it," said Junior.

"Says who?" asked Jess.

Junior looked at Amanda and she looked back at him. Who was going to answer that one?

"Again, we don't know," said Amanda.

"For crissakes," Jess said. "What *do* we know?"

"I wish I knew," said Junior.

Jess felt BB's arms wrap around his waist as he stood glaring at the two people who were responsible for this. They seemed to know a lot more than he did, but even then they didn't know shit. He felt

BB's hot breath on the nape of his neck. It gave him goosebumps and another erection. He felt he didn't have to hide it. Junior had seen it a hundred times and Amanda wasn't far behind.

"If we don't know who we're talking to, then who are we talking about? Who am I supposed to give my answer to?" he asked.

Junior dug a piece of paper from the pocket of his knit dress pants. He had written down a telephone number with a prefix he didn't recognize. He showed it to Jess.

"We're supposed to call this number by midnight with our decision."

"Who gave you this?" asked Jess.

It didn't add up. The whole thing hinged upon a note in Junior's handwriting? How simple was that?

"An anonymous caller. I received it this morning about ten o'clock," Junior said.

There was more to that phone call, but Junior didn't want to reveal all of it. It wasn't the right time. He glanced at Amanda. She felt Jess needed to know everything, but she didn't know how best to tell him.

Frustrated, Jess opened a drawer and took out the spiral notebook, the novel he had been writing. He found a blank page at the back and scribbled his answer in large script. He handed the notebook to Junior.

"Here's my answer."

Junior read the note and handed it to Amanda. She glanced at what Jess had written.

FUCK YOU!!!!

"It's not that simple," she said.

Jess raised his hands in the air, the posture of a man held at gunpoint.

"Okay, I give."

Junior felt maybe Harris was right, he *had* looked the other way and now it was something he had to fix—the consequences of his inaction.

"They say they're gonna blow up the pond," Junior said.

It didn't come as a total shock. Jess thought it might lead to something like this if he didn't sell. But he had sold. Or at least, he thought he had.

"Who didn't get the message? Didn't we settle on my terms? Take the rock and run with it. Build a fucking monument out of that airfield for all I care."

"If I don't get the bid, we don't get the gravel," Junior said, stating the case for the other side, whoever they were.

Junior wasn't in control anymore and it frightened him what they would do. Actually, he thought, they'd do about anything, and that's what frightened him the most. Dynamite stuck in the gravel ridge? Absolutely possible.

"That's correct," said Jess. "The ball is in your court. So you better put up a good number."

Junior looked down at the tabletop.

"I think that's what they're concerned about."

That really blew Jess' mind.

"*They*? Who the fuck is *they*, Junior? Come on, you know. I've been put through living hell over the last couple months, and some of it's my own fault. But now I'm thinking it's you. It's been you all along."

Here he looked at Amanda.

"Can you believe this guy?" he said. "Don't you think it's a coincidence that he's holding all the cards? Some phantom caller is pushing my buttons because of what I've offered—what I've *agonized* over? And now it's not enough for them? Think about it, Amanda. It's been him all along."

It was clear to everyone that he needed to vent, and they gave him room to do that. Even Junior, who in other times may have taken his brother to the woodshed for what he'd just said. Junior looked up from the trailer table and calmly said, "Are you finished?"

The big gulps of water had made its way to his bladder and Jess felt the pressure.

"I gotta piss," he said.

He chose to piss in the old job shack rather than in the bathroom of the trailer thinking it might give him an opportunity to cool down.

Jess walked out the trailer door and it left BB with a thought. It made perfect sense to her that Junior was holding all the cards. It shed a whole new light on the subject. She gave Junior a cold stare.

"Well, well, what do you know," she said, implying something.

Junior wasn't about to take any finger-pointing from her.

"He's just mad."

"So am I," she said.

"I could give a shit about you," Junior said.

BB grabbed the closest thing she could lay her hands on, the spiral notebook, and fired it at Junior's head. It connected with his cheek before he could raise his hand to stop it. Loose pages flew everywhere.

Her reaction startled Amanda. It had come at a point where Amanda felt she needed to interject, a reminder that it was Jess' decision, but it was obvious she was a little behind.

"Hey, hey, c'mon now!" Amanda said, getting up from the table and spreading her arms in each direction.

She did her best to arbitrate.

"We've got to stick together. It does us no good to fight."

BB wanted a piece of Junior. His smug and superior approach to life grated on her. Over the years, they had tolerated each other, and that was about it. Each had an axe to grind. Junior didn't like the way she had left town without saying goodbye and breaking his mother's heart. For BB, the mere thought of Junior pissed her off. She could easily see him orchestrating this whole thing to benefit his wallet. BB took a step forward, brushing Amanda's arm aside.

"You fat fuck!"

"Hey, hey!" Amanda shouted, putting her hands on BB's shoulders and backing her off.

Back came Junior's reply. "You fuckin' *bitch*."

BB flung Amanda aside and took a swing at Junior. Junior ducked and caught her arm. He looked at BB like he wanted to break it off, which he was fully capable of doing, and that's when Amanda grabbed BB by the waist and pulled her away from the table. Amanda

"Okay, here's the deal. I've had the entire area searched. We've found a couple sticks but I'm sure there's more. We can only do so much with limited resources. How long have you been gone?"

"I left Friday afternoon."

"That would give them time to hide as many sticks as they wanted. I just got a call from a state engineer who says if the pond blows it could send a wall of water eight feet high across the pit floor. It'll drown anybody who's near it. I've asked Junior to move the trailer just in case. We have to take this threat seriously."

Jess thought Harris should have his own TV show—Detective Harris, EPD. He imagined the graphics blazing across the screen.

Harris continued.

"I've asked Ms. Hunt and Junior to put up the pretense of negotiation. It'll buy us time." He looked at his watch. "We're still trying to track down that phone number. It's an Ohio prefix, and my guess, it's a number that'll be hard to track."

Jess tried to take it all in, but he was way too tired to be thinking clearly. Junior spoke up.

"The sticks are in the gravel, Jess. There's nothing we can do about it. If you would have stayed home, maybe they wouldn't have done it."

He was accusing Jess of something but Jess' thoughts were all jumbled up, he was so tired.

BB shouted back at Junior.

"If your guys had an ounce of respect for you, we wouldn't be in this situation. So lay the fuck off!"

Amanda had to laugh at BB's brass. She would love to tap her potential, to get this dynamo pointed in the right direction. Junior bit his tongue. He wanted to say something, but Amanda placed her hand on his knee underneath the table.

"This is all your idea?" Jess asked Harris.

He nodded.

"After I got the call from Junior this morning, it seemed the best way to proceed. They're nowhere to be found."

"They?"

The detective looked at Junior. He was surprised that he hadn't explained the situation to his brother.

"The men walked off the job at ten. Nobody has seen them since," Junior said.

Uh-huh. Jess figured as much. Actually, it was a good move on their part. Outta sight, outta mind.

"Why don't you sit down," Harris suggested.

Good idea. Jess was exhausted in a way that you only get from being outdoors, exposed to the elements for days on end. He was bone tired. He hadn't taken inventory of his physical state until now. Plus, he hadn't eaten since last night and he was hungry as hell.

"I need to eat and I need sleep."

Harris had a suggestion. "Good. We'll order out. Make 'em think we're really working at it."

"Who's paying for it?" asked Jess.

He surely couldn't. Again, it was Harris who spoke up.

"The department will handle it. I can send a man out. You're in my hands now. We don't move unless I say so. This is a dangerous situation, Jess. We're doing everything we can to verify the threat. I believe it's serious."

Jess recalled the events of the recent past and agreed. Actually, to blow up the pond would solve a lot of problems. Their problems.

"I do too."

He sat at the table with Amanda and Junior feeling that feeling of vulnerability all over again. He was in the hands of an unknown element, and Jess didn't like that BB was there. But what was he going to do, ask her to leave? *Right.* He looked to Amanda, seated across the table.

"Okay, counselor, what do we do now?"

Amanda gave his hand a big squeeze.

"We wait," she said.

From a distance, BB admired them together. They seemed like such opposites. Amanda with her movie-star quality and Jess dressed in a Zeppelin T-shirt smelling of fish guts and campfire smoke. BB handed him a plastic bag with ice in it and motioned to the bruise on his cheek.

"It's swollen."

BB was worried about Jess. Through this whole ordeal she hadn't seen him look as defeated. Jess loved that pond. It would kill him if something happened to it.

Amanda suggested an elegant plan, as only she could suggest.

"If we're going to be here all night, let's do it right. What do you say, Junior? If we were going to the eleventh hour, what would we order?"

She knew his answer.

"Steaks."

"Easy enough. Make *them* pay for it," Harris said, pointing to the parking lot where the crowd had swollen to hundreds.

"How about some candlelight?" BB added.

To Jess, it was the kind of scene that all gravel pit epics should end with: the sunset in the rising action, the proverbial lull before the storm just before all hell breaks loose.

The tension seemed to bring out the best in everyone. Junior and Harris decided the restaurant—the Dockside, where else?—while Amanda and BB planned the evening's ambiance. Amanda hinted that candlelight was out.

"People don't do deals by candlelight. That's the way you get fucked."

All this while Jess staggered off to bed. The voices of those who would protect him droned on in the hum of the wa-wa dynamic. The needle on the sound recorder receded and the volume turned slowly into silence.

Later, Jess woke when he heard Amanda and BB talking. Pleasant chatter. He sat up. It was dark outside except for the moonlight. He wiped the sleep from his eyes and walked out to the kitchen for a drink of water. By all appearances, he had missed dinner.

"It's alive," Junior announced.

Jess opened the trailer door to catch some air but there wasn't much to catch. He looked at his watch, 10:16, and all was still. A hyperbolized quiet hung over the pit. Even the crickets seemed to hesitate. BB got up from the table and kissed him.

"I didn't want to wake you."

"Where'd they go?" he asked, looking out the window and seeing nobody in the parking lot.

"Who knows?" answered Junior. "Probably back home. The bastards."

BB heated his plate in the microwave while Amanda and Junior sat at the table playing crib.

"Where's Harris?" Jess asked.

Junior spoke up.

"He walked out just before dinner and we haven't seen him since. He told us not to do anything until he got back. We have to hook up the trailer at some point and haul it out of here."

Jess couldn't believe that no one seemed in a hurry to do much of anything. They lounged around like it was the Fourth of July waiting for the fireworks. He felt better after the nap. He walked outside and sat on the stump and considered this strange silence. He wasn't concerned for himself as much as the others. They had to leave.

He listened for the falling rocks. Nothing. The full moon shined through the trees like a large parking lot light beaming down on them. He knew strange things could happen under such a full moon.

Junior came out with a couple of beers and handed one to him. He sat down in the director's chair next to the stump. BB brought out his dinner, but Jess wasn't hungry.

"I'll eat later," he said. "Thanks."

"You gotta eat, baby."

"In a bit, okay?"

BB took the plate back inside. Jess couldn't eat after he'd slept.

"I've got a bid day tomorrow," Junior ruminated, casually.

He had meant to say "big." Junior got sentimental when he was drunk. After six beers he had become aware of his actions and his inactions throughout this entire ordeal.

"I'm sorry," he said to Jess.

Jess heard the tone of his brother's voice and realized it was heartfelt, as much as his brother was capable of. But it meant a lot to Jess to hear him say it.

On this surreal night, they could hear the traffic going by on the highway in the distance. Every so often someone would open it up on the straight section headed out of town, just past the mini mart, and the sound could startle anybody, even the gravel animals. The two men couldn't feel a breath of air.

The act of living, to guess when you would die, was a strange set of emotions with unusual side effects. To Jess, everything had become the antonym of what it should have been. Junior should have been amped up, but he looked ready to fall asleep.

"You awake?" asked Jess.

"Just thinking," said Junior, shifting in the director's chair. "We should hook up the trailer and pull it outta here."

"Yup. You and the girls have to leave."

Jess looked at his ten-dollar watch. It had stopped on 10:25. He knew it was later than that. The watch had served him well over the last couple of months. But time seemed so incidental to him now. It was a question for his soul. Will I stay or will I go? He knew the answer, but he thought he should check his better mind one last time before he would go down with his dreams.

Jess got up from the stump and walked inside the trailer. BB and Amanda sat at the table, talking.

"Ready to eat, baby?" asked BB.

"You have to leave, both of you," he said. "If something bad happens, I'd never forgive myself. It's time to go. This is no bluff. We're in some real danger here. If that ridge blows up, we'll all drown."

His plea stopped them cold. He had tried to muster up a better speech, a Knute Rockne kind of speech, but words failed him. But at this point, it was the best he could do. He put his arm around Amanda's shoulders.

"Tell BB why I'm right. These guys are for real. Junior will back me up on that."

Jess then put his arms around BB and lifted her up in a big love hug, pressing his body against hers. Amanda got up and went outside. She sat on the stump next to Junior. She'd had a few glasses of wine, yet she knew Jess was right. The alcohol had made everything seem less dangerous than it was. She looked to the gravel bank, the eastern rim of the pond, and from a distance she spotted a silhouette, a human figure sitting cross-legged and rigid on top of the gravel bank.

"Look," she whispered to Junior, pointing.

In the moonlight, Junior recognized the unmistakable profile, the hat on the head of a person who lived with a sense of purpose, however righteous it may have seemed to others.

Junior called to Jess inside the trailer.

"Jessie, come here."

It was bad timing since Jess and BB were getting all worked up. She had pulled her sweater off and Jess was working on her bra. He wasn't good at unhooking it without looking at it, so BB finally just slid it of her shoulders, leaving her *Playday* boobs out in the open for anyone to see. If he was going to die, Jess wanted one last reminder of how good it could be with BB.

"What?" said Jess.

"Come look at this."

Jess buckled his belt, zipped up his pants, and stuck his head out the door.

"Look, on top of the ridge," Junior said, pointing.

Jess spotted the figure, but didn't recognize who it was. He jumped down in his stocking feet and glanced at his brother.

"Shorty," said Junior.

Of course, thought Jess. It was the final stand. If they were going to blow the pond, it would take Shorty with it. BB slipped on her shirt and came out to look.

"Let's invite him down to join us," she said.

Jess gave her a look that made her feel like she had said something really stupid.

"I think we should leave him alone," he said to her softly, grabbing her butt.

BB had a butt like no other. Her muscular ass cheeks molded into her blue jeans so you could see the shape of each cheek clearly defined through the denim. If he drowned, he would miss those cheeks.

Junior shouted up to the figure, shattering the eerie silence.

"Good job, Shorty!"

Jess cringed. What did this have to do with a job? It had everything to do with courage and valor and respect, all that the Brotherhood wasn't. He recalled the shot as it had awakened him. The patter of running feet. The pickup pulling away in the moonlight, leaving the finality of Dierdre's death and its repercussion: the stillness.

Shorty's presence cemented what Jess already knew—that this was the real deal. The Brotherhood meant business, and Shorty's stand on the ridge guaranteed it. If the hill were to blow, he'd die with it.

"You guys need to go *now*!" Jess shouted, once he saw Shorty and realized what it meant.

"Not without you," BB said.

Amanda, however, was more pragmatic.

"I think we all should go."

Fair enough. But to Jess' mind this wasn't about fairness. It was one thing to blow up the pond. It was entirely another to take lives in the process. If everyone cleared out, he felt they would blow it for sure. If he stayed, maybe they would think twice about killing Shorty and him.

"I'm staying," said Jess.

Junior considered the situation. Would they do it? Undoubtedly. Did he want to die? Not much.

"I agree with Amanda. We all should go. Hell, I can't swim."

Jess delivered the final salvo. He threw his keys to his brother.

"Get in and back it up. This ain't the *movies*!"

Jess went inside the trailer to put away anything that might break or fall in the move. BB came in to talk. She placed her arms around his neck. He could smell the scent of her skin, the BB smell that he loved so well.

"Please," she said. "We'll go to Pop's house and everything will be all right, you'll see."

She whispered in his ear, a promise of what she would do for him if he would come. It was nasty as hell.

Jess looked at the time on the microwave, 11:17. They had time to pull the trailer out and get away. He grabbed the blanket from the bed when he decided he would sleep in the old job shack. Then he realized he had all his camping gear in the back of the truck. He would lend his blanket to Shorty since it would dip into the thirties later on.

When Jess looked up, they all had assembled in the trailer staring back at him. Before anybody could say anything, he told Junior, "Get out and take them with you. Please," he begged.

Jess didn't have to plead any longer. Headlights came whipping into the parking lot. The patrol car slid to a halt in the gravel. Harris got out and ran to the trailer.

"It's Harris," Amanda said, watching him hurdle the steel cable like a cop on TV.

Harris shouted as he approached, "Let's go. C'mon, that means everyone. Now!"

When he got to the trailer, he stuck his head inside.

'He's not coming," Junior said.

Harris tried to remain calm, but there was a definite sense of urgency in his voice.

"They're gonna blow it, Jess. We just got the call."

Jess laughed out loud.

"Did you think they wouldn't?" he said, his voice trailing off as he imagined where they placed the dynamite.

If it were him, he would load up a string along the bottom of the ridge on the eastern rim. If the bottom blew out, it would be like a house of cards folding in on itself. An eight-foot wall of water would swallow up the trailer, and the water would carry him away. It would barrel down on him in a second, and he wondered if he would have any forewarning, knowing that he was gonna have to swim, *now*.

"I'm not going," said Jess.

"Then I'll arrest you," said Harris.

"You can't."

Jess knew this because of Spirit Lake Harry Truman on Mount St. Helens. Old Harry wouldn't budge off his property and there wasn't anything the authorities could do about it. He went up in the blast.

Junior had come to his senses. He recognized the situation for what it really was.

"If they blow it, so what. We can rebuild it. You, Jessie, we can't rebuild. If you stay here and die, we all lose and they win. C'mon, let's go."

It was a good speech, and BB seconded the motion, then Amanda. They were all aligned against him—the good ones, the ones who wanted to protect him. But who was going to protect the pond?

"What about Shorty?" Jess asked Harris.

"What about him?" asked Harris.

Junior pointed to the figure framed in the moonlight. *Christ, that was all he needed.* Harris took off on a dead sprint and scurried up the bank. When he got to the top, while he caught his breath, Harris took note of the way Shorty was dressed in battle fatigues—the boots, camouflage pants, coat, and hat, the full regalia. He felt sorry for every veteran who couldn't let go, who couldn't mend.

"Shorty, they're gonna blow it whether you're here or not. You've done all you can. Come on, let's go."

Harris was referring to that little birdie on his shoulder, the voice he had listened to over the last few weeks. He felt he owed this man something. To save his life might be a start.

Shorty turned his head away and appeared to be in a trance. Harris knew it was no use. He looked at his watch. 11:34 and counting.

Harris slid down the slope, and when he reached the old pit floor he motioned for his backup, Officer Skip Nelson. The detective told him to escort the women to the police car. They weren't going to die on his watch, not today.

Amanda helped Officer Nelson with BB. They had to drag her away kicking and screaming. She was a big muscular girl and it was difficult hauling her off. Harris told Junior to get in his car and start driving fast. Junior hesitated.

"But what about the trailer?"

Harris wanted to punch him in the mouth.

"Too late for that."

"Get out, Jessie," Junior shouted, as he ran to the Lincoln.

Harris turned his attention to this stubborn man. It was one final attempt to save him. It was the role of a lifetime.

"Jess, they're the monsters of our time, and we can't let them get us. So they blow up the pond. It's nothing compared to your life. Take your fiancée in your arms and go live happily ever after. But do it somewhere else. You can't do it here. She needs you. Think of her."

It was a good speech, but Jess wouldn't budge.

"Please, let's go," said Harris.

Jess barely heard what the detective had to say. The detective couldn't possibly understand what the pond meant to him. Yes, he would die for it.

"Then they win," Jess said.

Harris didn't see it that way. But he didn't have time to argue.

"Maybe. But I'll get the guys who are doing this."

Jess looked at the clock on the microwave, 11:52.

"You better get going. Time's running out."

Harris knew Jess was right. Time, indeed, had run out.

' Okay, Jess, have it your way. Good luck."

The detective ran out of the trailer and sprinted to the car. Nelson had the motor running, pointed down Old Pit Road. Harris jumped in and Nelson peeled away, headed for higher ground and the highway intersection. Inside the police car, the doors in the back were locked, and BB had nowhere to go. But she was an amazingly strong girl and Amanda took a beating as she tried to restrain her.

Officer Nelson drove as fast as the dirt and gravel would allow. He could feel the back end of the car swing back and forth, the wheels turning faster than the ground they gripped. Harris rolled down the window and listened for the explosion.

They made the intersection and turned into the mini mart

entrance where Harris had set up camp. The other patrolmen had put up barricades, sealing off Old Pit Road. The police were still trying to locate Melvin Banks, or anyone else in the Brotherhood for that matter, but nobody was home.

Then Harris watched a Cadillac Seville drive right by the mini mart, right by the roadblock, past the barricades, and on down Old Pit Road. Two patrolmen stared in amazement at how somebody could so brazenly dismiss the yellow barricades. They had simply driven right around them.

"Marie!" screamed BB from the back of the patrol car.

Marie had lay awake for about an hour before she got up and decided she should do something about tomorrow's bid. If she had to intrude on her two son's business, so be it, such was a mother's right. And if it was a question of money. . . perhaps she could do something about that too. She had talked to Junior, and now she needed to talk to her youngest son. Even at this late hour.

A police car pulled alongside her with its lights flashing. Marie wondered what she had done wrong, which of the traffic laws she had broken. She checked her speed. She was doing twenty miles an hour. She hadn't seen any new signs posted, and from her many years of driving up and down Old Pit Road, she knew it was twenty-five.

Marie steered the Cadillac off to the side of the road and stopped, her heart pounding. She rolled the window down. She could see BB in the backseat of the police car and she didn't know what to make of that. A man in a long black leather coat got out of the car. She could hear BB yelling her name and crying hysterically. Marie was confused. Harris immediately recognized her confusion once he opened the driver's side door.

He spoke calmly.

"Ma'am, slide over please."

He waited for Marie to unhook her seatbelt but her hands were shaking so bad she couldn't manage it. Harris opened the door, pushed the button at the base of her seatbelt, and herded her over to the passenger side. Marie couldn't believe that a man was climbing into her car, and he was even gonna drive it. Harris jammed the shifter into Drive and spun the Cadillac around, put the pedal to the metal, and headed to higher ground.

When they pulled into the mini mart parking lot, Harris looked at his watch, 12:01.

Maybe it was all a bluff. Or maybe their watches were off.

In the trailer, Jess looked up at the digital timer on the microwave. The red numerals read 12:01. He didn't know if it was accurate.

He wondered what to do with the last moments of his life other than clean up after the guests. He poured a full bottle of beer down the kitchen sink and thought, what does one do at zero hour? Jack off? Have an orgasm at the moment of deliverance? He thought better of it. He would hate for his body to be discovered with his dick in his hands.

Play the guitar?

He imagined playing in the best band in the world, all hooked up in synchronized perfection, where time was strung along in brilliant sophistication.

He didn't want to die. He didn't want Shorty to die either. He looked out the window. The figure on the hillside framed an indelible picture in his mind: Shorty in the moonlight practicing, always practicing, the rite of compassion.

Chapter 27

At eight o'clock the next morning, once all the Brotherhood had been accounted for, Harris thought it was safe enough to remove the barricades blocking Old Pit Road. BB had stayed at the mini mart all night long, and Officer Nelson escorted her back to the trailer in the patrol car.

She woke Jess with her hand pushing down his jeans. They made passionate love in celebration of his being alive. Afterwards, she dozed off while he made coffee. He went outside on a cloudy morning to contemplate the new dawn. How to proceed with the rest of his life.

Harris drove up as Jess stood outside in his bare feet with a cup of coffee in his hands. The detective walked toward him and Jess thought losing the coat was a big improvement.

"Sleep well?" Harris asked.

Harris could only imagine the night Jess must have had. Every second could have been his last. They shook hands, a meaningful shake when two men grip the soul of the other firmly.

"Not bad," Jess answered. "But you look like you could use some coffee."

Harris still had things to do.

"Mind if I get a crew in here to make sure there's no more explosives?"

"Do whatever you have to," said Jess.

"BB was pretty upset last night," Harris said with obvious envy.

Jess smiled, imagining the scene.

"Yeah, I've got a tiger by the tail," he said, quoting the famous Buck Owens song.

"It's plain to see," Harris smiled, finishing the line.

As the detective walked away, Jess stopped him.

"Harris?" he called out to the cop.

Just before Harris stepped over the cable, he looked back at Jess.

"You're a good cop," Jess said.

The four words rang like Mozart through Harris' thirsty soul, for it was recognition of something he had known all along. He *was* a good cop.

"Thanks," he said humbly.

Shorty abandoned his vigil shortly after sunrise. He went home to put on his work clothes and made it to work at 6:30, the final act of defiance. He didn't say a word and neither did any of the other guys in the shop.

Shorty called his wife at work to say good morning. The day before, he had told her that he might have to work on an all-night pour.

"You're tired, I can hear it," she said.

She would pray for him to feel better.

"A little," admitted Shorty, but only to his wife.

After the bid opening, Junior drove the two miles out of town to the old pit and spotted BB's Mustang parked in the same place. If he was interrupting, too bad. This was important. He knocked on the trailer door and Jess answered fully clothed, having eaten a late lunch.

Junior looked up at him.

"I got the bid."

The words struck Jess' heart like sledge to sternum. He really didn't know how to feel. But now it was real. The old pit was going under the knife and his home would never be the same. In one sense he was happy for Junior. It would also be income, money he sorely needed. But the ticket to paradise had come at a very steep price.

BB came to the door.

"Congratulations," she said, offering her hand.

This was good news to her. Now their lives were going to be different. They would finally have some money.

"Thank you," Junior said, graciously.

Junior noticed the disappointment written on Jess' face. It could be said that he didn't take total pleasure in this victory, but it had been a good bid, and without Jess he would have lost it sure as hell. His second number, the one where he had to barge the gravel in, would have been third low.

"I wouldn't have gotten the bid without you. I wanted you to know that," he said to Jess.

There was nothing more to say and Junior turned and walked away.

Jess called out to him, "Wait."

Jess jumped down onto the gravel in his bare feet and walked towards his brother.

"No, it's terrific news," he said, offering his hand.

Junior would dismiss the handshake and instead hugged his brother for all he was worth.

"But I'll never forgive you," whispered Jess in his brother's ear.

Junior straightened.

"Why?"

"I know you were behind all of this. The fire, the shots, the garbage, the swan, the jets, and whatever it was last night. Jesus, what a show."

Junior exhaled loudly. He knew Jess wasn't stupid. He needed that rock and there was nothing that was gonna stop him from getting it.

"I had nothing to do with last night, but the other things . . . yeah, I was behind it," Junior said, meeting his brother's gaze. "I figured if I call the shots, you live. If they call the shots, you die."

Jess scraped the ground with his toe, weighing the sum of Junior's honest response. He'd have to think about that before he could forgive his brother. After a pause, Jess added, "Do you think they would've done it?"

Junior smiled a knowing smile.

"I've seen 'em skin an elk when it was still alive. So you tell me."

Junior looked up at the large-batch barrel marked in white two-foot lettering, *Buchanan Construction Est. 1929.*

"Damn, I love this place too," Junior said.

Jess kicked a pebble at his brother with his big toe.

"Go easy on her," he said.

Junior reached into his back pocket and took out a wad of bills from his wallet and handed it to Jess.

"Go buy some groceries. You're too damn skinny."

As Junior walked off, Jess shouted after him, "Thanks for supporting the arts!"

Junior waved.

"Go fuck yourself," he said, once he climbed into the Lincoln.

Jess walked back to the trailer feeling defeated by the forces of charge and compromise. Would it always be that way? Would he always have to accept terms that were meted out to him as a condition of life? And to what end? What was the moral of the story as he stumbled forth in this juggernaut of acts and their consequence?

But, as was fate's habit, it was exactly this moment when Jess heard a familiar refrain, an echo off the trees that stopped him cold. He listened for it again. He must have imagined it. The sound.

But inside the trailer, BB heard it too. She stopped the potato chip midway to her mouth, listening.

Silence.

Then they heard it again, the melody so sweet that nearly all could be forgiven. BB stood in the doorway of the trailer and looked to where the sound had come from, the eastern rim of the pond. Then she looked at Jess. Their eyes met and neither could believe what they just heard, nor what they saw, when moments later they were tossed into the fray, the river of joy.

"Come here, boy!" Jess shouted.

At the top of the gravel bank stood the ending too poetic for **BB** to withstand.

"Legs!" she cried, blubbering through **BB** tears.

Jess felt himself moving outside his body again but he fought it off. He wouldn't let the movie guy have this moment; this was his moment, his dog, his ending.

Legs posed for the still shot in a spot that Shorty had occupied only a few hours before. He looked well cared for, healthy, and happy to be alive. He even wagged his tail to prove it.

"Come here, boy," Jess repeated, as Legs ran down the gravel bank toward him.

Jess cried tears of happiness. They were the kind of tears that seemed to work its way into his life without warning, without notice, without preparation. They were tears of joy . . . *Because you just never know*, his dad was so fond of saying.

Lightning Source UK Ltd.
Milton Keynes UK
UKHW012030230421
382556UK00008B/428/J